ISRAEL RAIN

By

M. A. Cole

ISRAEL RAIN

All rights reserved © 2022 M. A. Cole

ISBN: 979-8-218-02342-3

To My Greatest Blessing

Table of Contents

Key to Life

John Lennon once told a reporter about how when he was a young boy his mother taught, and often reminded her beloved son, that finding happiness was the true key to success. He then spoke about how later, after he started school, he was given an assignment where he was asked to answer the question, "What do you want to be when you grow up?" John, became almost giddy as he remembered his mother's persistent life lesson. So, in absolute certainty he answered that question with one simple word, "Happy." His teacher and classmates more or less made fun of his seemingly over-simplistic answer. They told him he must not have fully understood what he was being asked. He then, in his purest conviction harshly defended his mother's teachings by telling his classmates and his teacher they were actually the ones who didn't understand life's real assignment or its true purpose.

My younger brother Samuel—Sammy, as we called him—definitely understood what that later-to-be-famous Beatle was saying, even if at times it didn't seem like he understood much else. Sammy was the middle of us three brothers. There was me, Israel - I am the oldest, then Sammy, and lastly Jacob, our youngest brother. Unlike Jacob or me, Sammy was born with quite a few more challenges to deal with early on. During the first ten or eleven years and quite a few unexpected times thereafter, his life consisted of one hospital trip after another. They were mostly geared towards trying to fix a heart abnormality but he also had quite a few other fairly severe intestinal problems as well. When Sammy became old enough, for some reason he started calling his trips to the hospital visiting the White House.

I guess to him, every hospital was either painted white or mostly decorated in white so that must have been where he thought he was going. Believe me, in his early years he sure did visit that stupid white house a lot too. But, regardless of any of his health issues or really any other characteristic that some would define as not-so- normal, he was definitely the glue that held our little family together, and the light that always led our way. There is an absolute beauty and a definite innocence in people that are born with what Sammy was born with. Not many people speak about it, or they may not know that kind of wholesomeness is possible, but it's there, and it's there without question. In Sammy's case, to confirm these thoughts, he always had this one particular look in his eyes. It was a look that signaled to the world that he was so much greater than any problem life could throw at him.

That look was also to let everyone know that he had something very special inside of him and that special something didn't have anything to do with an extra chromosome. Sammy's surgeries and the majority of his other health problems eventually subsided and once they did he was more or less free to be that gleaming light, not only to our family but to everyone he ever met. Our parents never let us, or really anyone treat him any differently from anyone else. At times, we all may have had to be a little more patient but for the most part, Sammy was just as much of an adventurous little boy as any other knuckleheaded kid would have been at that age. All of us brothers were a little more than a year apart and when we went to school, Sammy had his classes and we had ours but either Jacob or I would get Sammy for lunch and after school every day. We did this not only to make sure he was okay but also to ensure he wasn't getting into any more trouble than we were at the time.

No one ever picked on Sammy or treated him poorly either, I mean no one, not around the neighborhood or in school. I guess one reason was everyone knew Jacob and I were never too far away but I think it was mostly because everyone just loved Sammy so much. Whenever anyone interacted with him in any way they themselves seemed to brighten up afterward. I can't fully explain it but Sammy had such a genuine and caring personality that it seemed to literally rub off on anyone he was around. He did have a funny little quirk though. It drove me nuts at times but whenever he'd greet someone for some strange reason he would always warmly say, "Good Day, Good Day." I don't know where in the world he got that from. I'm guessing he just picked it up from a movie somewhere along the way but for whatever reason it stuck.

What was even funnier was many of those people he welcomed so Britishly often copied his refreshing salutation and fired it right back at him. Sammy just made everything special and enjoyed life more than most allow. Although he liked to do just about anything, his absolute favorite thing to do was to go fishing. His love for fishing was something that he and I definitely had very much in common. What made it easier was we lived near the James River in Richmond. So, to say that we often partook in our favorite pastime together, was quite an understatement. The second great commonality Sammy and I had was painting. For a long time, it seemed like all we did other than school was either fish on the bank of that beautiful river for hours on end, or either enthrall ourselves in whatever painting we were working on for what seemed like days at a time. No matter what we did though, we always included a ton of laughter and some of the most profound and enjoyable conversations of my life.

Sammy always threw in a few flexes from his miniature biceps each time too. Even when fishing or painting I think he thought he needed to pump up his little arms as a professional wrestler would before entering the ring at a big event. Sammy had such an ease with life that I've never seen with anyone else. I always admired his peaceful soul and to be truthful, I was probably even a little jealous of his relaxed disposition about pretty much everything. My youngest brother, Jacob and I, definitely didn't share Sammy's tranquil life experience. We often acted our grievances and frustrations out on each other and as much as Sammy and I got along, my youngest brother and I did not. I don't know what it was, I guess Jacob and I were just born to be polar opposites, but regardless of the reasons, we fought all the time growing up. I never knew what I did to make my youngest brother dislike me so much but for whatever reason, he just didn't want anything to do with me from the very beginning.

My parents thought our little youthful squabbles were funny at first, but over time, they became worse and even more serious. It's not that we never got along. We did have our moments of toleration, but for the most part, any full-fledged sibling peace or affection was quite a rarity. Even though Jacob never liked fishing or painting, or really anything else I did, he would participate in another favored past time that Sammy and I had. We would all lay on our backs looking up at the sky pretending that the clouds were animals, or people, or really anything else we wanted them to be. In fairness, Jacob had his own special relationship with Sammy, but his way of doing things always seemed to be very different from mine. I must have done something very wrong to that kid in a past life or something because I couldn't ever figure out what his lifelong beef with me was.

To make matters worse, we all shared a bedroom and my bed was located right in the middle of where both of my brothers slept. I can remember rolling over in the middle of the night and looking over at Sammy. Sammy always had this look of contentment and happiness on his face, which always warmed my heart, but then I'd roll back over towards Jacob. Even though I knew early on he probably didn't know what it meant, he still, for some reason, slept with his middle finger stretched out in the air, and that finger always seemed to be pointing directly at me. Being the oldest, I was often left in charge, if you could call it that. Sammy had so many medical bills, my parents really didn't have any other choice but to work a lot. Both my mother and father had two jobs all during our youth and many times, from an early age, I was left to watch over my two younger siblings simply because they couldn't afford to get anyone with better qualifications to do the job.

I can't say that responsibility was always fun but I will say, whether it was Sammy, Jacob or even myself, something unexpected always seemed to happen. My mother really didn't have a lot of rules for us back then but the one rule she did have was she expected all of us to sit down to dinner together each night as a family. This was a chance for her and my father to catch up on whatever their children were getting into and, of course, a time to interject some parental guidance before their boys did something else stupid or disappointing once more. My mother never allowed the television on during our forced family time either. She didn't want anything to distract from our little group therapy sessions. That was okay, though, because it seemed like one of her boys always provided plenty to talk to about. Our parents spent as much time as they could with us, and understandably, a little more with Sammy.

They really did the best they could but we were still three boys that were left alone probably a little more than we should have been. I really felt for my father back then. He worked what seemed like all the time. Looking back, I can't ever remember a time that we went without anything. He just had to work so much to make it that way. My father was a proud man who was bound and determined to work his way out of his family's financial hardships, even if it cost him so much precious time away from those he was working so hard for. He was a meat cutter by trade. He worked in the most winter-like surroundings almost all the time. He'd come home with his hands so swollen from the constant cold, and he'd be so tired from the long-exposed hours to the freezing elements. Many times he could barely make it through our family meals before he'd have to go back to work again. The only part of any day that I can ever remember him taking off from work was on some Sunday evenings. Most of that time he'd try to catch up on his greatly deprived and much needed sleep.

Being that my father was either gone or asleep most of the time, my mother was our definite and declared disciplinarian. It's not that we were ever but so bad, but they had two boys who had a great dislike for one another and another pretending like he was in the world wrestling federation flexing all-around all of the time. Simply put, things were bound to happen, as they often did. Many times, that something had to do with Jacob and me fighting. One of our long-lasting skirmishes started when Jacob would often wait until he saw our mother's old green Monte Carlo pull in the driveway. Then he'd go towards the coat closet by the front door. When he heard our mother's key enter the door knob he'd start hitting himself. Sometimes it was to the point of drawing blood and then he'd lock himself in the closet until she actually came in the door.

That little jerk would jump out of the closet blaming me for hitting him and putting him in the closet in the first place. I think Sammy thought it was a game that Jacob always played on me but it wasn't. We had an old-school mother; eye for an eye, butt whipping for hitting a little brother kind-of-mother, and that's often what I got. I must have gotten a hundred whippings because of Jacob's theatrics, all while both of my brothers just sat there laughing at me and my pain. I always retaliated to Jacob's trickery though, whether it was a wise idea to do so or not. Sometimes it was immediate and other times I'd take a week or longer to plan out my next actions. Either way I always got him back regardless of the cost. One of my favorite acts of retaliation was during one of the coldest days of the year. My mother left her usual chore list for all of her sons. One by one we had certain things to do each day and we all knew we better have everything on our respective lists finished before she got home.

Sammy's list usually only included putting the dishes away. Those were the same dishes that we dared not leave in the sink from the night before but he was included nonetheless. My chore list was always the longest. I guess because I was the oldest, but Jacob's chores always included taking out the trash, so I did feel a little vindication. On this one particular day, I decided to reciprocate some revenge on my least favorite fan. My father always made us take a shovel and push the trash down as far as it would go. This was so we could pack in as much trash as we could. He really did this so the trash could be picked up every two weeks instead of every week like most people. If it saved him a little money, that's the route he was going to take, or make us take anyway. That day, I knew Jacob was going to have to lean all the way over to push that nasty trash way down to the bottom of that big can.

It was no more than ten degrees outside and the stage was set because I knew my mother would be home soon and that meant Jacob had to be on his way outside shortly. I wrapped Sammy in his warmest jacket and then opened the upstairs window in our parents' bedroom. We both climbed out on the roof laughing and chuckling all of the way. That past Christmas, whether it was smart or not, I received a pretty strong BB gun and that day I decided I was going to use it to inflict some pain on my brother who so often was the source of mine. I guess you could say I made up my mind to hunt me some retaliatory Jacob butt. As Jacob leaned way over in the trash can following my father's wishes to compact it down as much as he could, I fired off six rounds. I know for a fact each of them reached their intended meaty target. I could tell every pellet peppered each butt cheek with a fierce and unexpected equal bite.

Jacob was screaming and jumping around holding his backside as if he was stung by a million bees. Sammy was laughing so hard I thought he was going to fall off of the roof and, in truth, so was I. Jacob didn't see where the sneak attack came from but he definitely knew without a shadow of a doubt who unleashed its malicious wrath. As comical as that was, I fully accepted the logic that what I delivered on that cold winter day would definitely bring a spanking that was very much worth getting. Jacob and I had so many of those back and forth interactions that they really were commonplace in our household. When we were bad enough, my father would get called in as back-up but from my memories of whatever punishment we got it must have never lasted too long because we were always back at it again almost each and every day. I will say there was a time that almost scared me as much as it did Jacob. On that day it was raining outside, so the three of us were stuck in the house. Jacob and I were fighting, as usual, over some video game or something stupid.

Sammy was once again laughing at his ignorant brothers and watching our tensions grow. Jacob, as he always did, waited until the last minute to take out the trash and since I had my BB gun taken away a long time ago, I felt I had to do something at least on a similar scale as before because he had been one-upping me for a while. As he went to the back yard to complete his daily chore once more, I went to the front yard to try and quickly figure out something to do to him. I'd been fishing earlier in the week with some of my friends and someone left an oar in our front yard. I then had the final draft of my newly concocted plan even though I could have never guessed the actual outcome of such ignorance. I thought it would be a good idea for some reason to throw that oar over the house to hopefully scare Jacob or maybe just hit him a little.

Even I didn't think the oar that flew over the house so easily would hit him directly on his forehead with such a great and damaging smack. The outcome of my hasty plan resulted in Jacob being completely knocked the hell out lying motionless in the back yard. It was a little comical seeing him lying there with his arms and legs spread out as far as they could stretch until I realized he wasn't moving at all. I wanted to get back at him for all of his constant crap but I never wanted to actually hurt him. Once again, Sammy was cracking up, but I wasn't this time. I was scared that Jacob was hurt pretty bad. Even though he didn't like me, I really didn't dislike him and I definitely didn't want to seriously injure him—especially right before my mother got home. Sammy and I shook Jacob over and over again. Eventually he did wake up but as he sat up, he didn't say a word. He did, however look at me with these squinty devilish eyes which seemed to say, "It's really on now." That was the first time Jacob didn't tell on me about something, but he didn't have to.

When my mother got home, it wasn't Jacob waiting at the door, it was that daggon Sammy, and his first words to our mother were, "Israel knocked the hell out of Jacob with an oar." He was a little more explanatory but my mother knew her boys were at it once again. This time, though, instead of getting after me as she usually did, she was more worried about Sammy saying "hell" and she spent the majority of her efforts correcting him. I felt like I kind of got away with that one but, in truth, I think that scared Jacob and I both to the point where we took a little break from our shenanigans towards each other for a while. From that point on, more so than messing with each other, Jacob turned his efforts to trying to outdo me in everything instead. If I scored a touchdown in a football game, he'd score two. If I got a B on a test, he'd get an A. One time, I broke my finger and that kid broke his wrist a few weeks later. I don't think he did that on purpose but I definitely wouldn't have put it past him either.

There was no limit to how badly Jacob wanted to beat me at everything. It was simply unexplainable but for some reason, that's just the way our relationship went. Lying on our backs, looking up at the sky with Sammy was the only time we all had any sort of common ground when it came to each other. Because of our ridiculously immature teenage minds, our favorite sightings in the clouds were those that we told Sammy were "sky boobies". When he'd spot what he knew to be a pair, he'd yell out, "Look at those big ones!" Or, "Man, oh man, I see them shaking all over the place now!" Jacob and I would almost cry laughing at Sammy's cloudy and colorful "mammarian" descriptions. Those were times when it was our turn to laugh at Sammy and with him too. When Jacob and I fought, Sammy never really took sides. He was just there rooting both of his idiot brothers on.

He didn't care who won or lost, he was just amused by watching his two dumb brothers half-kill each other every chance we got. Sammy was so different from us. He just didn't seem to experience the anger, frustration or even jealously that Jacob or I did. Sammy had such a peaceful nature that even his embattled brothers would take a break every now and then from fighting to make sure we weren't doing anything that may upset him. He didn't realize he was any different from anyone else but he definitely was. He was better; especially better than either one of his ignorant brothers. After experiencing as much of a truce as Jacob and I ever had, Jacob, out of nowhere, thought it would be funny to throw a fire cracker down at my feet. It wasn't any sort of ordinary firecracker either, it was a ridiculously loud and powerful M-80.

He could have blown my foot off, but unlike the oar incident where I didn't try to hurt him, I was mad enough to put his lights out that time. I never hit Jacob with my fists until that day and when I did, I beat him pretty good. Little to my knowing and since our backyards butted up next to an elderly couple's house who seemed to always be outside watching everything, I did it right in front of them too. The old man stumbled over to the edge of his yard as fast as he could. When he finally got there, he started yelling at me to stop. I stopped when he asked me to even though I thought Jacob deserved a little more. I was mad at Jacob but I was more scared about what that old man was going to tell my mother when she got home. As I followed the old man's wishes to stop beating my brother, Jacob was looking for a weapon that he quickly found and started using himself. He got that damn shovel that he so often used to push the trash down and began beating me with it in his own attempts at pay back.

He hit me with that stupid shovel to the point that I couldn't just stand there and get beaten to death by a garden tool, so I started fighting back again. It was so bad that the old man's wife called the police. As luck would have it, the men in blue and my mother arrived at our house at almost the same time. Jacob and I weren't grown men at the time but we weren't far off. We were both in high school and fairly stout and could have very well hurt each other pretty badly if we would have kept going. I still didn't think whatever we could have done to each other was going to be anything close to what my mother was going to do to us now that her and the police were in our driveway together. When my mother pulled up, seeing the look of absolute terror in her eyes was probably the worst punishment that we could have ever received.

She was definitely not a crier by any means; I've probably only seen her cry one time before that day, and that was at my grandfather's funeral, but this time, she was bawling from fear for her boys. She got out of the car and went rushing around looking for Sammy first. When she realized he was okay, she then came over to Jacob and then me. She spun each one of us around one by one to make sure we didn't have any bones or shovels sticking out of our bodies. Once she realized we were somewhat okay, her facial expression completely changed to one of absolute disappointment. A bad beating would have been better than that look of shame she gave us. To make matters worse, my father arrived in that crowded driveway a few minutes later. I'm sure my mother called him and he probably wanted to see for himself what his almost grown sons had done this time. My parents spoke with the policemen by themselves for a few minutes and then at least the policemen left.

My parents may have kept us out of the pokey that day but what we got was much worse. My mother had always been so quick to respond in some kind of physically-whipping-sort-of-way, but not this time. We'd long since been what most would consider too big to get whippings, and in truth, they stopped hurting a long time ago, but that's what she was taught, so that's what she usually gave. This time, however, there was none of that. She didn't want to talk or even look at me or Jacob. She was so upset that she didn't bother with the normal questions about who started it or what happened. She and my father just took Sammy in the house and slammed the door behind them. That move left Jacob and I very much locked outside. This was as serious as anything we'd ever done. We hurt her so much, and in truth probably have been for a long time but on that occasion, she'd had enough.

As Jacob and I sat outside on the porch waiting to see if our mother would ever let us back in the house, Sammy was at the window waving at us. He'd throw a little flex up every now and then trying to get us to smile but he knew we were in trouble. Our little buddy was missing us though. He was missing us not being inside with him. While outside, Jacob and I both agreed that we didn't have to like each other but we could never hurt our parents like we did that day anymore. Regardless of our differences, seeing our mother so disappointed broke my heart and I know even though Jacob probably blamed me for everything, it probably did his as well. At that point I knew I'd be graduating in another six months and hopefully off to college soon after, so all of those years of that constant battling and sibling rivalry would finally be over anyway.

Puddles

Christmas wasn't too far off and after our mother's disappointment eventually subsided she fully engaged herself in the holiday season as she did every year. She loved Christmastime. Now, we never per se wanted for anything, but we didn't have all of the nicer new things that many of our more well-to-do friends had either. Christmas was the one time that my mother would treat us all like kings. Sometimes I thought that was the real reason that her and my father had to work all of the time. I honestly felt they worked so hard throughout the year so they could give us such wonderful things on that blessed day. I know it might be weird to say as a kid but none of us ever really cared about what we got, we were just happy to get to spend so much more time together during the holiday seasons. Sammy always woke up first on Christmas morning and his job was to wake everyone else up.

This was a job that he mastered throughout the year so it was a simple duty for him to accomplish on that day as well. Just watching Sammy animate the Christmas songs while opening his gifts would have been enough for any of us, but not for my mother. She always went over the top. She had a certain way of doing things and everyone knew not to mess with her holiday rhythm. She'd make everyone unwrap their presents one gift at a time so the others watching could participate in the excitement of the recipient as she described it. I think in reality she was just trying to extend the day that was so precious to her. Sammy always went first on the smaller gifts, and like most kids, along with the stuff he really liked, he'd also get some necessities like underwear and socks. When Sammy got to those types of presents even he couldn't pretend to be but so excited. He'd open those presents up in full excitement and if something like that was inside, he'd say, "Oops, next up."

He wasn't fooling anyone. He wanted everyone else to hurry up so he could open something else that he might like a little bit better. As we opened our gifts, Sammy always kept us running as efficiently as possible. If he thought we were taking a little too much time with our own presents he would once again yell out, "next up." Out of respect for our most seasonally excited, yet sometimes demanding brother, we'd hurry along as he directed. My mother always felt she needed to be completely fair to all of her sons for some reason too. She had to spend the exact same amount of money on each of us, as if one would feel less loved if she didn't. The other thing that our mother did every Christmas would be she'd pretend like all of the presents were opened and then she'd start cleaning up. When she was almost finished cleaning, she'd say, "Boys, I believe I forgot something."

This happened every single year so we always knew that statement would eventually come. When Sammy felt that time was near, his "next ups" became a little louder and more frequent. My mother would always hide our last gifts--"the big gift," as she called them—somewhere strange around the house or in the garage. That year, Jacob got a used car. It may have only been an older Toyota Corolla but it was every bit as nice as what my mother or father or even I was driving at the time. They bought me a Jon boat that year. They knew I loved fishing, as did Sammy, so I couldn't have asked for a more thoughtful and useful gift. Unlike what she called the smaller gifts, my mother always made Sammy wait until last to open his big gift. I think that's the way she truly wanted to remember our Christmases each year. When it was Sammy's turn that year, he discovered his present wasn't large in size like Jacob's or mine, nor was it hidden in the garage like ours was either.

My mother told Sammy to go check in the bathroom for his last and final gift of the year. We all laughed as Sammy looked back at our mother in shock because he let everyone know he never had to look for a present in the bathroom before. He wanted to make sure she told him the correct location, so he said, "Are you sure it's in the bathroom, mom?" My mother giggled and then confirmed that she was absolutely sure where she hid his last gift. Sammy ran down the hall to the bathroom and came out less than a minute later with another very confused look on his face. He then yelled out, "You got me poo?" No one until then realized that he was the last one in the bathroom before then and unknowingly left his own self a present, but it wasn't the one that my mother was talking about. As Sammy flushed the toilet even my often stoic father was laughing at his colorful and very animated middle son.

My mother then made her directions a bit clearer as she told Sammy to look in the tank of the toilet. Sammy used to play in the toilet tank for some reason so he knew exactly where to find his big gift of the year. This sounds like a crazy place to hide something but for my mother, believe it or not, places like that were more of the norm. When Sammy came back in the living room, he was holding a plastic bag with two tickets inside. When he opened the bag he noticed a picture of Mickey Mouse plastered across the front of the tickets. He knew then exactly what his big present was, as he yelled out, "We're going to Disney World!" He was so excited because my mother decided to spend a little time with just him. The happiest kid in the world and his mother were going to the happiest place in the world. My mother always surprised all of us like that, even if at times we had to look in the toilet to find the surprise. I don't care what age you are, everyone loves Disney World and his favorite part of it was Animal Kingdom.

Ever since Sammy was small he loved all kinds of animals. Even with that BB gun he'd never let me shoot anything but targets and of course Jacob's butt. He even made me throw all of the fish we ever caught back. I don't think he thought about what happened to the worms but I never had the heart to tell him either. While they were away, Jacob and I for the most part stayed away from each other. We still didn't want to take a chance of hurting our mother again but also because my father was a little more in charge than usual. Our parents did so much for us for Christmas, and really the rest of the year too that we were going to at least try to act grown while she was gone. We missed our mother the week she was gone but all of us secretly missed Sammy even more. The house just wasn't the same without either one of them there but especially without Sammy.

When they finally returned, Sammy excitedly filled us in on all of their magical adventures, especially those that were related to animals in any way. He told us about the safari they went on and all of the exotic birds and giant fish they saw. My mother knew at least one of her boys was totally grateful and extremely happy. Sammy definitely enjoyed himself but we were just as happy that they were finally back home. When they were gone I did realize however, that it would soon be spring and then I would get a chance to use my Christmas present as well. Fishing season was right around the corner and that was another thing that Sammy was going to be almost as excited about. This time, instead of fishing from the bank, we got to go out in my new Jon boat. I knew life jackets would be a must, they even were when we fished from the bank, but Sammy never minded. I think he kind of looked at wearing his as some sort of fisherman's badge of honor.

I knew we didn't have many trips together of any sort left because I wouldn't be around much longer. I wasn't sure how he'd handle me being away and truthfully, I didn't know how I was going to handle it either. Sammy wasn't just my brother, he was my best friend and in a lot of ways I looked up to him as much as he ever did to me. He made me and even Jacob better people, that is, all except towards each other. So many outsiders thought Sammy was the one with the problems but it was never him at all. He was just like John Lennon said and more so of how we all should be more often. He was happy, and he was happy all of time. Our childhood was filled with many things. Some of which many would consider bad or even challenging but in reality it was mostly wonderful. Our lives at times didn't feel so easy but my parents always made it work. Most of the time they found a way to make it work well and with Sammy around, it was a lot of fun too.

When fishing season arrived, I, as promised made plans to take Sammy out on my little boat maiden voyage. Before I did though, I told him that it was bad luck for a boat not to have a name so I was bestowing that great honor upon him. He told me that he had to think about it for a while and he'd let me know. I wasn't expecting a delay in his decision but that's what I got. Anytime any of us thought we knew what Sammy was going to do or say, he'd surprise us with something we never thought of. Along with a true happiness, he had a creativity that was simplistic yet brilliant at the same time. In this case, this trait caused me to barely be able to wait to hear what he was going to name my big Christmas present for that year. I don't think either one of us slept a wink waiting for daybreak. It was finally our time to catch some of those much sought after fish from the James River on a boat this time.

We had the life jackets, worms, fishing poles and boat all loaded up and ready to go. When I thought it was the perfect time we left out on our first adventure in my new boat. My mother always made Sammy ride in the back seat even when he was older but because I had an old pickup truck, there was no back seat. He always seemed a little nervous sitting in the front and when Sammy got nervous he talked a lot—even more than usual. Everything we drove past, he'd quickly relate to fishing and some other aspect of his life. I felt like I was listening to one of the great philosophers of the past as I just drove and dared not to interrupt this young Socrates spurting out such wisdom. When we arrived at the loading ramp, Sammy got out to direct me into the water. As usual he forgot what his duties were and instead stood by the pier greeting everyone that was around with that ever-familiar "Good day, Good day."

After finally launching the boat, I realized that I had forgotten the oars. A Jon boat doesn't usually have a gas motor and I didn't have a trolling motor at the time either. The only way we could really go anywhere was by rowing the best we could with our hands. So basically, because of my forgetfulness we could only get as far as where we usually fished from on the bank. At first, I thought about going back home to get the oars, or maybe even rescheduling the trip but Sammy already had his line in the water and it was already bouncing back and forth with the first fish of the day on it. Sammy's eyes lit up even more than usual as he started telling me how to fish from that point on. He was now not only the first one to catch a fish but evidentially now a professional fisherman and fishing tour guide for the day. I reluctantly listened to his guidance while shaking my head at that cocky little turkey.

His knowledge, however, whether I originally doubted him or not, was proven when my rod also started jerking back and forth. We caught so many fish that day and we weren't even twenty feet from where we usually fished from on dry land. It must have been something about being in a boat because we'd never caught that many fish on shore before, and especially not as many of those blue whiskered catfish. After about an hour of pulling in one fish after another it began to drizzle. I asked Sammy if he wanted to go home and I'm sure since we were catching so many fish, he said, "No way, I'm killin 'em." Of course, that wasn't literal because he still made me throw all of the fish back, but we did catch a lot of fish that day. The drizzle became a rain, and then almost a downpour but Sammy dared me to move the boat an inch toward the dock until the fish stopped biting.

It seemed like the more it rained the more fish we caught. After about thirty minutes of catching a bunch more fish in what most would consider a downpour I noticed my feet were getting wet but not directly from the rain. Puddles were building up around my feet from a few tiny pinholes in the bottom of the boat. That problem is easily fixable on dry land but we weren't on dry land. I had a big cup so I began scooping the water out as fast as I could. After my third or fourth scoop Sammy yelled out, "I got it!" I thought he caught another fish but that's not what he "got". Sammy then yelled out "Israel I have the perfect name for your boat". He wasn't worried about how it was raining so hard the boat was filling up as fast as I could scoop it out or about the tiny holes that were pushing just as much water up into the boat. He named my little boat and wanted me to know exactly what he came up with right then and there.

Sammy giggled and yelled out again, *"Puddles, Puddles the Boat!"* I laughed with him as I thought in the maritime history of boats I doubt very seriously that any boat has ever been named *Puddles*, but it was definitely fitting at the time. I didn't want the boat to live up to its new name too much that day so we both laughed at the ingenious name Sammy came up with and began to pack up for the long twenty-yard hand paddle back to the dock. It took about ten times as long to get back as it would have taken with oars but Sammy enjoyed the wet ride and he was very proud of how he came up with such a clever name. Since the clouds were darker and more fluid than usual, he was also enjoying the sky boobies that he claimed he saw everywhere. He proudly let me know that he thought they were much more jiggly than on most days. When we finally made it home similar to how he excitedly told everyone about his time at Disney World, he did the same about our first day of fishing on my new boat.

He was once again proven to be a true fisherman because every time he told someone about his day, the waves, the fish, the puddles and even the sky boobies became bigger and bigger. Before long, he was speaking as if he had caught Moby Dick from the deck of the Titanic during a monsoon right before it sank. After that trip I began to realize that it wouldn't be long until my graduation time would finally arrive. There were many times that I didn't think I'd make it that far, but I did. I know even Jacob was happy for me, possibly for no other reason than I'd finally be leaving the house at the end of the summer. On my graduation day everyone dressed up in their Sunday best and they all made their way to the high school auditorium for the event. Sammy had a little bow tie on with the word *graduate* written across the front in my honor.

With graduation being at the high school, he was very comfortable being there. He was so comfortable that when the principal asked him to be the school's graduation greeter he had absolutely no problems obliging at all. That boy sat at the entrance and must have said, "Good day, Good day" five hundred times or more that day. He greeted every single person there in his comical yet ever so special way. When all the graduates sat down and he had welcomed each and every attendee he then came and sat down right beside me instead of sitting in the stands like everyone else who wasn't graduating that day. Nobody minded though, and I was honored to have my best friend sit right next to me on the day of my greatest accomplishment thus far. When they called my name to receive my diploma, I think Sammy was happier than I was.

He stood up on his chair and clapped and cheered. He even ran down to meet me at the foot of the steps as I was getting off of the stage. The whole auditorium rose to their feet and cheered with him. I knew it wasn't for me but that made me even more proud to graduate in such a way. Later that night, Sammy's mood turned to something quite the opposite though. I knew he realized I'd be leaving soon but I don't think it fully hit him until after we got back home that night. The one thing Sammy always had trouble with was the concept of time. I was leaving but not for two more months, so we still had time to check out some more sky boobies, do a few more art projects and go out on a few more fishing trips. Once I let him know that, he didn't need to hear anything else because that was enough to change his mood back to where it was earlier in the auditorium. At the time, whether you call this using him or not, and even though it wasn't meant that way, Jacob and I taught Sammy how to go up to the cutest girls in our school and flirt with them.

One of his philandering trips gained me my first real girlfriend, April, and like most people, I think she liked Sammy more than she did me. I didn't really mind though because heck, I did too. She was a very nice girl and she would often come over our house to play Uno or Yahtzee or some other board game with us several times a week. I think Sammy had a little crush on her too so we often took him with us when we went places or did certain things. One of those times was the day after graduation. April was going to the SPCA to pick out a new puppy. I knew Sammy would love to go along so we planned to take him with us. I always knew Sammy had a nurturing, even healing side to him. He always took such care of everything he touched, especially animals, so I knew he'd love visiting the kennel. The next day when we got there Sammy walked by each and every cage. One by one, he wanted to spend a little time with each and every dog so none would feel left out.

The dogs actually seemed to calm down quite a bit when Sammy said whatever it was he was saying to them. I thought I was watching a dog whisperer but then I just remembered—no, it's just my brother, my very, very special little brother. April finally picked out a puppy and called Sammy over to get his seemingly all-knowing approval. I think Sammy thought he still had to flirt with her because he winked at April, as to say, "That's the one, babe." April giggled and off we went—me, April, April's new puppy and the newly-crowned prince of puppies. We took the puppy back to our house to play with it for a while and being that Sammy was so good and loving with the dog it gave me an idea. The only problem was, it was an idea that I would definitely need to get approval on before ever enacting. We never had a pet growing up but after seeing Sammy at that kennel, I knew Sammy would definitely give any animal everything it could ever need.

After I told my mother how Sammy reacted when he thought I'd be leaving sooner than I was and how he so lovingly treated all of the dogs at the kennel I don't think my mother had any other choice than to agree with my planned departing gift. Once my mother gave her permission I asked Sammy if he wanted to go back to where April got her puppy from. He could hardly say yes fast enough. During this trip in my truck, all of his enlightenment and philosophies were about dogs. When we got back to the kennel, before we went in, I told him that I wanted to talk to him for a minute. He was excited to go in but he also at least pretended like he wanted to hear what I had to say. I told him that I'd be leaving soon for college. Once again, his face dropped in sadness but I also told him that I talked our mother and she said he could have a puppy, more or less in my place.

Whenever he missed me he had a buddy kind of like I was to him to help make things a little easier. I was a little hurt because he definitely heard the part where our mother said he could have a puppy and then he jumped out of the truck and rushed in the kennel as if I had already said all that he needed hear. As he looked through the dog enclosures this time he was even more involved. He took all of the time that he needed to pick out just the right one. I don't think any of those dogs realized how blessed they'd be if they were the one that he chose. As he got to the cage of one of the scruffier looking older dogs, I tried to keep him moving. He wasn't having any of it though. He had to give that little ruffled guy an equal and fair chance too. As Sammy held that previously unwanted dog the darn thing started peeing on him. I just knew Sammy would move on then, especially after he yelled out, "Yuck" several times. Sammy didn't do that though.

He picked that little pee-er up and once again winked but this time it was at me as to signal that he had made his choice. I've learned not to doubt any of Sammy's decisions so this time it was me, Sammy and that lucky dog on the way home. Sammy was happy after fishing, he was definitely happy after returning home from Disney World. In truth, Sammy was happy all of the time but I've never seen him as happy as he was that day with his new dog. This time he didn't have to take any time considering a name. He knew what that dogs name was from the minute it sprinkled all over him. When Sammy got home he proudly introduced me and everyone else to Puddles, Puddles his new dog. I, as I so often did back then just shook my head and laughed at my younger brother. I did realize though, with a boat and a dog named Puddles, there was no way to forget either one of them now.

By this time, Jacob and I had for the most part been doing our own thing for quite a while, but for one last time before I left, I planned to take both of my brothers out to the field down the street from our house to cloud gaze one last time before I left for college. This time, we'd have to take Puddles the dog with us. Since Sammy had very much made him an equal part of our family from the second we brought him home, that was more than fine with me. On that day, while we were lying there, Sammy didn't call out a single sky boobie. He was seeing things like dog bones and dog toys in the clouds more so than anything else. I knew for once I had made a good decision in helping him find something that would be very important to him, but also something else that he could take care of like he did with me without even realizing how much he actually did. Jacob and I were on common ground under the sky looking at those clouds. Basically, he just wished me well, and because Sammy didn't do it, he called out the sky boobie sightings for the day.

Sammy may not have found them himself, but he and I still laughed every time Jacob did. That night, I packed up all of my stuff and put it in the back of my old truck. I wanted to be ready to leave the next morning. As I was packing, I looked up and saw Sammy looking down at me through the window. Just like when our mother locked Jacob and me out of the house, I knew Sammy was going to miss me and I definitely knew I was going to miss him right back. As Sammy was waving and comically throwing a few flexes up, I saw Puddles jump up and lick him on the side of his cheek. I thought to myself, *Puddles is doing his job as planned,* so as Sammy disappeared from sight most likely chasing Puddles I finished loading up and started feeling a little better about my own new adventure.

When the next morning came, I left early, long before anyone else woke up. I had already said my goodbyes and I didn't want my going to college to be any sadder than it already was, besides, I didn't want Jacob throwing a party that early in the morning either. On the six-hour drive to my new college I think I spent the most time thinking about how appreciative I was that my parents gave up so much of their own lives so we could have the lives we had. Over the next few months I also realized that unknowingly I took many things for granted back at home. Things like toilet paper and food. Those things were so expensive that when I wasn't at school, I had to work all of the time myself just to have the necessities. I really didn't have time to do anything else, but I was bound and determined to make it work just like my parents always did for our family. Regardless of my busyness, I did make sure I was always around on Sunday evenings. That was the time that either I called my family or my family called me. Everyone, including Sammy, seemed fine with me being gone and besides, Puddles was obviously still doing his job.

Armageddon

My first semester roared by and before I knew it, it was time for spring break. Now, the rich kids may have been going to Daytona Beach or Mexico or some other exotic destination but us working class students were going back home for the break. Other than not being able to afford to go anywhere else, I wanted to go home anyway. I missed my parents, Sammy and maybe even Jacob a little bit. I even missed both of the Puddles—the dog and my boat—so in response to my newly found maturity I headed home the very second my last class was over. When I got home, it was as if I just got back from a war or somewhere more important than where I actually was because everyone was so happy to see me. My father even shockingly took a day off from work that week. What overwhelmed me the most was almost as soon as I got back Jacob told me that he wanted to go fishing with me and Sammy the week I was home.

I definitely thought to myself I need to go away more often if this is what happens when I come back. I told Jacob I knew he really didn't like fishing, but he insisted. I also knew it was supposed to be drizzling again around the end of the week. Remembering back to how many fish Sammy and I caught on our last rainy trip, I thought maybe we could try to duplicate our efforts then. Like life seems to do, that week flew by and Saturday, our planned fishing day was upon us. For the first time in history, Jacob and Puddles would be joining us too. This time when we got to the dock Sammy once again duplicated his rounds of "Good days" but Jacob did help unload the boat. I not only managed to remember to bring the oars this time, I also had an electric trolling motor that I bought from that nosey old neighbor whose wife called the police on us that time. My plan was to roam the river until everyone caught a bunch of fish. That strategy worked to perfection for quite a while.

The rain, as it did on the last trip brought the fish in once more. This time, however, with Jacob joining us, it looked like we'd catch even more than we did on the maiden voyage. Once the fish took a break in one place, I'd crank up that little electric motor and chase them down again. I know if Puddles could have held a rod with his scruffy little paws he would have caught a few bass or catfish that day. Once our arms became sore from all of the reeling, we deciding to head back in. As we headed towards the pier something got my attention. I probably should have been more aware of it earlier, but I really wasn't. It was a large boat that had been racing back and forth across the river the whole time we were out. I first noticed it because of its size and speed, but later because of its name. Sammy named my little boat *Puddles* because of all the puddles that built up under our feet during our last rainy fishing trip, but I had no idea why that big boat was named "*The Armageddon*".

It wasn't necessarily following us at any time. It was just so big and fast that when it sped up and down the river, it seemed to be everywhere all at once. My absolute acknowledgement about that big boats presence came as we were headed towards the dock to put my boat up for the day. That huge boat was heading right for us and this time we were the ones being ignored. Its captain obviously didn't realize what he was getting ready to do. Jacob started screaming first, as both of us tried to grab Sammy and Puddles to help them jump to safety. That didn't work though. *The Armageddon* ran completely over my little Jon boat with all of us still inside. The collision threw me under the water for what seemed like forever, but when I finally resurfaced, I saw Puddles and Jacob swimming towards the shore, but I didn't see Sammy anywhere. My heart sank like never before.

I knew Sammy had his life jacket on but I didn't know where he was or whether that huge boat's propeller tore him to pieces. Jacob and I started screaming out for Sammy over and over again but there wasn't even a peep as to his whereabouts. Absolute terror set in as the man in that big boat finally realized what he had done and turned back around to check on his negligence. As he drove up next to me, an older shirtless tanned man pulled me out of the water and into that big boat. I couldn't get the words out that my little brother was missing because before I had the chance, the man pointed at something bobbing up and down in the water. My heart all but disappeared in my chest this time because I already knew who it was. What would have taken me a half an hour or more to get to in my little boat only took him seconds to arrive at. It was Sammy and he was covered in blood floating face down in the water. I jumped back in the river again to retrieve what I thought was only going to be the lifeless body of my little brother.

When I rolled him over he wasn't breathing so I quickly handed his limp body out of the water and up to the man leaning over the side of his boat. The man frantically started pumping on Sammy's chest and breathing into his bloody mouth in regulated intervals. Almost as soon as I climbed back into the boat Sammy started sputtering up the water that had so viciously settled in his lungs. An absolute heartfelt relief came over me but it was plain to see that he was still pretty torn up. *Another damn trip to the white house for him, I thought, but at least he was still alive.* Jacob, in his fear and caring, had already called the police. Thankfully the rescue squad was waiting for us at the dock within minutes of us getting there. The team of men snatched Sammy from the big boat and directed us to follow close behind. As the ambulance sped off, Jacob, myself and Puddles hurried to my truck as fast as we could.

Jacob wisely had already called our mother at work to tell her what happened. I know that was a terrible call, but we knew her and my father were already on the way to the hospital by then as well. Almost as soon as we got into my truck, Jacob started screaming at me. I didn't respond because I felt I deserved it. I didn't see how I could have prevented any of the events of that day but a guilt came over me like never before. Jacob kept asking me why I ever had to come back home but I just kept driving because in truth I was asking myself that exact same question. As I drove, I kept thinking back to the time that our mother locked us out of the house. I remembered her absolute disappointment, especially in me. To me, that was the worst punishment she ever issued but this time I felt I deserved much worse. I wasn't worried about getting in trouble this time though, I was just praying that Sammy was going to be okay.

It was my responsibility to make sure he was that day, and simply put, I didn't do that. As we pulled into the emergency room parking lot, as expected, both of my parents' cars were already there. Jacob jumped out and ran inside right after we parked but I couldn't. For the first time in my life I just sat in my truck and prayed. I prayed so hard and so loud that Puddles started howling. I was pleading with God as hard as I knew how and I guess that little fluffy black dog was as well. When I thought I had begged enough I finally gained the courage to go inside that stupid white house myself. Once inside, my mother and father ran up to me, as I'm sure they did to Jacob when he went in earlier. They didn't seem to blame me, or have anything negative to say, but it didn't matter. I blamed myself enough for everyone. Sammy was back in surgery for what we later found out was a broken arm and some other pretty serious lacerations. Other than that, thank God, he would be more or less okay this time.

The thing about my parents was, even though they always treated Sammy the same, they knew he wasn't. We all knew in many ways his life was more delicate and all of us had to protect that fact. I really thought I had done that up until that point, but not this time. This time I failed him. Sammy spent the night in the hospital but he did get to come home the next day. After he went to sleep that night I overheard my parents talking through the thin walls in our old house. I know they thought they were having a private conversation but every word still stained my soul. My mother was talking about how scared she was and how they needed to protect Sammy now more than ever. To them, that protection meant even if it was from me, his oldest brother. I was supposed to look out for him no matter what, and regardless of the situation, I didn't do that and evidentially they felt that way too. What made matters worse was all through the night I heard my mother crying again but this time it was about what could have happened.

You can call it shame or even cowardice but I didn't think I could look any of my family members in the eye the next morning, so I headed back to school in the middle of the night. I don't know what I would have done if that fishing trip would have killed that boy. I took all of the precautions, I did everything I knew how to do, but it wasn't enough. I was so thankful that Sammy would be okay, but I wasn't so sure of how long it would take for me to get there. The next day, my mother called about four or five times and multiple times throughout my first week back at school but I wouldn't answer. I was just too immature and too ashamed to talk to any of them. This overwhelming guilt went on for well over a month. During that time, I don't think I slept for more than a couple hours a night or went to class but a few times. My grades dropped to the point where I was in danger of failing out, and I didn't care.

I did eventually schedule an appointment with my academic advisor to see if there was any way of saving my faltering college endeavor. When I met with the advisor she suggested a study abroad program for the summer to try and boost up my GPA. I knew if I went, I could possibly make up for my academic shortcomings, but also wouldn't have to go back home for the summer either. I did talk to my family after that original avoidance, but it was never on a regular basis and quite frankly, it was never the same. Sammy did eventually heal and he definitely didn't blame me or hold any grudges. Just like with the life jacket, I think he looked at his new scars as another fisherman's badge of honor but I still have to say, from what almost happened and the guilt that followed, I was still bleeding from the incident. Sammy and I piddled around with painting so much growing up that I eventually became pretty good at it.

Someone else evidentially thought the same because I never thought I'd go to college on an art scholarship, but I did. Now, to save my academic standing and the money that the school gave me, I had to go to another country for the summer to have a chance to bail myself out. As irony would have it, that other country was Israel. Before my parents had kids, and I guess when they had a little more money they actually visited the country. They obviously liked it there because they named me, their first child after the place. I guess this time, the word irony was a massive understatement once again. This unexpected journey had me going to Israel with two other guys who were also art students. When the three of us arrived at Ben Gurion, Israel's national airport, the first thing I noticed was the massive amount of armed security. Some of which approached our little group while we were waiting for our bags.

They started asking a bunch of questions. At first, I thought we may end up in jail, if for no other reason, than unknowingly being Americans in the wrong place at the wrong time. We told the men that we were college students from the U.S studying abroad for the summer and we'd be staying at the Waldorf Astoria in Jerusalem. After the men verified our story and checked our credentials and rummaged through our luggage thoroughly they let us go but we were still very much experiencing that suspect-vibe throughout the airport. About the time our original caustic greeting to the country wore off, it was time for us to get off that old double decker bus that took us to the hotel. Once we arrived I realized I'd never seen a building quite like that. The outside of the building had a pronounced Middle Eastern flair. It had these huge sand-colored stones for walls and large hourglass shaped windows with that mystical Saracenic Arabian point at the top. It was impressive and really big, but the inside of that place was even more majestic.

One of the first things that grabbed my attention were all of the wrought iron clocks on every wall. The man at the hotel that helped us with our bags told us the clocks represented all of the different languages of the world and the great diversity of their country. There was also a giant rotunda with a sky light at the top and nine floors of the most elegant rooms of any hotel anywhere in the world. I may have still been running away in a sense but I can remember thinking I have ran to somewhere pretty darn nice. If there was anything negative about the hotel at all it was having to share a room with my two new traveling companions. I laughed about that though because heck, I've shared a room with two other people pretty much my whole life. The other student's names were Theodore and William.

Holy Land

Sarcastically, once I got to know my two new roommates a little better I started calling them Bill and Ted after the movie *Bill and Ted's Excellent Adventures*. Their nicknames seemed to stick too because I know we were all hoping this trip would be our own version of an excellent adventure. Back at our college, before I left, my professor submitted one of my paintings that actually came in third place in a national art competition. I was told that the art from the top five students was going to be advertised and used as collegiate promotional material throughout the country and probably around the world. It was an unexpected honor, but by the suggestion of my professor my time in Israel was to be spent figuring out why my painting didn't do any better than third place. I always thought to myself that was a much better prize than I could have ever wish for but my professor evidentially didn't feel the same way.

I really didn't know how to do any more than I did with that first painting but I definitely knew that I didn't want any more inspiration coming from any other hurt family members, especially if it was Sammy. During our first week in Jerusalem we were more or less free to roam our new surreal surroundings. The first few days we saw the majority of the most commonly visited places. We went to the Dome of the Rock, the Sea of Galilee, the Mount of Olives, the Wailing Wall, and the Church of the Holy Sepulcher, where Jesus himself was crucified. We even ate at a two-hundred-year-old café named Zalatimo's. They served these crispy cheese desserts that none of us could get enough of. Those scrumptious things were called Mutabaks and they were absolutely addictive.

Our classes were at Jerusalem University in the heart of the city. It was specifically located on Mt. Zion. That was the resting place of King David—the same guy who stood up to Goliath in the Bible. We definitely felt we had a lot to live up to say the least. Bill and Ted, unlike me, jumped right in to their work and often finished what they needed to do each day way before I ever got started. Because of this, they often left me by myself, staring at an easel with no clue of what I was going to do next. It's not that my first painting couldn't get better, I just didn't know how to make it any better at the time. It was on one of those evenings alone that I kept feeling like I was being watched. I didn't see anyone around but I just felt like there was someone watching me from somewhere. When that feeling became too great I'd look around in each of the nearby classrooms and down a few halls but I never found anyone. Being summer, there were only a few students around anyway so I just wrote it off to my imagination and returned to basically wasting time in front of that easel a little longer.

Another hour of confusion went by on this one particular day when I just gave up. I realized that I wasn't going to make any great breakthroughs that day or probably ever, so I decided to pack my stuff up and head back to the hotel. It was getting late and being that some of the areas that I had to walk through to get back to the hotel were pretty sketchy, I decided to take a bus back. I waited at the bus stop for about thirty minutes but when no one came I didn't have any other choice but to grab all my stuff up and start heading back on foot. As I began walking an old taxi pulled up beside me. There was already someone else in the back seat, but I had all of my art supplies almost falling out of my hands—to include that big dumb easel—so I accepted the drivers offer without a second thought.

I'd seen similar cars driving around the city but I didn't know what kind it was so, if for no other reason than to make small talk, I asked the driver what it was. He proudly told me we were riding in a 1970 Sussita. As he was telling me about how that particular model was the last car ever to be manufactured in Israel I tried to politely listen until I noticed that we were headed in what I thought was the opposite direction of the hotel. I didn't say anything at first because I figured he knew his country's roads better than I so we went on chatting for a little longer. It wasn't until after we crossed a long stone bridge that I knew something wasn't quite kosher. My instincts were proven correct because that once nice man pulled out a small hand gun almost as soon as we reached the other side of the bridge. The once jovial driver now had one hand on the steering wheel while the other was on a newly revealed chrome revolver pointed directly at my ribs. In the movies you always see the good guy knock the gun away from the criminal. Then the so-called hero would roll out the door to safety but in real life it simply isn't like that.

I figured whatever was happening wasn't a robbery because they would have done that long before then. I just didn't have a clue what was going on. As we made our final turn down a long dirt road, I tried to at least pretend like I was a movie star and started opening the passenger door as gingerly as I could. Ignorantly, I was hoping not to be noticed but that old door squeaked so loudly from just the attempt that the gun that was once pointed at my side was now raised to my head. To confirm their control of the situation, the man in back seat followed suite when he pressed his own gun against the back of my head as well. I knew then, with two guns pointed at my poor cabeza that I was doomed if I didn't follow whatever directions they gave me. As we reached the end of that bumpy dirt road we stopped at what looked like an old abandoned factory.

By the looks of the place it must have been out of business for as long as the Sussita Motor Company had been out of the automobile industry. As the car stopped, the driver directed me to stay where I sat and the man in the back seat made sure his gun was still pointed at my head just in case I had any other ideas. The driver that disappeared into the building wasn't gone long, but when he returned, it was my turn to go inside. The main thing I noticed once entering the building was the stench. With no exaggeration, that place smelled like death. It must have been some kind of old meat processing plant or something similar because the rankness was so abusive that my nose started running profusely. After we were inside, the man who had been driving led me into an old meat locker. After he forced me inside that pitch-black metal box he slammed the door shut. I heard chains being wrapped around the door handle, and soon after, a click from a padlock ensuring my entrapment. It was as dark as death in that dingy makeshift prison.

Slime was dripping from whatever inhabited that place before me. I couldn't see anything at all so I felt my way around until I found the driest area to sit down. I wanted to try and figure out if there was any way out of that unexpected and terribly pungent confinement. What I'm guessing was about an hour went by, and since I didn't hear anything from the outside any longer I got up and slammed my shoulder against the door a few times. That thick, insulated metal door didn't budge an inch, even though I rammed it over and over again. Once I realized I'd be in that dark and dirty place until someone decided to let me out I almost laughed thinking about if my capturers wanted a ransom, they definitely picked the wrong person. I knew there was no way my parents could pay any type of bounty.

My parents didn't have any money and obviously neither did I. Again, I almost chuckled as I thought, *Hell, I was just a broke and failing college kid studying abroad.* After I failed at even coming close to budging that huge metal door, what felt like another hour passed and once again I heard voices. This time however, it was a heated argument. It sounded a lot like the rants that Jacob and I used to have, but this one was maybe even a little worse. This was a feud that I could tell one man had the definite upper hand over the other. As the chains rattled once again, the padlock clicked in reverse this time. The same men who stole me earlier that day both grabbed me under my arms and led me down a long-carpeted hall. I didn't see either of their guns this time but I definitely remembered they both had one and both of them were pointed at my head not long ago. It was so strange because the further we went through that giant building, the nicer the carpet got and the less abandoned the building looked.

When we reached our intended destination, that same old factory building looked more like a modern-day office or classroom than the disgusting place we started out in. The room that I was taken to contained a long oak conference table surrounded by eight really nice black leather chairs. There was also a white board that stretched across half of one of the walls and a modern computer in the corner sitting on another little cherry wood desk. There was even a phone sitting on the conference table that looked to be still hooked up based on the amber light that glowed on top. The taxi driver who led me there, alone this time, didn't say a word. He just pulled out my chair like a waiter would at a fine restaurant. I think he was the one who was just scolded by whomever else he was arguing with. The reason those were my beliefs other than him politely pulling out my chair was the overly flushed look on his face.

That's a look I've postured a thousand times when Jacob would hit himself and then hide in the closet so I'd get a whipping when our mother got home. That man may not have gotten a beating that day, but he definitely lost some respect and it showed so heavily on his stubbled rosy-red plumply aged cheeks. As I sat there by myself for a few minutes, the original man left but another man entered the room and closed the door behind him. This guy looked nothing like the guys who started all of the craziness that day. Those men were middle aged and kind of frumpy with salt-and-pepper-colored hair. They both wore wrinkled clothes that definitely had a little stench of their own on them. They could have almost passed for brothers themselves but not this new man. This man was obviously wearing an expensive suit and he had a very sullen yet distinct look about him. He was definitely of Middle Eastern decent but he spoke without any sort of accent.

He seemed genuinely concerned about how I was so violently brought to that old building, especially how I was thrown into that terrible meat locker. Just by appearance this new man looked to have more money than I'd ever have, so again, I was doubting that he wanted any type of ransom from a college kid—as if it could be paid anyway. I was also almost sure that if anyone wanted to kill me, they would have surely done it by now. I kept thinking the only thing I was sure of was that none of the events of the day made any sense at all. As he sat down across from me at the table, this time both of the original two men came back in. Instead of carrying guns, they had some of those cheesy Mutabaks and that stout Israeli coffee from Zalatimo's. When this happened I thought to myself, this kidnapping seemed to be turning into some kind of civil business meeting that evidentially included snacks.

Regardless of his politeness, I had an overwhelming feeling that the well-dressed man who was now directly talking to me was a lot of things, but I doubted very seriously any of them included being someone who didn't get his way. There wasn't a great deal of beating around the bush on his part. He told me that he saw my painting somewhere, which he never disclosed where that actually was, and wanted me to paint something very similar for his son. I just about fell out of my seat. I almost laughed out loud because I knew full-well that I was far from a professional artist. I tried to tell him that but he hardly let me speak at all. I wanted to tell him that I was just a college student who, for the most part, was already failing at what he seemed to be demanding. I just knew he had to have me mixed up with someone else. Besides, why did he have his men kidnap me to do something I probably would have at least tried if he would have just asked?

As he spoke, he definitely relayed an urgency to his request. It seemed I had to do what he was asking, and I had to do it right then. The two men from before brought my original painting in and set it up on a wooden easel in the corner of the room. They also brought the rest of my art supplies and a fresh canvas in with them. My idea at that point was just to give the new man my other painting and hopefully that would be enough for him to let me go, but confusingly enough, that's not what he wanted. This request was so strange that it was almost comical, but the funniness ended anytime I thought about the ride there just a few hours earlier. This man was serious. I wanted to tell him that I originally poured my heart into my first painting because of what happened to my brother, Sammy, that day on the river with the Armageddon. By then I had somewhat realized that I couldn't have prevented what had happened, but I also had so much guilt. I had to release what could have happened out of my mind. I guess I chose to paint my feelings away.

That painting, and the way I threw myself into it was the only relief that I could create for myself at the time. To me, if anything, that part of my original work was the only thing that could have been so special about it. When my professor noticed there could have been more, the only thing I felt he could have been talking about was how much anger and fear I inadvertently expressed in the painting as well. As I poured my heart into the first one, all of my emotions came out and I think whoever judged the thing saw the love and compassion that was definitely expressed in it as well. My professor, on the other hand must have also seen the pain and anguish that may have been hidden a little better. In the art world that's called a diptych. It really was two pictures in one. I was secretly glad that I wasn't overly rewarded for that part of my work even though I didn't even realize it was there at first myself.

When I stood up to get started, I guess the well-dressed man noticed me looking at the phone. He openly assured me that it was functional however clearly told me not to use it. Originally, I thought, if I ever got a moment by myself, I'd try to call for help. The problem was, I didn't know if Israel had something like 911 or who I would call that could actually help in this strange situation. Soon after my warning all of the men did leave the room and once again left me locked inside. This was one of those times like in the cartoons where you see a miniature angel on one shoulder and a little devil on the other. If I listened to the angel I'd just get to work without asking anymore questions or keep wondering how in the hell I got in this ridiculous predicament. On the other hand, there's the little red guy. If I followed that daggon joker's advice I'd find a way to barricade the door and make as many phone calls as needed until someone came to rescue me.

I think it's obvious who I listened to the most growing up but those guys had guns and they were right outside the door. So, at least for the time being, I decided to try and paint something. The problem with true painting is, it's not something you can just do in an hour or two, or even longer in many cases. There are outlines and layers that have to be applied. I knew the last painting took me almost a week to finish and that was pretty much working around the clock on most of the days. I felt this one was going to take much longer and I knew damn well I didn't want to be in that place any longer than I had to be. In the first painting, I felt like every emotion that I was experiencing had to be put on, brush stroke by brush stroke, with such care. The kind of care that I felt I should have given Sammy. I honestly believed in many ways that painting was some sort of an additional apology.

Now I thought, how could I paint on demand considering what it took for me to create the last one? Regardless of any of my wandering thoughts, I readied the canvas and spread out my brushes and acrylics, if for no other reason than to pretend like I knew where this new forced project was headed. As I dipped my brush into the paint, I began about two thirds of the way up the canvas. I chose the darker colors for the outline, still not knowing where this attempt would go. I've always loved looking up at the clouds with my brothers and I really enjoyed painting them too, so I decided to start there with a cerulean blue. Now, cerulean blue was not only my favorite color but it was also my favorite shade of any color. That blue is almost as beautiful as the sky itself, and as I spread that magnificent color from one corner to the next I couldn't get that damn phone that I was dared not to touch out of my head.

****

I have to say, at least I thought about doing the right thing probably a little longer than I did when I was younger, but either way that little red devil won again. With my new misguided confidence leading the way I went up to the door and pressed my ear against it. I wanted to make sure I didn't hear anyone before following my old red friend's perceived advice. Once I didn't hear anything I remembered I had to dial 1-0-0 before reaching the United States. I may not have known how but I did know if anyone could help in such a ridiculous situation my parents could. Before I could overthink the specifics their phone started ringing. After four rings it seemed no one was going to answer. I thought to myself I'd have to leave a message that sounded something like, "Hello mom, its Israel and I've been kidnapped in Israel, I don't know where I am specifically, or what else to say, okay love you, bye".

The thought of leaving such an absurd message definitely didn't seem right to me, but what else could I do? The red man won again. As I was actually preparing to leave such a ridiculous message, thank God, I heard the phone pick up. I heard what I would usually consider the most welcomed voice on the other end say, "Good day, Good day." It was obviously Sammy and he was super excited to hear from me. I really wanted to talk to him too but considering my circumstances that simply wasn't the best time to catch up. I kept trying to ask him to get our mother or father or even Jacob but in all of his elation he just kept talking over me. He wasn't listening to anything that I thought I really needed to say. When I tried to speak he would just tell me about Puddles and Jacob. He told me about how his fisherman's battle scars had all healed so well. He even spoke about our parents even though he wouldn't let me talk to them.

The entire call couldn't have lasted more than three minutes but Sammy got so many words in I was almost dizzy from all of his stories. Unfortunately, the two men from outside obviously heard the sounds from my attempts at a two-sided conversation too. They came back in the room with more of a similar attitude as they had when they threw me in that nasty meat locker and ripped the phone cord out of the wall. It really looked like I was going to have to paint something for real then. When things simmered down I put the brush back in my hand and thought about Sammy's voice. I just heard it for the first time in a while. Thinking about him, a smile came over my face and my heart, regardless of where I was or what I was being forced to do. His voice, even though it was only for a few minutes, gave me all of the inspiration I'd ever need. Just like before, bit by bit and shade by line, I started building colors on top of colors until before I knew it, slowly but surely, a rough outline of an amazing landscape was developing.

It was becoming glaringly obvious to me the more I thought about Sammy, the more that painting started coming to life. If I was truthful with myself the more I felt him there in the room with me. Even though it was my imagination this time, it was just like when we were kids painting together. I knew the two armed men were outside the door sitting in folding chairs. I guess they felt like they had to make sure I didn't do anything else but paint, but I didn't care, I wanted to paint then. This new painting began to come together with an ease that I'd never experienced before, not even with the last. This time oddly enough, I painted without anger, guilt, or even fear. It still wasn't a fast process, but by the next morning without a single break or any sort of hesitation I was completely finished and even proud of how Sammy helped me once again.

I painted throughout the night without realizing any time went by but this time, unlike the last, I could tell this one was special myself. It definitely came from somewhere or someone else. When the well-dressed man came back, he saw what I, and now I guess he was blessed with. He then sat down at the table and placed his head in his hands as if to try and hold back his tears. He repeatedly apologized for making me paint in such a way but he also assured me his two men would take me back to the university very soon. He let me know he'd be back in an hour, and then I could leave. I guess as strange as it has been, this particular unexpected adventure would be concluded at that time. As he left, he told the two men to bring in some more of those treats and that rich Israeli coffee. The same men who threw me into that old, disgusting meat locker, and later who ripped the phone out of the wall, were now sitting at the table with me, eating snacks and drinking coffee like we were all old friends.

After every bit of an hour passed, the man in charge returned as he said he would. This time however, he brought a young man in a wheel chair in with him. This frail brown-haired young man was probably just a few years younger than me, maybe about Jacob's age. I could instantly tell he was born with the same chromosome difference that Sammy had. That was the difference that caused so many of Sammy's stupid trips to the white house, but this young man looked like he'd seen places like that even more. Once inside the room he struggled to roll himself over to the easel where the new painting rested. He eventually made it all the way, but he wouldn't allow anyone to help him over or out of his chair. After he finally reached his destination he stood all the way up and grabbed the painting with one hand at the top of each of the corners of the canvas.

He looked at that painting deeper than I knew how to look at anything. After quite a few moments of gazing he sat back down in his wheel chair and then looked up at me. He didn't say anything but a look of absolute gratefulness spread across his face. I could tell at one time this young man possessed a similar sparkle in his eyes that I always saw in Sammy's. There was a difference though, his was quite a bit dimmer as if it may not have much longer to shine. It's not that this realization made the situation make any more sense, it's just now the reasoning didn't matter. I knew I would do almost anything for Sammy even if it didn't make any sense to anyone else, and that's exactly what a father did for his son.   Like I've always said there is an absolute beauty and a definite innocence in people that are born with what Sammy and this young man were born with. Not many people speak about it. In truth, they may not even know that kind of beauty is possible, but it's there, and it was there in that young man without question as well.

My thoughts then flooded towards my brother, and all of the struggles he had, especially early on in his life, and then more recently with our accident with *The Armageddon.* This young man's health issues seemed to be much worse, maybe even to the point where he was on his own forced time schedule. As the well-dressed man turned to me, he nodded and grinned in appreciation. He then signaled for the two men to take me out of the room and back to that old Sussita. We sat outside in the car for a while until the grateful father from inside came out to meet us one last time. He walked over to the car and handed me a large manila envelope with strict instructions not to open it until after I was dropped off. He then patted the car as you would a horse to getty up and off we went.

While driving back to the university, the men were talking as if nothing ever happened, but whether on purpose or not they did add a little light on the events of the past two days. When someone turns in a painting for a competition or other types of academic projects, a summary of their motivation or inspiration usually accompanies it. Without me knowing where it was going I remembered that my professor made me do that very thing. I didn't lie or try to hide anything. I let everyone know in the description of my original work that my painting was for my own very special brother. I didn't get into all the specifics but that was the gist. That well-dressed man or maybe his son evidentially could relate to what I wrote and wanted the same for themselves. In his case, I guess,… well I now know, that young man had a father that could make almost anything happen, which as crazy as that sounds is exactly what he did.

What's even stranger, is I somewhat understand that now. I was feeling a peace that I hadn't felt in quite a long time. Listening to my now friendly kidnappers inadvertently filling the pieces to the puzzle helped a lot. Knowing a little more, and coming to an understanding that I really did create something without all of that anger, guilt and pain all mixed in was refreshing. The men finally dropped me off near the university, as if it was a real taxi ride. They wished me well and left as uneventfully as when they picked me up. I stood there dumbfounded at the past couple days knowing that no one in their right mind would ever believe such a tale. I knew I couldn't take any credit for that painting though. I was just the vessel for a gift that would continue to keep giving to others well into the future.

Old Gypsy Woman

I think at that point for the first time in a long time I was finally like Mr. Lennon said I should be. I was happy, happier than I'd been in a long time. Another reason I was quite happy was when I opened that big manila envelope there was $10,000 of cash inside. It was all in crisp, new American one-hundred-dollar bills. That thankful father, out of his gratitude, gave me an amount that I'd never seen before. I never had money like that and I doubted very seriously that my parents or anyone I knew ever had that much either. I immediately came to the realization that with such a blessing, I had to use it for something that would help my family in some way. There was no way I'd waste even a penny. Instead of going directly back to the hotel, I went into the school. Bill and Ted were already inside working. They must not have missed me very much because they didn't say a word about me not going back to the room for the past two days.

I guess they probably thought I was just inspired by something and had been working around the clock as artist sometimes do. If that's what they thought, they'd never know how right they were. I decided never to tell anyone about my kidnapping, mainly because if for no other reason, more good came from it than bad. The whole situation was so strange, and even scary at times but later I'd learn how helpful that event would be to my life, and to the lives of those I love the most. Even though I never told anyone about what happened in that old building, there was one person that I didn't have to tell. The day before we left Israel, I was once again visited the Wailing Wall. It was my favorite place in Israel and I realized I may never see it again in person so I wanted to spend as much time as I could there. While admiring the appreciation that so many were showing and receiving from that holy destination, an old gypsy woman walked up to me.

Surprisingly, she reached out and grabbed my hand. Having my money safely hidden in the room, I tried to tell the woman that I didn't have anything to give her. She didn't care about getting paid though as she began speaking as much as Sammy ever did. I definitely didn't want any more strange things to happen during my trip abroad but the more I tried to resist that old woman's grip the tighter she'd squeeze my hand, and unfortunately for me the more she spoke. My hand almost turned blue before she turned it over to get a closer inspection. At first, I was mostly just trying to be polite by letting her continue, but when she started inspecting the varied creases on my right palm she started saying things that she shouldn't have had any way of knowing. She told me about the secret that I was trying to keep, and almost every detail about what happened in that old building. I have to admit, I was a little more than intrigued because she described everything with such accuracy that the hair on the back of my neck stood up. At first, I wondered if she was there herself because of how detailed her descriptions were.

I also thought, since she knew about the money, down to the exact amount, she may have been trying to scam me in some way to get at it, but that wasn't it. She never wanted a penny as she spoke about my past but also about what she claimed was going to be my extremely turbulent future. That old lady spoke about how I and one of my siblings were at great odds and how that battle has lasted for a long while. That alone made me think she had some kind of insider information from somewhere. One of the most frightening things she spoke of was about how many great losses I would have in my life. According to her my losses would be so great that I would come to believe that death itself would be the unfortunate and unexpected perennial theme of my life.

The more that old woman spoke, the worse my life was going to be according to her. I don't know why I didn't just walk away. It was like she had me in some sort of hellish trance which left my hand stuck in hers and my feet concreted to the ground. One of the few positive things that she did say was I'd have a daughter and she'd have big beautiful hazel brown eyes and wavy hair. She said, she'd be my life's greatest blessing. But of course, that good news only came after claiming that I would be in a great war. That old gypsy lady would not let me go until she revealed every horrid thing she wanted me to know. When she finally released my hand, I think I was more scared than when I got kidnapped at gunpoint. Her words gave me nightmares for the next few days and many times thereafter. The dreadful images of her so called prophecies were absolutely terrible and haunting. When I got back to my college after the summer, her words still had a hold over me. I had no idea how she knew exactly what happened in the past but I prayed she was as wrong as anyone could be about my future.

I tried to shake her words but I couldn't. For months there were very few waking moments that her words weren't on the forefront of my mind. I did make my way through the rest of that semester but instead of doing so in guilt this time it was in fear. To describe this next part of the story breaks my heart as much as anything ever has. As far as that old witches prophesies go, when I finally made it back home for the next break, it didn't take long for me to realize that Sammy had been going back and forth to the doctor and had been doing so for quite a while. This all occurred without anyone telling me while I was gone. I guess they didn't want me to worry but finding out that way was worse.

The formal name for Sammy's newly discovered heart problem was an atrioventricular septal defect. That basically meant he was born with these small holes in his heart. As he aged, his heart was pumping harder, but all of the things that his heart was supposed to do was slowing down. Sammy's doctor's felt confident that with a small procedure they could mend much of his most pressing issues and he'd be fine again. Sammy's heart operation was on a Monday and according to his doctors he only had to stay in the white house a few days on that visit. The operation seemed to go well but on the Friday after his operation after Sammy got back home Jacob and I got up to start our day. I can't ever remember a time when either one of us woke up before Sammy so I went in to check on that little sleepyhead. As I went into his room, more than horror struck.

Every fear or terror that I'd ever had culminated to the point where I thought my own heart would explode. Sammy wasn't asleep and he wasn't breathing anymore either. His beautiful body was already cold and stiff to the touch. Puddles even knew all hope was lost, as he laid next to him with his furry little head on Sammy's shoulder. I'm sure that dog, in his own way, was also praying that he would just open his eyes and get up, but that's not what happened. I screamed out for Jacob and when he ran in the room, he had the same reaction I did, bone chilling horror. Our beautiful brother, the best of us was gone and we all knew how much we lost that morning. The greatest person I ever knew died in his sleep at the end of the first week I got home after being away for so long. Jacob and I both knew that call to our parents would almost be unbearable but we still had to do it. This time I couldn't ask Jacob to do it for us, I had to make it myself. I had to at least act like the oldest brother one last time.

There wasn't a part of me that wanted to tell my parents what happened but I knew I had to. My already broken heart crushed once more as I dialed my mother's work number and told her what happened. That was the only time in my life that I can remember dreading my parents coming home from work. I knew having to see their hurt and pain would be absolutely terrible, but when they arrived, it was worse. They lost their son and most likely the greatest part of their hearts that day. Before the coroner zipped Sammy up in that cold black vinyl body bag, I saw the scars that I helped create that day on the river. Those scars and his pitiful body would be a sight I'd never forget. I asked if Jacob and I could carry Sammy out to the awaiting hearse ourselves. If nothing else, I wanted to do one last thing for the person that did so much for me. I grabbed the two straps at the head of the bag and Jacob held the ones at the feet.

As we carried our beloved brother out, we both looked up at the sky. That sky that had given all three of us such comfort so many times growing up. This time, however, all I saw were scars in the sky. From that day forward, in my mind Sammy would be in that terrible sky and not with us. The brightest of bright lights burnt out way too early. For the rest of my life I will always be able to hear his voice, feel his skin, and know how much he blessed my life and the lives of my entire family. He was special, the most special person I ever knew. One of the hardest things to do after a loved one dies is go to the funeral home and pick out a casket. Not too far behind that heart wrenching event is deciding what words to put in the obituary. I realize it's a necessity, but it's like pouring salt on an already open overly fresh wound. Row by row, you have to walk by each line of caskets. The one's that seem to always be so perfectly lined up.

I kept thinking this choosing was for our Sammy, and quite frankly, there has never been a casket made that could come close to being good enough for him. My parents brokenheartedly did their best in their selection. They didn't take too much time picking something out because I don't think either one of them could have stood the pain of having to do so for too long. Everyone wants to give their loved ones the best final farewell possible. In this case, for Sammy, they wanted more. This may have been business as usual for the funeral home, but not for us. This was the most important sendoff that any of us would ever have. As the salesman calculated the cost, the price came out to exactly ten-thousand dollars, and my parents wept once more. My mother and father would have done anything to bury their middle son in the best way they felt he deserved—it's just they had no idea how they'd realistically ever get that much money at once. If my mother was upset about the cost, my father was absolutely crushed.

My parents didn't care about money, they never did. They just cared about providing for their boys. They both worked so much so we could have the lives we did—especially my father—but this time, my father felt like everything he had ever worked for didn't matter if he couldn't give Sammy what my mother wanted for him. I overheard my father tell my mother that he felt like a failure and afterwards he went over to the corner and appeared to be praying. After a few minutes, he came back across the room where we were and said, "I don't know where I'm going to get it from, but for my boy, I will." He then told my mother to sign the papers, agreeing to the amount, so we could leave". From the minute we arrived at the funeral home I already knew where they were going to obtain such an amount from. I just didn't know how to explain it to them so I never did.

After we got back home, I snuck back out to my truck and headed back to the funeral home. My father was a lot of things; he was loving, he was kind, and he was an extremely hard worker, but never a failure—not now and not ever. I made it clear that I never wanted anyone to know where the money came from. I just wanted the funeral director to call my parents after I left so that one worry could be taken off their already extremely overfilled plate. As I drove back home, thoughts of that old gypsy woman re-entered my mind. I yelled at her as if she was sitting in the seat right next to me. After Sammy's death and all of the aftermath that always follows, I tried to go back to school but for a lack of being able to describe it any better, I simply didn't care about painting or school anymore. Besides, almost everything I learned about art I did so I would be able to teach it to Sammy, but Sammy wasn't there anymore.

A few months went by after I returned from school when I realized I just couldn't sit around wallowing in my anguish any longer. The only thing I felt left for me to do was to join the military. They say traumatic experiences cause the survivors to become closer. It's not that we didn't try, it's just neither my parents, Jacob nor I were ever the same again. This time it was us that had the holes in our own respective hearts. Those holes were just too big for it to be any other way. Each of us seemed to walk around going through the motions in that numbness that death so often brings. Of course, we still loved each other and we all knew we needed each other probably more than ever but none of us, to include my parents, knew what to do to change it. The goal of each day seemed more about just getting through it more so than anything else. I began to have the same feelings about home as I did about school.

So then, I did what I learned to do best and I ran away once again. My beautiful parents fully understood that I had to do something to find myself again. They probably wished they could have done the same. As they sent me off, I knew I was going in the military with much more than a chip on my shoulder. When there's talk of someone having a chip on their shoulder, there's usually an assumption that they have something to prove. If that's the case, I had something quite the opposite on mine. I was smart enough not to disobey orders or any other directions from my superiors but the simple fact was, I just didn't care either. I didn't care about whatever they ordered me to do, and in truth, I didn't care about my own life. When I packed up to leave, I must have packed that deep dark numbness that death brings with me instead of a chip.

I had Sammy's death and my family's pain on my shoulders, and for myself and those around me, that was some pretty hazardous baggage. The limited regard I had for anything or really anyone actually helped me thrive a great deal in the military. It was also the driving force in me volunteering for any and everything that was ever presented. The more dangerous the assignment, the more content I was in taking it because I knew I didn't care if I lived or died. I fully realize that everyone has a story and everyone's story is just as valid to their lives as mine. In saying that, I must acknowledge that the military did eventually give me enough compassion once again to realize that fact. But before that realization happened, a habit of carelessly volunteering for everything eventually got me deployed to the Middle East for two long years and that deployment was smack dab at the forefront of a war. Once again I realized that old gypsy woman's words were ringing true. Webster defines a dream as something that you want to be, do or have for a very long time.

I dare say that everyone who has ever lived has had dreams such as these. You would think everyone wants to be, do, or have something, but I really didn't. I was just existing at that point. For me, death in one form or another had already been the unfortunate and unexpected perennial theme of my life, just like that crazy old fortune teller said it would be. So when I finally saw death coming directly for me it was welcomed and dressed as a SCUD missile. When I saw the ball of fire streaking in my direction, I truly began to feel relief... that is until it missed. I was twenty-years-old at the time, and 6,283 miles away from home. I was in a tiny foxhole that I dug out for myself, as I was ordered to do that day. I sat there almost pissed that stupid shooting Death Star that I strangely thought was so beautiful whistled away from its intended target, which was evidentially me and others in my unit. I've heard people say you have flashbacks when you think that you're getting ready to die, and you do, but my flashbacks were so terrible that I began having flash forwards as well.

Those are thoughts of what your life could have been. Maybe if I would have done certain things differently, or if different things happened to me. Even though I was somewhat inviting a different result, time seemed to stand still when that SCUD hit. Everything flew up in the air, to include me but for some reason I saw everything happening in slow motion. I was surrounded by this giant, fiery dust ball that dredged all of the breathable air out of my lungs, but somehow I knew it wasn't my time. I was thrown through the air for what felt like an eternity but when I finally did smack back down on the hard desert floor, the one thing I did know was I was still alive. All of the adrenaline set in at once and I used it to help ensure that all of the others near me survived that day as well. We were like a colony of extremely efficient fire ants.

This was a young colony that was definitely majorly disturbed for the first time of many to come. I may not have cared about myself but I was still the kind of person, thanks to my parents that cared about others. I, and the rest of my unit at least did all we could to prove it that day. As I helped with checking each bunker and the surroundings, we discovered on that particular day, the only thing that stupid missile delivered was sand, noise, and a gigantic hole in the ground. We didn't lose anyone on that first attack but I wasn't tricked. I knew we lost something, I just couldn't tell what it was at the time. In times like those your mind kind of travels everywhere and mine for some reason stopped at the months before that attack and back to when I joined the Air Force. I remember laughing as the recruiters gave me a form they called a Dream Sheet. The way it works is, you fill it out to tell the military where you would like to be based. From that point, and true to its name, the only actual chance you ever have to be based where you choose is in your dreams. Being from Virginia, I selected all East Coast bases.

I chose Langley and other places in Maryland, even some in Florida. I definitely wanted to get away again but I knew I didn't really want to go too far from my parents just in case we ever had another great loss. In true military fashion, they listened. They even sent me to the East Coast just as I selected. The only problem was, it was a little too far east, and of course, across the Atlantic Ocean to Spain. Being based there reminded me of that summer in Israel. Regardless of how shocking it originally was to think about, it really was somewhat of a paradise too. This was at a time where everyone there still seemed to love Americans and our dollar was worth three times what their peseta was. I was stationed at Torrejon Air Base, which was a very short distance from Madrid. Madrid was more or less known as the New York City of Europe.

This claim definitely lived up to its billing but in a strictly European sort of way. They had bullfights, siestas—which are these nice little naps in the middle of the day. They had a pub on every corner, huge nightclubs and shopping centers everywhere. They also have some of the most beautiful women in the world. Unfortunately, they have this ridiculously strong alcoholic drink there too. The locals called it Sol y Sombra. The actual translation of the drink's name is Sun and Shade. I guess that's because regardless of when you drink it, it would put most people's lights out. In reality, it was a debilitating concoction made with brandy and anise and to me that drink was the only bad thing I ever experienced in the country. Just like in Israel I was able to travel a bit. I saw swordsmiths in Toledo do their work as they did over a hundred years ago. I went to Valencia to see the most precious porcelain Lladro figurines.

I also traveled to Benidorm on the Spanish coast where clothes were very much optional to my surprise. I visited so many other surreal places throughout Europe too. Places like Paris, Luxemburg, Aviano and on and on. For a bit I almost forgot about that chip because I felt like I was living a life that could only be seen on the *Lifestyles of the Rich and Famous.* My broke twist to the show, however, should have been named something more like, *The Debauchery of the Young and Dumb.* I originally flew into Spain on a commercial flight and my soon-to-be new boss, Andy picked me up from the airport. About fifteen minutes after I settled in, he started force-feeding me some of those evil Sol y Sombra's. He told me he wanted to properly welcome me to the best place in the world. Drinking was somewhat of a new thing for me but what I soon learned was in reality, all it really was, was just another way to run away.

With that knowledge in hand I graciously appreciated everyone's hospitality and partook in whatever anyone ever offered. Later that night, Andy and some of the other guys from my new unit continued my welcoming party when they took me to some of the local nightclubs. Andy was a big ole country boy. He stood about 6'4" and he was probably only about four or five years older than I. He talked with that strong southern slang. I really had to listen carefully to understand what he was saying half the time, but I had a solution. The more I drank the easier it was for me to comprehend his extremely southern dialect. Regardless of his stature, he was a humble and somewhat of a shy guy. At that time, I didn't realize I would be making my best military career move the very first night I arrived in that awesome country. That night at one of the clubs Andy saw this absolutely beautiful Spanish woman. She was standing in the corner, swaying back and forth to some overly loud music.

Andy kept telling me, "Look at that woman, she's hot," she's this, she's that. I listened to him banter about her so long that I finally told him to go over and talk to her. I said that even though I ignorantly thought she probably wouldn't understand anything he had to say. At the time, my simple self-thought was that because we were in Spain, she probably only spoke Spanish. I had only been in the country a few hours but it didn't take long for me to realize that wasn't the case really for anyone there. With all my prodding, Andy still wouldn't move a muscle, so with my own Sol y Sombra-fueled courage, I told him I would go over to her for him. On the way over, I thought about Sammy, and how he used to do pretty much the same thing for Jacob and I, but in English. Andy's eyes lit up as if no one had ever done anything that nice for him before. To me I was just going over to talk to a pretty girl, besides, I still didn't know she spoke English better than I did at the time.

The only class I ever failed in high school was Spanish and again as irony would have it I was right there in Spain trying to get a few brownie points with my new boss by speaking Spanish. I knew I didn't have a clue what I was going to say but I headed over to her anyway. I fully expected to be back with Andy in disappointment in just a few minutes. That's not what happened though. For some reason she locked on to every word I was trying to say. I was fumbling around in her native tongue at first until she taught me that most Spanish people start taking English in school before Americans do. Cupid himself must have been in that club that night because I simply wasn't that smooth on my own. We talked for about ten minutes, and before I got too mesmerized by her myself, I had to turn the attention of our conversation over to Andy. I didn't really know him yet so I just made up some things that I thought any beautiful woman would like to hear, and damn if it didn't work.

I eventually waved Andy over and after he slugged his way from across the room surprisingly, he took over without any problems. This beautiful, sweet and somewhat naive Spanish woman would later become his wife just three short months later. From that point on, Andy was not just my boss; we were like the best of buddies. Sometimes life is simply comical in the way opportunities and Spanish woman present themselves. After Andy's wedding many of the same guys from that night went back to that same nightclub. While we were there this time, I kept thinking that I recognized this somewhat inebriated Spanish guy at the end of the bar. I didn't think I would have any reason to recognize anyone there but I did. Then I remembered we did have a Spanish exchange student from Madrid at our high school. All I really knew about him was he was the funny exchange student who always drank these crazy drinks at parties.

A few more minutes went by and I guess he recognized me too because he ran over and started hugging me. He said in his accent, "It's me, Alvaro," and it really was him. He, in fact, still lived in Madrid. Alvaro's family was obviously very well off and after that night not only did he start inviting me and my new military friends to meet his other richer Spanish friends, he also took us to the best and most expensive restaurants and clubs in Madrid on a regular basis. I don't know what the odds were that we would run into each other halfway across the world, but I know they weren't high. Alvaro and his family were wonderful people. They wanted everyone to know they were wealthy but they didn't seem to mind sharing their many blessings. Alvaro's family started inviting us to go out on their yacht, and other times, to their mansion for dinner. This was like my time at the Waldorf Astoria, it was a life that I couldn't believe I was living. We were very grateful for their hospitality but we never asked them for anything. They just kept inviting us places.

Alvaro also had a sister who happened to be a model. I mean, a real Cosmopolitan or whatever that magazine's name is kind of model. She was nineteen and completely off limits to Americans, especially those of us in the military. When you tell all of those youthful hormones that something is off limits what did they think was going to happen? Her name was Luz, and not only was she extremely beautiful, she was also very smart, much smarter than I have ever been. It was a little intimidating as we began to get to know each other and do things together away from our normal group outings with the others. It was kind of like a less serious modern day version of Romeo and Juliet because her parents did not approve of her spending time with me on her own at all. Before they found out about us, I thought they liked me, but it must not have been as much as I believed.

Mohawk Madness

In truth, especially back then, Luz's parents were probably right. We tried sneaking around for a little while, but she simply had too much pressure at home, and I guess I had too many places to go that served that damn Sol y Sombra. After Luz, Alvaro never really kept in contact any more so I decided to loosen up a bit in a country with no drinking age and really very few other limits on anything. I didn't have a lot of money or maturity but what I did have seemed to go a long way there. Make no mistake about it, we worked hard, but when we were off, we played even harder. I honestly think we went out at least six out of seven nights a week, and even on the seventh we were drinking somewhere. We could do that thanks to a little trick Andy showed me and the other young airmen. He showed us if we got to work feeling a little foggy from the night before, all we had to do was get in the cockpit of one of those F-16's and turn the oxygen on 100% full blow. From there, you simply breath in the magical pure air of sobriety. With Andy passing along his great sobrietal knowledge, it didn't take but a few puffs on the pilot's flight mask to completely clear whatever ailment we may have had from the night before.

Andy was a genius in many ways and he always looked out for me, especially since I was his very own personal matchmaker. Whether he was my boss or not, he had my back, and he always passed his appreciation on for what I did for him ever since the first day we met. There was one time however, that I pushed even Andy's limits of protection though. I truly thought I was going to get kicked out of the military that time, but Andy stepped in and at least lessened the blow. It was a heavy and evil Sol y Sombra night and for some reason, our portable party was on the roof of a three-story dorm building. The more I drank, the less attention I paid to the ledge and before I knew it, I fell off that damn building like an idiot.

My friends later said it wasn't the first fall that put me in the hospital, it was the second. Screwing up the same things more than once wasn't anything new to me, but this time, I was so ignorantly filled up with that stupid concoction that after I fell off the first time, instead of going back in the front door and up the steps, my dumb ass started climbing back up the outside of that damn building. I was told after making it about half way up I fell again. The funniest part of that story, again from what I was told, is that each time I fell off I kept yelling out, "I AM THE SKY! I AM THE SKY!" What the hell does that even mean? Falling off that building only qualified me to say, "I AM AN IDIOT! I AM AN IDIOT!" I knew me and my brothers thought we had a connection to the sky growing up. Subconsciously that's probably where it came from but either way, whether sky or idiot, that fall put me directly in the hospital. Yep, my own trip to the white house.

They pumped out my stomach with this nasty charcoal solution. It took weeks for my bowels to stop being angry at me. When I woke up the next morning, I wouldn't open my eyes for two reasons. One was, I had no idea where I was, but the second and more important issue was there was something extremely wrong with my manhood. There was a pain between my legs like I never felt before. I don't care about admitting it either because I was scared for my parts. There are a lot of things a guy will joke about but not about his stuff. Anyway, I didn't have to leave my eyes closed for long because I eventually heard Andy's voice. I didn't know if I should have been more scared or relieved at that time. As I slowly opened my eyes, I peeked under the covers to see what the source of my pain was. What I saw was something I had never seen before. I had never been in a hospital for myself and I damn sure never had what I'd later learn was a catheter invading so much of my personal space either.

I can remember thinking how in the hell did they even get that thing in there. I didn't really think too much about my other problems at the time because I just wanted that damn hose-looking thing out of me. I didn't come close to appreciating all of Andy's belly laughs and snorting either. He was laughing so hard I thought they'd have to admit him right next to me. Just when I thought all of the comedy subsided, a nurse came in and made a few more not-so-funny jokes at my expense and then thankfully took that damn catheter out. The whole situation was embarrassing. What do you say when someone is pulling a garden hose out of your parts? Thank you? Gracias? Feliz Navidad? I didn't know what to say so I didn't say a word. After a quick tug, I did however moan a great and humiliating sigh of relief. Once the excitement, if you can call it that, calmed down, Andy let me know he wasn't there just to check on me. He was ordered to bring me to our big boss.

Things seemed pretty serious, and I knew it was, but then that big country jerk pulled out a bottle of the problem from the night before and asked if I wanted a swig. Not only did I not want it then, I didn't ever want to see that stupid Sun and Shade crappy beverage from the Underworld ever again. After my refusal, I fully understood that Andy had to do his job. Our Master Sergeant's name was Tom Huff and he didn't play. He was a Vietnam Veteran and he was also known for running his unit with an iron hand. During my first week on the base, that fool made me paint the same damn curb three different colors in one week. I dare not ask why he was making me do that, but I was thinking it. No one ever mentioned a word about painting curbs to me in training.

When we arrived at Master Sergeant Huff's office, Andy knocked on his door and very formally, in his country version of a big boy voice said, "We're here, Sir, as ordered." I felt somewhat betrayed by Andy at first but I really shouldn't have because he was just following orders himself. I knew I was the idiot who fell off the building, not only once, but twice. As I walked into what I expected to be my final day in uniform, I was preparing to defend my ignorant actions as well as any slick city lawyer could. Master Sergeant Huff never gave me the chance though. Sarge, which is what we called him, scoffed and then looked me directly in the eyes without blinking and issued my sentence. He ordered me to go through an alcohol education program, which I unquestionably understood, but he also ordered me to attend an anger management class. At first I thought, *I wasn't angry, I was drunk, maybe stupid but what the hell?*

I almost verbalized those thoughts until I glimpsed over at Andy and could hear him subliminally telling me to keep my big mouth shut with his eyes. Sarge then pointed to the door and yelled for us to "Get the hell out!" As Andy and I were leaving, I could hear Sarge muttering the words that I apparently used the day before. I heard him say, "I am the sky, I am the sky," then he laughed, and said, "Damn idiot." Even he knew that alcohol and the military are somewhat synonymous. There were beer machines on every floor of the dorms. There were also two bars on the base that were open twenty-four hours a day, and no matter what time it was, they were always full of people. Now, these people may or may not have fallen off of their own building but they weren't making the world a better place at that time either. A few days later Sarge called me back to his office. He said he wanted to check on me but he also wanted me to know that my punishment was mostly to slow me down a bit.

Sarge knew his troops, and somehow he also knew more about me than I realized before that incident. He knew what happened to my brother and many other things that I didn't think I ever told anyone there. Those were the things I was still trying to run from. He understood how the military worked, but he genuinely cared about all of us and from that day on I knew it. He was tough and direct but he was real. There was nothing fake or misleading about that man. I did feel bad knowing there was a strong chance I'd let him down again but I was at least going to try to do better. Sarge was a dedicated family man too. He always said he had five boys by his wife and fifty from our unit. He often let us know that we were his blood too. I came to deeply respect that man as everyone else in our unit did as well.

Sitting in the desert on the day of that first missile attack, many others went on like it was business as usual but my mind was still all over the place. I thought back to the night before we left Spain to head for the desert. I still didn't drink that particular drink but as usual, a few of us went and stayed out way too long drinking other inebriating concoctions. Somewhere along the way, one of us idiots, a guy named Eric, decided it would be a good idea to get tattoos and mohawks before we left. Tattoos aren't anything new to the military; hell, someone in the military of yesteryear probably invented the process but not now or ever have mohawks been acceptable. As the four of us newly-scalped airmen arrived at the hangar for departure to the desert, the loudest, "WHAT THE HELL?" rang out from our boss', boss' boss, Colonel Jefferson Hughes. Now, Colonel Hughes was nothing like Sarge or Andy for that matter; he was a complete arrogant ass. During our final departure meeting the day before, he wanted us all to know that we were going to war as "expendable beings", as he put it.

I don't know who taught him how to give pep talks but it definitely wasn't Tony Robbins. When that man saw us and our new hairdos he was so pissed. He loudly demanded for us to get over to him immediately. All of the men who were loading up and getting ready to deploy stopped what they were doing to watch us get publicly and loudly berated. The spit from every one of his words drenched our faces as he was so colorfully explaining his disgust in regard to our newly revealed appearance. During his rant we not only learned a few new cuss words, we also clearly heard how ignorant our mothers were for having us. After his tirade lessened he made us shave every strand of hair off of every visible place on our bodies, right there in the hanger.

This order included our heads, face and even our freakin eyebrows. I thought to myself, "What the hell kind of sadistic crap is this"? I thought it, but again, I dared not say a word. In our world he was like a demi-god and we had no choice other than to listen to what this disgruntled old bastard said to do. To make matters worse, we only had plastic Bic razors and some dull kindergarten-style scissors to do the job. The Colonel did, in all of his kindness, provide a cup of water for each of us from the nasty, gnat-infested rain bucket that was formerly stationed outside of the hangar underneath a drain spout. When we finished, our already youthful faces looked as if we were all ten-year-old chemotherapy patients. If the punishment would have ended there, it would have been bad enough, but when we arrived in the desert he continued to torment us. Everyone else was allowed to wear their hats outside, as they should, but not us. We all ended up with severe burns on our heads and where our eyebrows used to be.

To continue the abuse, he then made us sleep in an old, rat-infested building a good distance away from the rest of the unit. This went on for about a week until Sarge intervened and told that angry bastard that we had suffered enough. I feel I should have seen at least part of that crazy mess coming but I didn't. I'm still not convinced that the eyebrows should have paid the price though. I could deal with the babyface thing, the sunburnt head and even the humiliation of not having eyebrows, but the rats were a completely different story. Those things weren't scared of anything and they were everywhere in that old bombed out building. When we laid down at night, they literally ran across our sleeping bags. They gnawed at the zippers and let out these blood-curdling screeches all throughout the night. We zipped ourselves in to limit seeing those monster rodents but I think they were actually trying to drag us around the floor, as to evict their unwanted new tenants.

After the rat motel, but before our tent city, we were actually assigned to stay in one of the poshest five-star hotels in the Middle East for a while. I remembered how nice the Waldorf Astoria was in Israel but that hotel was even nicer. It didn't last long, but for a little while we had personal masseuses, outstanding food, and, being on the Persian Gulf, some of the guys even took windsurfing lessons. Believe it or not, and I don't know if they were twenty-four carats, but we even had gold toilets in all of our bathrooms. For most of the time we stayed there I felt like I had hit another unexpected jackpot and I can remember thinking if this was war, I was all in. We had a good month planned out to be living in that Middle Eastern paradise without a whole lot to do other than take advantage of all of the amenities of that place. I knew this time I was going to be on my best behavior. Besides, my eyebrows were just starting to grow back and I didn't want any more trouble of any kind.

Regardless of the opulence and even the surprising kindness shown to us by the locals, our presence in the country was definitely not appreciated by everyone. On the second week there, the hotel was bombed and ten young airmen from another unit were killed. The unexpected blast tore through the hotel's fancy restaurant, where so many of us usually were. We should have seen it coming but no one did, not even that pompous Colonel. We had guards outside and throughout where we were but I guess there were just too many distractions. The only good thing that did come out of it was Colonel Jackass got transferred and was never seen again. I guess at the end of the day he was the one that was expendable even though ten others paid the price for him.

After that we all began to understand what we were dealing with. You could never really tell who you were supposed to help or who would help you. We began to separate completely from the locals and we finished building our tent city as fast as we could. We all knew we needed a living arrangement that was much more secure than where we were. The night before we were scheduled to occupy our new makeshift military town, we slept outside near the flight line. We had these big, puffy sleeping bags. They were even puffier than the jackets Sammy used to wear. At about two in the morning, the skies opened and what felt like an ocean's worth of water started pouring down on us. It only rained that one time in the two years we were there but now I really know what a monsoon feels like. After about six straight hours of a torrential downpour, everything was basically washed away under about three feet of rising water. I knew I promised Sarge I'd never get back on a rooftop but I had to break my word this time; hell, we all did. As many of us that would fit climbed on the roof of that same old bombed out building.

We couldn't do anything else other than hold on and wait to see if the river of water rushing below would ever go somewhere else. This flood was eerily biblical. I almost expected to see Noah and all of those animals floating by but I was only partly right. The only animals we saw were those damn rats again. They were everywhere trying to scratch their way up on the roof to join us. They were climbing, swimming and drowning all over the place. No one was thinking about how everything was being so forcefully washed away because we were all just trying to keep those nasty, despicable things off of us. The ground must have been so hard that once the rain stopped, the water and the rats disappeared almost as fast as they came. We soon discovered that just about everything that we built over the past month floated away as well. The only thing to do then was build the tent city for the second time. After it was completed and we were sure it wouldn't rain again, we were all assigned to specific tents.

Andy and Sarge were in my tent—or should I say, I was in theirs. They both took up residence near the back entrance. Both men, having more rank, may have been given an extra foot or two of space but that was about it. Twenty snoring and farting men in one tent was a far cry from the dorms in Spain with all the beer machines, the Waldorf Astoria in Israel, or that five-star hotel with the golden toilets, but we had no other choice than to make it our home for as long as the military said it had to be. We taped pictures to the walls in our parts of the tent. We hung blankets to add as much privacy as we could, but for the most part, we all had about a four-by-six-foot space to stay in when we weren't out on missions. Occasionally, someone would get a care package that had what we all wanted inside. Sometimes there would be liquor in a mouthwash bottle.

A few times an actual six pack would make its way, but for the most part, the source of most of our ignorance from Spain simply wasn't available. The one time that any type of alcohol was openly available to us was when a few of us were invited to the ambassador's complex. He didn't have Sol y Sombra thank goodness but he still fed us beer and spirits from the second we arrived. What happened next had to be considered, at least partly, his own fault. By that time I had done so many ignorant, stupid and even thoughtless things while drinking. This of course included falling off a building, not once but twice. But even I never considered doing what Eric did while visiting the ambassador that night. After we all had about six or twelve beers, Eric started talking trash to the ambassador for some unknown reason. None of us had drank anything in quite a while and he didn't handle it well when he did.

He was one of the other original idiots who got a mohawk, so I knew this wasn't going to end well. I kept thinking, if a colonel made us shave our eyebrows, what the hell could an ambassador do to us? I don't know why Eric did what he did but I do know it was extremely stupid and more than follically dangerous to our military careers. We all tried to shut him up but we obviously didn't do a good enough job because the ambassador's bodyguard quickly made his way to Eric to do it for us. The next thing I know, Eric tackles the most muscular man I've ever seen into the deep end of the Ambassadors pool. Long story short, that mammoth of a man couldn't swim and literally started to try and walk his way from the bottom of the pool to the shallow side with absolutely no success. With the bodyguard not being able to pull himself out, and Eric already out of the pool looking for another beer, I asked myself, "What the hell do I do now"?

Trying to help a very bad situation, I ended up jumping in the pool myself and somehow pushing that gargantuan to a place where he could reach the bottom. After quite a bit of wrestling around with him, he eventually made it to safety. I immediately thought to myself, *here we go again,* except this time I knew it wasn't going to be any anger management class or a forced shaving. It's probably going to be a firing squad, led by that mule that Eric tried to drown. This situation was a lot of things but I couldn't see any of it ending well for any of us. Very shortly after this happened, the security police assigned to the ambassador came to take us back to camp. It didn't take long to begin our escorted voyage back to our freshly-rebuilt tent city. Of course, this was only after a full-fledged assault on a United States ambassador and his Swartzenegger-looking bodyguard. I was guessing that fact added to the swiftness of our trip. For clarity, we were headed to a place that our boss was already at, in fact, he even lived there in the same tent with us.

I knew I'd been in some mess before, but this topped every list I ever had. The ambassador's complex was quite a ways away from our tent city, so the drive should have felt somewhat long but it wasn't. Before we knew it, we were back at our temporary home and we began preparing ourselves for what we knew was getting ready to happen. This time I decided to lead the way and as I opened the tent's vinyl flap to enter, we all barely took three fearful steps inside when the most blood-curdling noise started blaring. It was that SCUD and it was on its way to us. It's not funny but I can remember cracking a smile thinking if our new Colonel arranged this punishment it was even worse than we expected. The ignorance of beer, and thank God, someone other than me, simply wasn't very important anymore.

I'm glad we didn't have the time to let Sarge know what happened that night, but I would have much rather told him that his guys were idiots once again rather than have a missile blow the hell out of everything. If maturity and responsibility had been lacking in my life, things were getting ready to drastically change in a hurry. A young person rarely understands the severity of the situations they're sometimes put in. I don't think I could or even tried to until that day. I had always been so careless with life because even though I enjoyed my friends and Spain I still had those holes in my heart. At that point, like so many others who leave us way too early, I just assumed life would always be there for me but again I still wasn't sure I wanted it to be.

When I heard the sirens I also heard all of the sergeants yelling out directions. I knew this was a far worse situation than I expected. I even knew that what seemed like twenty hours of watching all of those incoming missiles was in reality only about twenty minutes or less for some, but time stood almost still. My current situation reminded me of one of those many nights out in Madrid. As we were walking towards a nightclub I noticed a rusted out BMW parked directly in front of the entrance of the place. People were walking by, looking inside the car. Some shook their heads and others muttered to whomever they were with about whatever it was they were seeing inside. The sad thing is, absolutely no one was too shocked to stop or slow down. Everyone just kept going towards their night without any true regard. When I got to the car, I couldn't just look in and keep going. What I saw was a young couple that had both apparently overdosed on heroin.

The man still had the needle sticking out of an overly inflated vein in his right arm. The skin on both of their bodies was the most frightening shade of grey. That morbid color seemed to instantly absorb any thoughts of light or life that I was hoping was still trying to make its way out. This was a terrible thing to see but the worst part of all were their eyes. Their eyes left another haunting memory that I will never forget. I knew by this point that death in one form or another, had been the unfortunate and unexpected perennial theme of my life but I wondered why it had to be theirs as well. Their eyes were abnormally stretched open almost alien-like and they were pitch black. It was like looking directly into the nothingness of a black hole. There was no question that their souls were completely sucked out of their young bodies by the decisions they made, but no one deserved to leave or even look that way. I thought to myself, *how could people just walk by like they never existed?*

Even the security workers who were outside just a few feet away ignored what was going on. But I couldn't let them, or what was left of them, sit there to be gawked at or ignored any longer. I felt whatever life they had at least needed to be respected enough to help them find a final resting place. Not knowing what else to do, I called the Spanish police to hopefully get help in some way. When the police arrived, they were very professional, but just like the others, it seemed like this was a common occurrence for them. The police did however call an ambulance to pick up the dead couple and everyone eventually went on their way. Something absolutely came over me after they left, though. My friends went into the club but I couldn't. For some reason, even though I didn't know that sad couple, I felt like I had lost another family member. So instead of going with my friends I went home and sobbed myself to sleep.

M-16 Christmas

I don't know why seeing that poor couple outside that club hit me so hard but it did. They were so young and just gone like they never existed. Life didn't seem like it was very fair to them but I guess, like with everyone, life never promised it would be. As far as my own mortality, I obviously made it through many more SCUD attacks and I guess fortunately for me, I made it through many of the other evils that war always brings as well. Things were so serious at times, it didn't seem like we could even go to the bathroom without something absurd happening. My case and point was when I went to the bathroom with that damn Eric. It's not that I wanted to go to the bathroom with anyone, but as you'd expect, you never really went anywhere alone in a place like that. We jokingly called our uncomfortable relief pairings "Bathroom Buddies," and for lack of anyone else choosing him I was paired with Eric's crazy ass.

Truthfully, Eric and I were friends, but I damn sure didn't trust him at all after the incident with the Ambassador's bodyguard, and the eyebrows whether alcohol was involved or not. Where we were at that time, there were a lot of sand drifts. It wasn't exactly like a typical desert or a bathroom that most people think about, but that's where we were and that's where we went. These drifts often were pretty good hiding places for snipers and other people who just hated Americans being in their country. Sometimes those hiding would take an occasional pot shot but on this one particular day when Eric really had to go, it wasn't just a single attempt, it was a full confrontation with a whole enemy unit. The plan when we went to that area was always to do your business and then get back to where the majority of the other troops were as fast as you could. As Eric was finishing up that day, I was watching the area. I then suddenly saw a dust storm kicking up over one of the dunes.

A dust storm wasn't a rare occurrence, in this case however, it looked to be man-made. As I moved closer and peaked over the ridge, there were twenty or more armed soldiers less than twenty yards away. I couldn't yell for Eric because I didn't want anyone to know we were there, but I had to do something. I had to do it quick too because they were headed right at us. As my heart started racing, I whispered as loud as I could for Eric to pull up his damn pants and get over to where I was. Eric stumbled and tripped, and before he could be any help at all, I was in full sight of all of those soldiers. We all raised our rifles at the same time and I held my breath knowing that was the end. The same end that I only thought I wanted before. I knew I was doomed and began to question why I was ever so nonchalant about my own life. Out of pure fear, and still having no clue where I got the idea from, other than a silent prayer in my mind, I started pointing in different directions and yelling out as many different names of people as I could think of.

I did that as loudly as I could too. I was pretending I had a whole posse of soldiers hiding behind the dunes and positioning themselves to provide the much-needed firepower that it was going to take. After I yelled out, somehow, miraculously, all of those men threw their rifles down and fell to the ground. It was then just me pointing a rifle at twenty plus frail and tattered-looking men. Soon after, Eric finally made his way over to me. In his usual sarcastic way, he said, "Hey bud, way to go." I looked at him and just shook my head like I used to do to Sammy. Something had to be very wrong with that guy's medulla oblongata, besides, I didn't really do anything but yell out a bunch of names. They were all sprawled out across the desert, awaiting for some sort of instruction.

I strongly believe that if Eric was on watch instead of me, we would have both been killed that day but for some reason it wasn't my time to go again, both figuratively and literally I guess. Knowing Eric, he would have taken the first shot but thank God he had trouble getting his damn pants up. We quickly learned that those men were starving and they surrendered so easily in hopes of being fed. In reality, and contradictory to my ego, if I would have been a four-year-old girl with food, they would have surrendered just as easy. Their units were built up as one of the fiercest armies in the world but obviously, not without food. We marched the men back to our camp, which was about a mile away, and turned them over to the higher ups. The soldiers were allowed to shower and eat, and then I'm not sure what happened to them next because I simply didn't have enough rank to know. For a few months Eric and I were treated like folk heroes. I guess you never know what's going to happen when you go to the bathroom in the desert with your bathroom buddy.

The one nice thing that happened from that accidental encounter was it drew a visit from some of the top generals. They wanted to give Eric and I some sort of medal. You would think that getting a medal was a big deal for us but we got so many while we were over there another one really wasn't a great prize. We were originally supposed to be deployed for six months, then we got our first extension and we also got our first medal. It got to where every time they extended us they gave us all another medal. They always had some kind of exotic name for them too. That time I thought we'd be receiving the Bathroom Bravery Merit Badge or something like that. Either way, our chests were loaded with these fake medals but we were still stuck in that place long after most of the other units were sent home.

Before the generals arrived, our then commander built a field kitchen to celebrate his base capturing the twenty starving men. I guess he built it at that time to show how well he had been taking care of us. If that was the case, the first meal really should have been bologna, like I'm sure he was feeding those visiting generals, but at least we finally had hot food. Before then, for well over a year we only ate MRE's. MRE is an acronym for Meals Ready to Eat. They're dehydrated meals that come in these thick, brown plastic bags and all of ours were Vietnam's left overs. Most of ours still had Marlboro cigarettes and Chicklets in them which represented a very bygone era. Now however, with great thanks to Eric and me, the medal-winning heroes that we weren't, we had a field kitchen and hot food, and for that I was thankful. It was commonplace for us at the end of every week or upon the completion of a mission to have debriefings. Sarge, being the highest-ranking NCO, held the meetings which were in our own tent most of the time. I used to think there was nothing quite like working from home.

During those times, Sarge would not only go over what happened or what should have happened during our missions, he also checked-up on us personally. When you're away from normalcy for as long as we were, your mind and sometimes even your body starts playing tricks on you. I wasn't married and was still pretty young, so my experience over there was more like an extremely bad and dangerous vacation compared to many others', especially those with younger kids and wives back home. Sarge always seemed so much older and wiser than we were—and he was—but he himself could have only been in his mid to late forties. He did, however, know what extended tours in Vietnam did to so many families and what they were doing to some of ours. They often couldn't stand up to the stresses of war.

With being away for so long, certain and obvious emotional and even financial stresses set in. Sarge always made it a priority to make our problems his business and all of his adopted sons were grateful for his wholehearted efforts. Andy was still a newlywed himself and even he was worried about whether his pretty new Spanish wife would be there for him if he ever made it back. Most of the married men had some sort of separation issue in one form or another. Each time, Sarge's fatherly advice helped them in a way that nobody else's seemed to be able to. Sarge himself had been married for over twenty-five years and had five boys. Five is a lot of kids but Sarge had a lot of heart to go around. I knew Sarge's family had to be very close and, unfortunately, used to him being deployed like we were for so long. Sarge was a private man when it came to most of his personal issues, however, he would speak about his boys and his wife and what they were doing according to his letters from home.

That tough guy lit up like a Christmas tree when he'd read about his kids' achievements and their seemingly ever-growing activities. The debriefings were as much of a therapy session for all of us as they were anything else. Sarge was also a religious man. He was careful not to be too overbearing with his views, but slowly, through his actions he led most of us to believe similarly. He'd always end our meetings with a prayer and he always finalize his comments by asking God not to hard test his boys. Sarge's heartfelt prayers were greatly appreciated and no matter how well we were trained or how tough we thought we were, none of us younger airmen had ever experienced anything close to what we did in that place. War is so much like cancer. Some people die right away, some take a while to be hunted down, and others make it through. There is another category though, with them, they are dragged through hell and slowly deteriorate into nothingness whether they live or die.

Someone like Sarge leading us made all of those possible outcomes as bearable as they could be. There is a closeness that develops when you have to constantly put your life into someone else's hands. It's that commonality that could be considered a chemotherapy that actually works as long you stay together. However, as together is concerned, another issue with the military is that nothing ever stays the same. Somewhere, someone is trying to get a promotion and is willing to make random changes to get noticed while risking the lives of others to do so. For our unit, that was stage four, and it had arrived. As the main events of the actual war started to settle down, there were massive bouts of boredom. Make no mistake about it, we didn't want to fight anymore, but doing nothing was almost worse. Those were the times where the fights would rage in our minds instead of in the desert. We definitely weren't smart enough to appreciate those rare downtimes, so it didn't last long.

This caused our field kitchen building commander to start farming us out to search and rescue teams. He wanted to make sure we were busy enough to get him a different piece of hardware on his shoulder. I honestly think we all should have been happy enough with not doing much at that time. We should have all shut our big mouths, to include that colonel, but that's not what happened. Once again, life adjusted our restlessness and it resulted in the colonel breaking our unit up into smaller teams of six to go out on even more ridiculously dangerous missions that we really didn't know how to accomplish or survive from. I guess we had another commander remind us of how expendable we actually were. Colonel Jackass number two ended up being worse than number one.

We would have done anything for anyone, not that we had any other choice, but by this time, we had been over there way longer than any other unit in any branch by far. We were simply beat-up and tired and ready for some kind of relief. In proof of this being true, and even though it was not known by us at the time, our combined units were spoken about later by the name of "The Forgotten One-thousand" after the war. I guess we were promoted from expendable to forgotten without knowing it ourselves. Sarge heard us fussing about our new orders and the one thing you just don't do in the military is complain. In response, he called another group meeting. We all went and in a nutshell when it was over, we all pulled our proverbial head out of our asses and shut our mouths out of respect for him. Anything we didn't understand had to be put aside because our desert father had enough of his men acting like little boys who didn't get their way.

When a pilot gets shot down, of which our unit had seven, they assign teams to try to get to them before anyone else did. We— or should I say, I—was also assigned to scavenge all the black boxes that weren't blown to pieces from the crash. We'd get flown in on helicopters, jump out and get to work while many times being shot at in the process. Out of the seven pilots, we never got there first. That basically meant, we were sent on those ridiculous missions to save plane parts and of course to get a colonel a single silver star. Many times, these missions would occur in almost complete darkness but others would have a certain glow. The so called enemy often set their own oil fields on fire which created the blackest smoke that would almost completely lock up your lungs. The aftermath from their uncontrolled burns left what I think hell must really look like. Black oily blood spouting out of the earth while all of those smoky souls are released and swirling around its source.

This was another hellishly eerie sight that I pray I never have to see again in my life. When we went on those missions, extra equipment was required, both mentally and literally. In addition to fifty or more pounds of equipment, we also had to wear our chemical warfare gear. We didn't have the new bubble-type masks either. Just like with the MRE's we had Vietnam's leftovers. It was the kind that still used canisters and only had two little bug-eyed lenses to look out of. The mere appearance of that mask should have been funny enough, but it wasn't. In all of that gear, with all of those things to do, we had trouble breathing, moving and seeing, but we still had to do what some colonel told us to do. Out of the seven pilots that were shot down from our unit five died before we got there and the two that lived were captured. Those men were traipsed across the news after they had obviously been tortured. We launched those men to their final demise in all but two cases, but after what I saw, I think they wished they would have died as well.

Our unit had one television which constantly ran from a generator and it was always on the news channel. We actually watched the television on several occasions tell the world where our so-called secret location was. Sometimes they'd even draw it out like John Madden commentating a football game. I've even seen what we were bombing on TV before we bombed it. I think the worst thing I saw though was how they broadcasted our captured and beaten pilots. I hope their ratings were worth it because that never did anything but enrage everyone. Pilots are a different breed from the other officers. They appreciated those who kept them as safe as they could in the air and I know our unit was extremely proud of their bravery too. Even though I hadn't messed with painting or any type of art at that point for a long time I would doodle at times on their bombs or on a napkin or two out of appreciation for them.

This one day at the new field kitchen a pilot walked by and grabbed the napkin I was drawing on. I was just playing around but Jackal, as we called the pilot, asked me if I would paint something special on the bombs that were loaded on his jet. I didn't really have any plans to ever paint again but I didn't think I could refuse anyone that I respected so much. Per his request, I painted a Jackal on Jackal's bombs or at least I think I did. I didn't know what a Jackal looked like so I at least painted the meanest looking dog I could. Once the other pilots saw what I did for Jackal they all wanted something personal on theirs bombs or even in the side of their jets as well. I painted dragons, the American flag, naked women, and really anything else they wanted. Painting came back to me like I never stopped, it's just the only canvas we had this time was an F-16 and anything that could be attached to it.

One of the pilots that asked me to paint something for him was one of the ones who was later captured. As that damn irony struck again what he asked me to paint was a four-leaf clover. He was the only one out of the seven that survived the war. Five of our pilots must have died on impact. One died in captivity, and Lucky, the pilot that made it, was traipsed across the television until the end of the war. I remember seeing his eyes swollen shut from what I'm guessing was a continual beating. He also had several blood-striped lashes across his face, but just as the news advertised he was still alive. As Lucky was forced to speak to the world, no doubt at gunpoint, our spirits did more than enrage. We felt so helpless because one of our own was being tortured and paraded across the television in some sort of evil propaganda attempt. The worst thing is there was absolutely nothing any of us could do. There's a reason that pilots have certain nicknames chosen for them.

For Lucky even though he was alive I didn't know if whoever chose his was extremely right or perfectly wrong. That same pilot was eventually released at the end of the war. He was given a bunch of those fake medals, as the military gives, but he was never close to being the same ever again. His body healed for the most part but his mind never did. About six months after he returned home, he committed suicide. Lucky did for himself what his capturers spared him from. It's somewhat understandable when people die in war, but it's all the aftermath that war causes, to include additional deaths, that are so hard to get your head around. This was a horrible thing to happen, but for us and our unit, times were getting ready to get much worse. In fact, in many ways, it was going to be the final knockout blow.

It was Christmas day and Sarge called one of his meetings. Andy and his jovial ass decorated Sarge's M16 with socks and underwear just like sarcastic idiots do. We all sat down around the makeshift assault Christmas tree and talked about what we were thankful for. Eric said, "Beer," but most of us acknowledged that we were thankful for our families, friends, and still being alive. Sarge gave thanks for his wife, his boys and us, whom he once again let us know, considered as blood. I was feeling a little bold I guess because it was Christmas day so I took a chance and asked him why in the hell he made me paint that same damn curb three different colors that first week when I arrived at our base. He laughed and told me he wanted to see if I painted it the third time as well as I did the first. I smiled because I understood what he was saying. He was seeing if he could trust me to do whatever he asked, even if I didn't understand his orders. I knew he definitely trusted me by then, but more importantly I trusted him with my life knowing that he made me ready for whatever he had to tell me to do.

None of us could have done what we were forced to without him and I knew he was another great father, so I'd been blessed with two. There were many other units all around us and most of them lost a lot of troops, but not ours. I thought maybe he did have a direct line to God, or possibly his love for his desert family shielded us from what so many others had to face. We'd soon see that the greatness of Sarge, like with Sammy was like the brightest shooting star that burnt out way too early. Another one of the hardest stories of my life, one that will always bring tears to my eyes started when Sarge received his final gift of the year. He was as excited as we'd ever seen him when he called us all together. When the rare package would actually get to us, we usually didn't stray too far off so we could see what that person got. That system felt so familiar considering how my mother ran our Christmases when I was younger.

On this day, Sarge himself got a package from his wife. He quickly opened it as impatiently as Sammy ever was, and quickly discovered there was a VHS tape inside. I'm sure he was expecting it to be his kids playing sports or something like that but what he received was one of the most evil gifts anyone could ever get. As we all gathered to watch Sarge's tape, it didn't take long to realize something was very wrong. Since that time, I've seen similar plots played out in military-related movies, but I promise you in real life it's so much worse. Packages from home were precious but this was one pure evil. As we watched Sarge's tape, all of our hearts broke in shame. His wife sent him a tape of her having sex with another man, all while mockingly asking him for a divorce. If he would have ordered us to her house right then, we would have all went and there would have been nothing left. But that's not what he did.

I went to cut off the tape as fast as I could, but he screamed out, "NO! LEAVE IT ON!" Then he ordered us all to get out of the tent. We all left, too shocked to a say a word. Looking back, we never should have left, but we honestly didn't think it was possible for him to put that rifle that was decorated as a Christmas tree in his mouth and pull the trigger. As the single shot rang out, my heart immediately knew what had happened. I felt that feeling before. We all ran in as fast we could, but it was too late. Our father, our angel, our hope had killed himself. This death reopened wounds that I knew would never heal this time. Sarge was gone forever and we were instantly lost with no clue of what we were going to do next. In war, I don't think you really hate who you are fighting against. Most of time from what I saw they were simply like us, military men following orders trying to get some officer somewhere another rank.

But this enemy was different. This was the worst possible friendly fire of all. Sarge's death and the way it happened seemed to be the pinnacle of what any of us could endure. Personally, regardless of the missions, the bombings, or the raids, I'd never seen evil on this scale before. This evil came in quietly from someone who was supposed to love him the most and, unlike in the movies, we just couldn't switch to the next scene. I often thought about his boys even though I never personally met them. By the time we returned back to our base in Spain, his wife and family were long gone, heartbreakingly but also thankfully so. At the time of Sarge's death, none of us knew we'd be back in Spain within the next month. Not that it would have been any better but I often wondered why he couldn't have just waited until then to try and work something better out, but I thought even more, why couldn't she? If that situation would have been handled in almost any other way, he'd still be alive and with us.

It was always the hidden terrors that were the most dangerous in war and as I know from personal experience within families as well. I mostly thought about why we left him alone for a long time. He would have never left us, regardless of what we said. Guilt sets in stronger with suicide, more so than any other type of death, especially if you know it was preventable. This damn new guilt demanded answers. The problem was, those demands never had any chance of ever being answered. Sarge's death wasn't the first suicide while we were there, but it was definitely the one that hit the closest to home. Hell, this one tore my home down. Suicides aren't really talked about in the military. They're swept under the rug or fictionalized to some degree, but if I had to bet, we probably lost about five percent of our troops to something that was so ignored.

Life wasn't anywhere close to fair, but this wasn't one of life's subtle or even harsh adjustments or ironies; this was an atomic explosion that made a direct hit to our hope and faith in everything we thought we knew. After making it through all of those ridiculous missions and attacks, the cruelest type of death punch was thrown. This was too much to handle and we all knew it. There was just a true and unsettling feeling that we got to go home and Sarge didn't. A lot of that feeling came from knowing that we left huge part of all of us in that God-forsaken place. Those parts would be spread across that desert that gave so little but took so much. They would be on that flight line where we launched out so many jets. They would be in that tent where it all ended and they would be everywhere else that Sarge ever was. When the cargo planes arrived to take us back to Spain, I don't think anyone really wanted to leave. We all knew we were leaving with much less than what we arrived with.

Not knowing how else to handle this loss I realized my best bet was to run away again. Since you can't really run away from the military without getting arrested I decided to get to wherever I went with a bottle. When we finally touched down in Spain, I also realized that none of us had spent any money in almost two years. We were getting paid and it was going into the bank, but what were we going to buy, sand burgers? This was a forced savings system that none of us would have done on our own, but we had it, so it made us all feel pretty damn rich when we got back. In addition to money, we all had accrued sixty days leave over the course of the two years. Our little unmarried group decided to take the first thirty days to travel together throughout Europe and the last thirty to go see our actual families back in the States.

At this time I really did need a little time to decompress. Even though we were back, we really weren't anywhere close to being mentally back at all. Our minds and souls for that matter were somewhere else and they were as discombobulated as they could be. A military ID in those days allowed us to travel from country to country without any issues, so along with drinking that's what we did for that first month back. We went to Germany, France, Belgium, Italy, and of course, the Netherlands but my favorite place was the Rock of Gibraltar. That place was overrun with monkeys, tail-less Macaques to be exact. There were more monkeys there than rats in that old bombed out building. Those animals were funny too. They would steal peoples' food, pull women's shirts up or their skirts down. They would dry hump almost anything that moved, to include my leg. It was their little island and they weren't shy about letting everyone else know that we were the visitors.

MY MIA

From Gibraltar, we took a cheap and very dated cruise ship to Morocco. Morocco was my least favorite place for many reasons. By this time, we had female company join us on the trip. I took a blonde hair, blue-eyed Spanish girl. Everyone seems to think all Spanish women have olive-colored skin and dark brown eyes, but in truth, it's about fifty-fifty. Just as many have fair skin and blonde or even reddish hair but anyway I had one of latter with me. When we arrived in Morocco, it seemed like a very formal country. Even though they had huge sandy beaches, everyone was still all covered up in robes and scarves. Hardly anyone was on the beach itself. Morocco was one of the countries that we were warned against visiting, but since we were so close, we couldn't pass up the opportunity. Besides, they had a McDonald's just like we did, or so I thought. We went into what we thought was a McDonald's and ordered what we thought were hamburgers.

I should have known something wasn't exactly the same because, even though they had the golden arches and the same name, there were rabbits, chickens and I think some parts of a lamb hanging on a cord strung across the main dining area. After I took my first bite I knew this wasn't like any Mickey D's I'd ever been to before. The burger itself tasted like what I could only describe as a warm tongue. We didn't stay there long because, other than the food being inedible, we were only on a day trip and wanted to see as much of the country as we could. After we left, we started walking through the bazaars, just taking in the country. I honestly felt that Aladdin was going to jump out at any minute and try to sell us a magic carpet ride. I didn't see Aladdin but there were Persian rugs hanging everywhere for sale.

Those bazaars were like huge flea markets and it looked like it was where everyone in the city worked and happened to be at that day based on how crowded it was. As we were walking around, a villainous-looking man came up to us. He was wearing a décor that I'd never seen anybody wear outside of a cartoon. He had on red-and-white-striped pants, a pink puffy pleated shirt and he smelled like rotten tobacco. He asked me if I was interested in one of his rugs. Again, this really did feel like a bad Disney movie with no exaggeration. If I was the hero of this story though, I felt like I was getting ready to get jacked. When I told him, "No, thank you," he then wanted to talk to me around the corner alone. I just got back from a war and I didn't trust people directly in front of me, so I knew I didn't want to go around the corner with this character, but reluctantly, I did.

As he spoke, I thought I heard him say he wanted me to trade the blonde girl that was with us for one of his fine rugs. I soon found out how serious he was about that too. First of all, I didn't own her. Hell, I didn't even know her that well, but I did know we needed to get back to that ship as soon as possible before something worse happened. On the way back to the ship someone even tried to steal the camera off of my shoulder. I just held on tight and kept walking, blonde girl and all. Our trip may have ended on a weird note but all of it was an experience of a lifetime. Now it was time to get ready to go back to my real home in Virginia. Flights to the States were always on commercial planes and we flew for free if we wore our uniforms and had our military ID. By this time, I had spent most of my two years' savings, so free was the way for me. After our whirlwind thirty-day European vacation, I was finally really ready to go home to my real family.

Originally, it wasn't that I didn't want to see my family right away, I just wasn't ready. None of us were. Pieces and chunks were torn from my soul again and I never thought anything could ever fill that void for a second time, even if the attempts were from those who loved me the most. Saying I was confused wasn't anything close to what I really was. With everything we went through with Sammy, I didn't want to take a chance in bringing all that death anywhere close to my family once again until I felt I had a better handle on it myself, if that was possible. I will say, a good thing about the war I was in, was that America really stood behind their troops. It was the first war since Vietnam and unlike Vietnam, we were treated like heroes rather than criminals. I was extremely grateful for the appreciation but I definitely felt unworthy of such praise, even if I had a chest full of fake medals.

One of those demonstrations of appreciation was on the long flight home to Virginia. I never talked about any of the actual happenings, but I did confirm to the other passengers who asked that I just returned from the desert, and I hadn't been home at that point for almost three years. As soon as several of the businessmen on the flight heard my story, the free drinks of gratitude started pouring in. I think almost everyone on that plane bought me at least one drink and many bought, two or more. I was so polluted when I reached the terminal at Dulles that I had to have help getting off the plane. I knew I had to catch a connecting flight into Richmond an hour later to meet my thirty-or-so awaiting family members but I didn't make it. Instead, after I found where my next flight would be leaving from, I proceeded to lay down with my head on my duffle bag and woke up six hours later.

I woke up with a headache but also with the realization that I had missed my way home once again. I did manage to find the military office in the airport and I told the sergeant on duty exactly what happened. Regardless of my faults, I learned a long time ago that lying never helped so I fessed up to why I really missed my flight. The sergeant didn't care once he saw all of those fake medals across my chest and he quickly booked me on the next flight to Richmond. That sergeant also contacted the other airport to have them notify my family and let them know that I was detained for a day. I don't know if my parents ever really knew the story behind the real reason of my tardiness but I do know I was always too ashamed to tell them. When I finally walked down the ramp at the passenger gate in Richmond, half of those who were originally there the day before weren't there to welcome me home this time. I guess they didn't know if I'd actually make it home or not either.

I didn't care, though, because my parents and Jacob were there and that was enough for me. After I got to my parents' house, I stayed in my old room and slept in my old bed, and even though I'd been there what seemed like a million times before, it didn't seem familiar at all to me. Death had come in so many forms that I think it was blocking most of my innocent youthful memories out. It was somewhat of a welcomed numbness this time but it still didn't touch the sting from Sarge or the fact that even though it had been four years, Sammy wasn't there either. I tried to think back to my childhood but those mostly wonderful memories were hiding from me. I knew that my new assignment would be coming in while I was on leave, and this time, the Dream sheet pushed me a little further East to Tokyo, Japan. Once again, I'd be thousands and thousands of miles away, but this time, as military people do, I'd be starting completely over again.

There would be no Sarge, no Andy; not even Eric's crazy ass would be there. I had a lot to think about and only had a month to do so. I stayed fairly low key during my month at home. I enjoyed my family and I'd like to think that they enjoyed their time with me too. I knew if I accepted my assignment to Japan, I would have to re-enlist or end my military career and return home for good. I had no idea what I was going to do but my old friends from home knew what they wanted me to do right then. The weekend before I left to go back to Spain, they wanted to take me to the beach. I hadn't really spent any time with them while I was home, so I reluctantly agreed. I soon realized that my old high school friends were now every bit as wild and ignorant as any of my Air Force buddies. I had to be home by Monday for my re-going away party and then I was off again early Tuesday morning, on my way back to Madrid seemingly for the last time either way.

I still didn't know whether I was going to re-enlist or get out but I wasn't going to worry about it then. My friend's drink of choice wasn't Sol y Sombra, it was Tequila, a drink that was absolutely just as evil. Friday night I hung right in there with them, but Saturday, realizing my departure was coming up soon, I kind of took it easy. I told the guys that I was getting ready to head back to the hotel room and I headed towards the door. All of a sudden, before I reached the exit, I just happened to look left. As corny as it sounds, I caught the eye of this beautiful woman sitting with some of her friends and I couldn't stop staring. I felt strange because, for the first time in my life, I couldn't take my eyes off of someone myself. That must have been what Andy felt like when he first saw his wife. There was just something about that girl though.

It was like somehow I knew her without knowing her. She had strawberry blonde hair and big, round innocent-looking hazel brown eyes. She also had these little, soft, yet extremely sexy freckles that blended into her skin. They looked like they could have been punctuations to her absolute cuteness. She realized that some jerk was staring at her, and probably a little too much for her to be comfortable with. For the first time in my life, I felt like Andy, too frozen to make a move. Once again, and for some reason, life adjusted to my rare meekness as she began to walk my way. As she passed, she looked me in the eyes again and kind of flipped her hair to the side. I thought to myself, if this was some kind of hot girl mating ritual, I liked it. She then walked right by me heading towards another bar in the place. Halfway there, she turned around and nodded. She was probably thinking, *dumbass, aren't you coming?* I timidly followed my subliminal orders and we sat down next to each other.

She didn't ask my name or give me time to ask hers. She simply said, "So, what's your story?" *Oh crap, I thought to myself, my story, where do I begin? Umm, I'm going back to Spain in two days, I just carried the body bags of some of my closest friends for the past two years. Hell, what's my story?* I've always been somewhat subtle and to the point, but with this girl, I didn't want to take even the slightest chance of putting her off or showing her just how much of a dumb ass I actually was. I thought for a second and said, "My story is, I just met my future wife." I didn't mean to sound like too much of a cheeseball but she gave me a little cute giggle and scooted her chair closer, so something was working. With this newly-found approval, I gained back a little confidence and told her my name was Israel.

Then she let me in on the secret that her name was Emily. There we were, Israel and Emily, not knowing where this particular magic carpet ride was going to take us. She laughed at my dumb attempt at being funny, but once we started talking like adults, we just couldn't stop. What started in the bar, ended on the beach. After hours of nothing but just getting to know each other, I realized I had never been so smitten with anyone like I was with her. We exchanged numbers and by then, I was completely honest in telling her I'd be leaving in two days, but I'd be back soon. That one chance meeting finalized my decision about ending my military career and coming back home for good. She wasn't the only reason, but this mystery girl was definitely a big part of my final decision. This girl glowed, I tell you. Maybe it was my eyes but there was just something so special about her. I simply can't explain what she did to me almost immediately after seeing her for the first time.

She was soft-spoken, confident and built like a Sherman tank, but in truth, I didn't even notice what I usually do in a woman because of her glow. I almost thought that glow was a signal from above because I was simply too slow to recognize any other signals on my own. Maybe I got a little divine help, I don't know. We had full access to the phones on the base in Spain, so once I got back, we talked almost every night. We also created some pretty big phone bills over the next month. As everything else in my life has, my remaining time in Spain flew by. A week before I was supposed to make the final trip home, I started getting cold feet. I thought, *what the hell am I doing getting out of the military?* Reality started setting in. I knew I didn't really know this girl, glowing or not. I even went as far as going to the commander to see if I could still accept my orders to Japan at the last minute but he said it was too late.

My orders had already been filled by someone else. My feet turned from cold to frozen in a hurry. The last week on base, I wouldn't take Emily's calls. I was actually questioning every decision I ever made in life, especially that one. Regardless of all my confusion, I ended up on that same plane headed back home again, but this time, I wore civilian clothes, drank Pepsi and showed up on-time. It's hard to explain, but as I saw my family and started hugging them, Emily's glowing ass popped around the corner, too. All of my fear about her or getting out of the Air Force seemed to subside, at least for the time being. Either way, it was done, and I had to move on. I felt if she cared enough about me, someone she barely knew, to surprise me at the airport with my family there, then I had to at least give it a try. I thought to myself, they don't make a lot of women like this, so maybe we'll see. It was as if she was always a part of our family from that point on, she just fit in.

Over the next month like a whirlwind, and way prematurely, we decided to move in together. We both knew we were still getting to know each other, but by then, I was a little older and hopefully a lot wiser than before I left for the military. I still went out sometimes with my friends but I was a lot more conservative and respectful than ever before. This one night, I had already gotten in the bed when something was pecking at my bedroom window. I got up to see what or who it was. What I soon found out was it was my old high school friend, Eddie. Eddie and I were really good friends in high school but I had no clue why he was outside throwing rocks at my window that late at night, so I had to let him in to find out. Once inside, he excitedly told me that he had just enlisted in the military himself and wanted to go out to and grab a drink to celebrate. Emily wasn't a jealous woman, so she didn't have any problems with it, so I went.

I told Eddie as much as I'd tell anyone about the military and about some of our missions as we drank a few rounds. It got to be about 1:30 a.m. and an old high girlfriend came in for last call; it was April. She didn't know we were there and we didn't know she was coming in. We hadn't seen each other in years, so when saw me she ran over and gave me a big hug and then kissed me right on the lips. Just then, I looked up and saw that Emily was also coming in the other door and saw the kiss. She had come looking for us to make sure we were okay, but when she saw that other girl kiss me, she ran out crying. I never reciprocated and didn't know it was going to happen but it didn't matter. Emily went home and locked herself in the bedroom. I tried to defend myself through the door, but she wasn't having any of it, and made me sleep on the couch that night. When she came out the next morning, I told her what happened and I could tell that she was pretending to believe me. False or not, I knew if I didn't do something drastic, I'd lose her before we ever really got started.

So, even though I knew we were nowhere near close to being ready, I asked Emily to marry me. Emily seemed to forget about any hurt that I caused, whether it had been real or imagined, and she excitedly said yes. From there we began planning a very premature wedding. We didn't have a lot of money, so we got married at a small church with just our friends and family in attendance. I did get Andy to come and be my best man and Eric's crazy ass was also there as one of my groomsmen. I was so happy that they were able to be a part of our wedding. It was a nice and very informal and I felt if Emily was happy, so was I. I managed to save a little money to go on a honeymoon after, so off to the Bahamas we went. It was fairly cheap, and we met at a beach, so we decided to go back to one for our own little escape.

The resort was kind of dated but it was on a lagoon that was amazing. As with most things, nothing can be completely normal with me, so unexpectedly, it rained every day we were there. I don't know if all that rain was a warning from the rat gods of the desert, but if it was, they were a little too late. Since we were stuck in the room so much, we talked a lot. We talked about a lot of things we really should have talked about before we ever got to that point. I loved Emily but some of the things she told me really were shocking. I knew she had a much tougher childhood than I but not to the level that she waited to tell me about until after we were married. Emily was abused by two older male family members, to include her father, when she was a child. She never felt like her mother helped her as much as she needed, so Emily basically had very little contact with her, except on rare occasions. Her mother was at our wedding but she didn't stay long and really didn't talk to anyone. I've been around her mother a few times, but Emily always said she worked a lot, so I just took her for her word about the matter.

Now, I'm not going to pretend that I know anything about abuse or the terrible things that she went through when she was younger, but I did know I was going to do everything I could to help my new wife. Even if my pain was from a different source, I felt I could directly relate to a lot of what she was saying. At first, I was selfishly mad that she didn't tell me all of what she did that week earlier, but I didn't tell her about my heartaches before then either so I guess we were unfortunately even. I didn't even tell Emily about Sarge and the way he died until that week. Maybe getting stuck in the hotel room with my beautiful wife wasn't that bad after all. Our conversations got deeper and deeper, and I think we both told each other all of what we thought our deepest and darkest secrets were.

When I thought we already let everything out of the proverbial bag, she added that she also had past drug and alcohol problems. Again, not the best thing to hear after you're already married, but even though it wasn't drugs for me, I could definitely relate to the alcohol thing. She laughed almost as hard as Andy did when I told her about my catheter incident and that toxic Spanish drink, Sol y Sombra, and all the other curses I faced when I decided to drink it. Upon returning, I finally felt like we knew enough about each other to possibly make this marriage thing work. We both knew we weren't anywhere near being ready to be married, but we were, so we just had to do whatever it took to make it last. Emily set me out on a new mission. That mission was to help her take all of her pain away instead of worrying about mine any longer. I knew how to love. My family loved me and I loved them, and it was my turn to pass on what they taught me to my new wife.

Two broken souls were going to try and create one full and whole union. I loved Emily and I honestly believe she loved me, but about six months after we were married, her father died and all of her old feelings of betrayal and hurt came to the surface on a daily basis. Her emotions often came out in ways that were completely unexplainable to me. I would have done anything to help her, but she wouldn't let me. In six short months of marriage, she changed into this completely different person that I couldn't talk to or touch and, once again, I had no clue what to do. I told her that I was in it for the long haul and remembering how we left Sarge, I would never make the mistake of leaving someone I loved again. As a month or so longer went by, Emily simply didn't have that glow anymore. She had more of a foggy hue of frustration. It was so hard to love someone when they wouldn't let you in at all. One afternoon, after we had a long talk she asked me to leave.

I can't say I didn't expect it, but I would have never done that to her. I still didn't want to give up on her. Heart breaking, I thought about it for a while and made sure that was absolutely what she wanted me to do, and since it was, I decided to go. I couldn't judge her, I had my own demons, but like Sarge, she was hurt by people who were supposed to love her the most. With that understanding, I decided to let her have what she asked for and leave. I know I was greatly tested in my own prior life but I was always taught that love and faith can conquer all. She simply wasn't taught that and she definitely didn't experience anything like that in her early life. I felt it came to the time where I was forced to live with her decision. Just when I thought we had everything we needed to actually have a great start, life changed again, and I couldn't do a damn thing about it. The day before I was planning to leave, she called me into the bedroom and showed me this plastic stick with a red line across it. Like it or not, and together or not, we were going to have a baby.

At first, I was worried that she'd want an abortion but thank God that wasn't her decision regardless of her state of mind. I never blamed Emily for a lot of things because my heart broke for her. In many ways, I felt like I failed her too, but now that we were having a baby, we just couldn't dare pass any of our damage on to our child. If the thoughts of being married ever scared me, the thoughts of me being a father scared me even more. Emily and I were actually breaking up when she found out she was pregnant and I had no other option but to sit in a holding pattern until I saw which Emily I was going to get. From the second I found out I was going to not only have a baby, but a little girl, I changed. I mean, I changed forever.

I wanted to be a person that my daughter could be proud of. A father she could depend on. A dad that would always be there for her and make sure things like what happened to Emily would never happen to her. I know somewhere deep down, Emily wanted the same for our daughter, but she just couldn't find her way. Emily made it through the pregnancy, even though at times I really didn't think she would. She just kind of separated herself from life and it was all triggered by her father's death and the terrible life that he provided for her in her early years. I prayed, I tried to go to counseling and church, I even talked to her mother, but Emily had her mind made up. This time she was going to leave after the baby was born. There was nothing I could do about it and it killed me. As God as my witness, I did absolutely everything that she let me do, but it still wasn't enough.

I've been to some low places before but where Emily was seemed even lower. It was almost like she felt she didn't deserve love and not I or our little girl could change those thoughts. When I got to the point that I felt I was beginning to hurt Emily as much as I was helping, I had to stop and just let her go. What made matters worse was that Emily had a great deal of trouble delivering our daughter. She was a smaller woman and other than false alarms exhausting her, the delivery from start to finish took about twenty hours. Emily was torn and damaged once again, but this time, it was from our daughter's birth. She had profound problems before she got pregnant but now they were even worse. I wanted so badly to take her pain away but I couldn't. My Mia was born on February 22nd and Emily left us both on April 1st. That was an April Fool's Day I will never forget but it wasn't a joke. I cared about Emily, but now, with a new infant who needed so much, that baby had to be my top priority.

I may not have known what I was doing before with certain things, but this time, I knew without question that my little girl deserves all of the love that I can muster. I loved that kid from the second I knew she was coming. For her, and for my own sake, she had to be the only thing I thought about. When I looked at my daughter, I often felt remorse that I couldn't stop her mother from leaving us. I even sometimes felt sorry that she got stuck with only me but I was bound and determined not to let her down. When Mia was really young, we'd often just looked in each other's eyes as if to say, "Okay, now what?" It was funny, many times, our eyes locked together very similarly to how her mother's and mine did the first time we met. But with Mia, there was no question about the realness of the stare. Being a dad and the only person that little girl had was so different from anything I have ever experienced. Without a doubt this time, I felt like we knew each other ever since the beginning of time.

This caused me to rationalize that if Mia was the sole reason that Emily and I ever met, then it was more than worth it. I spent so many hours just looking at my baby and she did the same with me. It was as if our souls were linking up in those daddy-daughter stare-offs where the prize was unconditional love and trust. I couldn't blink when she looked up at me—hell, I couldn't move because my heart was so full and heavy at the same time. My child and I had some of the warmest and most tender moments before she could really do much of anything. I often wondered what she was thinking, but she was probably just asking herself, why is this big dumb idiot always staring at me? I was so happy to be that big dumb idiot, too. I didn't feel an ounce of my past or of that deep-seeded pain or loss when I held her. Mia took it all away by simply just being herself. This little girl was taking care of me every bit as much as I was her, even more so than Sammy did. That old gypsy lady was right about this too, this kid is and will always be my life's greatest blessing.

It was so hard for me to believe how much my life had changed. Just a very short time ago, I was dealing with things that I never thought I could get any sort of relief from. Now, and honestly, thanks to Emily and her great gift to me, almost all of my own pain was somewhere else, as if it never existed. I still felt Sammy and Sarge and the rest of the guys in my heart. I still hurt at times for Emily too but Mia needed me to put all of that aside, and I can't ever thank her enough for placing that need upon me. I was so happy at times that it almost made me feel guilty and even unworthy. I often wondered what Emily was doing and prayed she found the same kind of peace that I was truly experiencing for the first time in my life but I honestly felt she walked away from the one thing that could have given her what she needed the most.

At first, Emily called occasionally, but it wasn't the same; she wasn't the same. After a while the calls stopped altogether. I think the calls were made out of guilt more so than anything else but I'd never question her motives. She gave me my greatest blessing, so all I could do is wish her well and keep her in my prayers. In a selfish way, I was glad Emily was gone. Mia deserved so much more than abandonment from her mother. I still can't or won't dare judge the hurt and destruction that Emily's parents put in her life. I don't even know what triggered when her father died, but regardless of the reasons, I had a child to raise. Our little family was far from what most people would call normal, but it was great. My life as the single father of an infant never felt challenging at all. My family helped when I needed them to, especially my mother, but for the most part it was just Mia and me.

She's Back

I will say that Mia was an easy baby. She didn't cry a lot, but when she did, I'd rock her in an old rocking chair that my mother gave me while singing the worst rendition of Bob Marley's, "No Woman, No Cry" until she stopped. She must have eventually realized that she didn't have to listen to my terrible voice if she didn't cry, so her crying really was a rarity. I don't think back then I ever really slept very much myself though. At night, after Mia went to sleep, I would check on her about a hundred times just to make sure she was breathing, or to see if she needed changing. In truth, I think what it really was, was I could hardly wait until she woke up again so we could spend some more time together. This big, ex-military guy was becoming a big wuss but that was okay for that little girl. One evening, Mia and I were playing with building blocks in the middle of the living room floor like we did so often back then when the doorbell rang.

I thought it was my mother who may have forgotten something from her visit earlier in the day, so I opened the door without asking who was there. As I opened the door, it was as if I saw a ghost. It was Emily. She was all of a sudden back and she didn't look so good. Of course I didn't tell her that, I just invited her in and she sat down on the couch. She timidly watched Mia playing on the floor as if she was too scared or ashamed to go over to her. Emily left when Mia was just over a month old, so neither one of them really knew each other. By this time, I hadn't heard from her in months, and to be honest, it was more of an out of sight, out of mind thing for me. Since she didn't do it on her own, I told Emily to sit down on the floor and play with Mia. She slowly slid off the couch and made her way to where Mia was stacking blocks. Emily really didn't talk or interact with her a lot at first, she just sheepishly watched our daughter play.

You would think I would have had a million questions for Emily, but I didn't, I only had a one. I wanted to know why she was in my living room then. That was all I really needed to know. In the back of my mind, I knew we never went to a lawyer to finalize anything, to include a legal end to our marriage or any kind of custody arrangement, and this was something that always made me nervous. It's not that I didn't care about Emily, I would have still done almost anything for her, but I also didn't feel I could trust her or those demons that made her leave either. I know how lawyers work, and although we talked about it, she left town too fast after Mia was born to secure anything and my contact with her had been sporadic at best. Either way, she was there, sitting on my living room floor. I went over and sat down beside them and asked Mia if she knew who Emily was. In normal one-year-old fashion, and taking nothing away from Emily, Mia was playing with her blocks and really didn't care.

I then found myself awkwardly introducing Mia to her mother when I said, "Mia, this is your mommy." Mia had been around other kids, so I think she knew to some degree what a mommy was but I didn't know. She may have just thought it was a daddy with long hair. I knew this day would come, and I even felt like it had to for the sake of both Mia and Emily, but I wasn't ready for it. Emily stayed until after I put Mia to bed and I could tell she wanted to talk. After I returned from Mia's room, I made a pot of coffee because I knew that night had the possibility of being a long one. That conversation was probably going to be too important to miss anything. Once the coffee finished brewing, I poured both of us a cup and we sat down at the kitchen table. Once again, it took Emily a minute to start talking, but when she did, she told me what I feared. She was moving back and would like to start seeing Mia.

This was Mia's mother, I couldn't or didn't want to say no, but I knew my world was getting ready to change again and it was just when I couldn't have been any happier. I honestly felt bad that what I was actually feeling was defensiveness against my daughter's mother. She already had so many issues but this time I was having a rollercoaster of emotions. Even though I did care about Emily, and I knew she had been through so much, my little family was working, and we were perfectly happy without her. I didn't want anything to disrupt our lives, and selfishly, that included her mother. As we talked, I felt like I was talking to a stranger, and even though she had every right, I didn't want a stranger asking to take time away from me and my child in any way. I didn't ask her where she had been or what she had been doing. In many ways, it was none of my business, but it was Mia's business to me. Before she left, she told me she was moving in with a friend not too far from my apartment and would be fully settled in about two weeks.

All of these thoughts were running through my mind but I proceeded with the utmost caution because I knew Mia's mother was going to be back for the first time in a long while. Now she evidentially wanted to be in Mia's life on a regular basis. After beating around the bush for a while, I just came out and asked her how I could help her without disrupting our lives. She broke down in tears and told me she didn't know herself. This was kind of a relief because I knew she was telling me the truth and I guess that was a start. This was new territory for both of us and regardless of my fears or preferences at the time, we agreed that when she moved back, she could start visiting Mia. Emily moved back two weeks later as she said she would. She also started visiting Mia a couple days a week at my apartment as we agreed upon.

Most of those times, I would leave the room so that they could have their time together to get to know one another. From Emily's visits with our daughter, you could tell Mia was having the same effect on her as she had on me. In no time Emily began looking happier and much more confident than she did on her first surprise visit. I was happy for her, I really was, but I was used to that being my time, and although I realized I was being selfish, I couldn't help it. I never had to share Mia before and it bothered me. I think what bothered me the most was that I didn't know where this new reunion was going. Emily couldn't continue only seeing Mia at my place and I knew it. The day I knew was coming came. It took about six months after Emily's first visit for her to ask me if she could start taking Mia out with her on her own. By this time, we were already processing our divorce and trying to figure out what the most sensible thing would be as far as custody went.

Everything was amicable and really, once again, I had no choice but to let it happen. I have to give Emily some credit though she realized what I did when she was gone and really never treated me any other way than with appreciation. I was trying to help Emily while accomplishing my most important goal of making sure Mia had the best possible life I could provide. The sad thing about this is, I would have done the same for Emily, but she wouldn't let me. No matter what some of my stray thoughts were, it was too late for us, and I didn't want that situation to ever enter my mind again. The day soon arrived where we had to go to court for someone else to decide how we were going to work our custody arrangement out in the eyes of the law. The outcome of court was that we both received joint custody of Mia, which meant I lost more time with my daughter. Emily now had the legal right to get Mia fifty percent of her life and I basically lost my daughter half of the time.

This was an unsettling time for me because I didn't do anything to lose any time with my daughter. I was far from perfect but I did all I could for everyone in this messed up situation and I felt I was the only one who that lost anything. A few more months went by and Emily became much more confident in her actions and interactions with Mia. At first, on the days I didn't have Mia, I thought I'd go crazy wondering if she was okay or what she was doing. What made me feel better but worse at the same time was, almost every time I picked her up from her mother she was so excited to see me, but she'd often try and hurry us to the car and back to our home almost as if she was hiding something. Very carefully, I tried to talk to Mia about her life with her mother to see if she'd give me any clues to what she was experiencing, but she was too young to play along. The biggest thing I noticed after our new arrangement was that Mia didn't ever want to go to sleep when she was with me once the joint custody situation began. This bothered me to the point that I asked Emily if there was anything I needed to know but she told me she didn't really think so.

I didn't have a definite reason to be overly concerned, so I pretty much wrote it off to possibly being normal for her age. My instincts still often flared up when Mia started to have fits when I dropped her off to Emily. For the life of me, I was trying to figure out what I was supposed to be learning this time, but I just couldn't. I only saw that something was off and I had to know what it was. I knew what happened to Emily when she was young, and I didn't think that was it, but if it would have been, I'm pretty sure I know what I would have done. Just like in the military when you don't know what's going on, your mind begins to fill in the blanks with its own answers. Emily and I had to talk about this, so I invited her to the apartment and, once again, we sat down at the kitchen table.

Emily acknowledged my worries and said she fully understood my concerns and assured me there was nothing wrong. She did say she was trying to work some things out, whatever that meant, and told me if there were ever any issues she'd let me know. Regardless our talk, I still knew something wasn't quite right with the situation. Mia eventually settled down a little bit, so I did too. My baby girl really was starting to become a neat little person. We were best buds, as Eric used to say. She definitely had an outgoing and strong personality herself. Many times, I think she thought she was my mother. If I cooked something she didn't like, she'd eat it, but at the end of the meal she'd say, "Daddy, you can do better." I was getting cooking lessons from a two-year-old at that time and every other type of life lesson as well. I still missed her so much when she wasn't with me, but I know that absence made me never take our time together for granted.

That kid cracked me on a regular basis too. If I worked on the car, she worked on the car. If I cleaned the house, she'd pull out her tiny plastic vacuum and do the same. Hell, she probably did a better job than I did. If I did anything, she was right there doing it with me. Since I so often disappointed her in the food department we went out to eat a lot. Her favorite place, as many other kids' just happened to be McDonald's. I thought that kid would turn into a McNugget. It may not have been the healthiest of options, but I made her eat vegetables for her snack, so to me, her cuisine of choice was acceptable on many of our days together. Thank goodness none of the McDonald's here tasted anything like the one in Morocco with the warm, nasty tongue burgers. This time, instead of life adjusting to me, I adjusted it, or at least I thought I did. I still wanted to be with that little girl every second of the day, but I had to work, and like it or not, I had to share her with her mother.

Emily and I really didn't talk a lot about anything other than Mia and the normal niceties but things seemed to be fine again for quite a while. Emily had a pretty good job and seemed to be handling her own life and past fairly well and that did comfort me. I knew Emily was my daughter's mother and regardless of almost anything, she will always keep a special place in my heart, even if it would never be as husband and wife again. One day, right around Mia's third birthday, Mia came home talking about a guy named Joe. I didn't think a lot about it because she could have been talking about someone at daycare or really anywhere, so I kept doing whatever it was I was doing. Mia was at the age where she could have some pretty good little conversations as long as it wasn't about my cooking. She definitely seemed older than what she was and often understood things better than I did most of the time. Later that night, when I started reading her a bedtime story, she told me she already knew the book.

I asked her if they read it at school but she told me no, Joe read it to her. Joe again, I thought, *who the hell is Joe?* This was the second time I heard this guy's name out of my daughter's mouth so I was more intrigued. Emily and I had been apart about twenty times longer than we were ever together, so I knew she had to date or go out at times. Every now and then I even did the same, but I never really wanted anybody around Mia and hoped that she didn't either. I'm the father of a little girl, so there are some inherent worries, especially when it comes to men around my child. With Emily's past, she had to have some of those same fears. I didn't want to jump to conclusions or make myself crazy again, so I left it alone until I saw Emily, but this Joe-whoever was still on my mind. Even though, in essence, I lost Mia half of the time when Emily came back, for the most part, we didn't have problems with each other.

It took me a while to get used to our arrangement but eventually, I did. It was like Mia had two entirely different lives but she was loved and taken care of in each. I eventually came to think that the more the love, the better, and in Mia's case, the more birthday parties and more Christmases, too. That little girl kind of made out like a bandit in a backwards sort of way. Double Christmases or not, I may have learned how to live with the situation, but nothing changed about how to keep me sane. I always needed to know that Mia was okay. I found out who Joe was by telling Emily a little white lie. I said, "Mia asked me if I knew a guy named Joe," and asked if she knew what our daughter was talking about. Emily nonchalantly said, "He's a guy I have been dating," and that was pretty much all she said as she continued greeting Mia and helping her take her jacket off to get in her house.

We hadn't been together for a long time, so again, I knew this was going to happen someday but I wanted to know a little more than what she told me. I didn't want to do it in front of Mia, so I waited and called her that night. Now, I would never say that Emily and I came to the point where we were overly close friends after she left, but we cared about each other and had somewhat of a mutual respect for one another by then. We never really fought about anything and if either one of us needed to get Mia on the other's time, there was never an issue. We just functioned together pretty amicably. Emily and I lived almost completely separate lives. We didn't talk to each other about how our days went, work, our life goals or really anything other than Mia, and things were working that way. We got married way before we really knew each other, and even then, with a child together, we still didn't know each other so well.

She had her life, then her life with Mia, and I had the same on my side, but relationships that included other people around Mia were a bit different to me. To my knowledge, she never had anyone around Mia before and I knew I didn't either, so there was definitely a need for that talk. So, I called and we talked about Joe. There were no problems or resistance in our conversation. Emily said that she thought she and Joe were getting somewhat serious and he was around sometimes when Mia was there. I didn't like hearing that but like with so many other things that had happened prior to this, I just had to find a way to deal with it. I was a little tired of being helpless in my own life, but again, things like this are bound to happen and dammit, I'll figure it out one more time. I, in a way, was even somewhat defensive of Emily to myself by thinking that someday I'd probably like to have a real marriage, too, so maybe this won't be that bad. I asked myself, When I was ready, wouldn't I be doing the same thing?

When we talked, she didn't seem to hide anything, so I got my answer about who Joe was, whether I liked it or not. I did ask Emily if I could meet the guy if she felt their relationship was moving to the next level. After another two or so months, that damn Joe asked Emily to marry him, like I figured he would. *Son of a bitch*, I thought, I now had to live up to all of that peaceful crap I was trying to make myself believe. It was definitely much easier to say than to actually do. We decided to go to Mia's favorite eatery, McDonald's, so I could meet my daughter's soon-to-be stepfather. I thought to myself, where the hell did the word stepfather come from anyway? Did it mean another step away from the real father? I was so inexplicably frustrated that I Googled what "step" actually meant. Google said it was an Old English word for when a widow remarries.

This time I thought, *what the hell, Google, I'm still here!* There's no widow, or widower, or widowee, or whatever you call it. I then wondered what the New English dictionary said, hopefully something better than that crap. I was obviously a little sensitive on the topic. As absolutely selfish as I could be, I really wished Emily never came back and that it was just me and Mia like it used to be. I was a little embarrassed of myself for thinking it, but I did. I had to hide all of those feelings but I still felt them. I knew this was self-pity but how can I have peace in anything when everything keeps changing so damn quickly right after it becomes really good? As soon as one thing gets straight, functional or not, something else is added or taken away and I have to start the whole damn game all over again. There's never a rule book or instructions for any of these important things in life either. We all just have to learn as we go. It just doesn't make any sense, and I was not only expressing it, but fully feeling all of that confusion while getting dressed to go meet this damn Joe, the step guy.

Mia was already with her mother that day, so, once I stopped all of my internal whining, I got in my car and headed towards the golden arches. On the way there, my mind was everywhere but it settled on the time when we were similarly whining about being broken up into those search and rescue teams. I remembered when Sarge called the meeting to straighten us all out. I began thinking about his words. When our Sarge spoke, we listened, and I needed to hear his voice so badly for a little direction once again. Even if it was just a whisper of guidance from the wind or from anywhere. I knew his voice would calm me down and help me understand what I couldn't on my own. In truth, I really needed this to happen before I pulled into that restaurant so that I would act like an adult towards this guy who hadn't even done anything wrong yet.

I realized I was working myself up for no reason at that point but I still needed what I thought only Sarge could provide. I don't know if I expected the seas to part or the angel of Sarge to come sit down next to me on the ride that day but neither happened. I did, however, remember what he said to us in our meetings. We knew we were being used in getting assigned to go do something we weren't trained for. We knew that it was happening for the wrong reasons, which did, by the way, help that other idiot colonel become a general. But we still had to do what we had to do. Sarge reminded us of that, and that we had to do it well and survive from it. Sarge didn't talk a lot, but when he did, man did he speak the truth. This was another one of those cases that I didn't have to agree or even like it but I had to do it well and survive from it. I had to give Joe a chance and be happy for Emily, because in a way, Sarge told me to. As I pulled into the parking lot and began to get out of my car, I was now equipped with some of Sarge's last orders, so I stopped whining to myself and stepped forward.

I opened the door to the restaurant, and before I was fully engulfed by the French fry aroma, I heard Mia yell out, "Daddy! Daddy!" Sammy's "Good Day, Good Day" was close but nothing warmed my heart like Mia calling out "Daddy, Daddy" when she saw me. I picked her up and looked in her big, beautiful brown eyes and smiled. As I always did, I said, "Hi, baby girl. She giggled and led me by the hand to the table where her mother was. We always had to sit in that room with that dumb ball pit. I'm pretty sure, in actuality, that's why McDonald's was her favorite restaurant. Every time Mia and I went there, I had to take a huge bottle of sanitizer and almost bathe her whole body with it after she finished playing in those dumb balls. I've seen more than one diaper lost in that abyss.

I expected to see some dude sitting at the table when I got there but Emily said Joe would be there in a few minutes and for us to go ahead and eat because he wouldn't eat at McDonald's anyway. I didn't say a word but I was thinking it. I went to the counter and ordered Emily and myself two Big Mac meals, and for my little turkey, her favorite, chicken nuggets and French fries. As we were sitting at the table near those damn balls, I saw this nice bright red convertible Corvette pull in beside where I parked. This older guy got out and headed inside after looking at himself in his side view mirror for what I would consider way too long. He was dressed in a suit and tie and wore some kind of fancy pointed patent leather shoes. When he came in, the first thing he did was grab a napkin from the counter and wipe his hands. I guess he was worried about germs there as well.

Mia looked up and then over at me, and before Emily could tell me or before he could introduce himself, Mia said, "That's Joe, Daddy." She didn't seem overly enthused but that was more than okay with me, I wasn't either. When he got to the table, he made sure that I saw him give Emily a hello kiss. I thought to myself, I don't give a damn. I haven't touched that girl in almost three years but I just smiled and stood up to shake his hand. He introduced himself, as did I. I complimented his car and we talked about the weather for a bit. I, through small talk, quickly learned he actually lives in one of the nicer houses directly across the street from my apartment. I can actually see his front yard from my balcony. *Great, were neighbors*, I thought. Overall, our short visit wasn't too bad and Emily seemed happy so I guess I had to be as well. Mia was playing in those balls, so she was good. I guess this was just the next step in the *As the World Turns saga* of my damn life. One that I wish would stop spinning around and around so much most of the time.

After we said our goodbyes we went in our own directions. Of course, my direction and Joe's were the same, except he got to go in a shiny red Corvette while I had to go back in my old Truck, but off we went nonetheless. Mia was still with Emily, so I was at the apartment alone. I was trying to figure out what I was actually thinking. I started looking out of the balcony window now that I knew who lived across the street. Joe must have gone somewhere else before getting that Corvette home because he got to his house about thirty minutes after I did. I felt creepy watching this guy, but I wanted to know more about him, and this crazy life made this whole situation way too convenient for me not to achieve that mission.

I shook my head at myself that time and turned on the television to try to take my mind off the fact that my daughter, ex-wife and some rich old guy may actually end up being my new neighbors in a very short amount of time. It was almost comical like one of those cheesy soap operas, but damn, so much of my life had been that way anyway. Too bazar to ever fully explain or understand. I damn sure didn't want to be one of those people in everyone's business—but when it came to Mia, I didn't mind so much. Over the course of the next few months, I saw Emily's car at my older, richer neighbor's house a little more. That was expected, even if not wanted. I wasn't checking up on Emily, or even him necessarily, I just still wasn't very comfortable with anyone around my three-year-old daughter other than us and probably never would be. I felt like I was fighting a losing battle but in reality, I didn't fight it at all... yet.

Hey Joe

One Saturday when Emily had Mia, I had just come in from the gym and was headed towards the shower. As I walked past the balcony door I saw Mia outside in this guy's front yard. Whenever I saw my child, my heart pumped a little harder and seeing her through a window across the street was no different. Now, being nosey about the guy or Emily was one thing, but seeing Mia was another. She was almost four at the time and I didn't see anyone else outside with her. Our homes were split by a sometimes busy road, so I went downstairs to make sure Mia was okay. As I made my way closer to the road Mia saw me and as she always did, yelled out, "Daddy! Daddy!" I started heading towards her faster because she was getting ready to cross the road to get to me. I screamed, "Get back, baby! Stay there! I'll come over to you!" She listened but I was shaken a little because I really thought she was going to try and cross to get to me and once again in a way it would have been my fault.

I made it to Joe's front yard and I was right, there was no one outside with her—she was outside all alone. I picked her up in my arms and went to his front porch to ring the doorbell. As I started to push the button, the door flew open and it was Emily. Before I jumped into my intended interrogation, I noticed she had a towel with ice in it over her right eye. I was still mad and wanted answers, but mostly, I was grateful that Mia was okay and that Emily was there to take care of her. I could tell Emily was shaken too as I told her I found our little girl in the yard by herself heading towards the busy street. Emily then took Mia from my arms and hugged her tightly herself. Emily said she must have snuck out and she didn't know she was outside by herself.

Once things settled down, I asked what happened to her face and she told me she was in a car accident on her way home from work. Of course, I asked if she was okay and if she wanted me to take Mia. She said yes to both. I felt Mia deserved some McNuggets after that unplanned and unsupervised adventure so off we went. Mia ate and played in the balls for a while. Her being in the yard by herself was a bad thing, but I knew little Miss Mia was at the age where you had to watch her almost all the time or she'd be gone. She always listened when I corrected her but she was a very adventurous little girl at least part of me understood how something like that could happen. I'm just grateful her attempts at freedom didn't lead her into that busy road with all of those cars flying back and forth. I was scheduled to keep Mia for the next couple of days anyway, so we just did our usual things. We played and I cooked bad meals.

We watched that stupid purple dinosaur show about twenty times a day and enjoyed each other's time together like we always did. The more she grew, the more she looked like her mother but I honestly believe she was starting to act like me and whether that is a good thing or not is still to be determined. She was never a rude child but man was she direct for such a little thing. She always knew what she wanted and didn't mind verbally expressing those desires. Her little rotten butt got about everything she ever wanted, but even at her age, she was so appreciative that it was just so hard for me to ever say no. I even had her read to me at night. It's not that she could read perfectly yet, but she did pretty well and on the words she didn't know she would just make something up and turn it into a story. Her imagination took us to wherever it was she wanted us to go. Most of her renditions were even better than the original versions too.

In her stories, she often spoke about how her, and her Daddy were floating through the sky, chasing birds or clouds or something like that. I dared not ever tell about that one time in her ignorant Daddy's life, he called himself the sky while falling off a building not once, but twice. Her stories were so cute. I was so honored to be in her imaginary adventures taking us wherever it was she wanted to go. We went to so many places, and did so many things without ever leaving her room. She was also fascinated with the stars. That big-headed kid even made me greatly overpay for a star for her once. One day, when she let me watch something other than Barney, a commercial came on that was advertising the ability to buy your very own star. I thought to myself, *how the hell do you buy a star?* I didn't have to think too hard about it though because the television told us if we'd just pay the low-low price of $99.99 it could be ours, and for an extra ten dollars they'd even name it after you.

My dumb ass paid a hundred and ten dollars plus tax for a picture of a star that had the name Mia on it. I could have cut out a picture and written her name on it for free myself, but no, I didn't do that. My little manipulator had done it again by just saying, "Daddy, Daddy." She waited for weeks to get that thing and when it arrived I think even she was a little disappointed when what was just a piece of paper with her name on got there. I laughed remembering her reaction. She opened the cardboard tube that her star came in and then looked at me and then back at the poster a few times and said, "Daddy, they could have done better." I definitely laughed at her words then because, yeah baby, they certainly could have — especially for a hundred and ten dollars, plus tax. After my days with Mia, when Emily picked her up she couldn't apologize enough about how Mia was in the yard by herself.

I believe she was still truly scared of what could have happened herself after that kid made a break for it. Emily's eye was still a little blackened from the car accident but it looked like it was getting better. I asked how she was otherwise and about the car. She told me everything was fine and Mia hugged me, then they left. Mia didn't put up half as much resistance when she left with her mother this time like she used to. Selfishly, that tugged at me a little, but I took it as she was doing fine and enjoying her time with her mother too. Emily still lived with her friend, thank goodness. She was at Joe's more often but the road incident was the first time I actually saw Mia at his house, and being the sleuth I was I would have known. I didn't like it, but it looked like my daughter and her mom were going to be my new neighbors in the not too distant future after all. I sarcastically thought, at least I'd be close to her. That was definitely not the most ideal of situations but, once again, it was what it was, and I had to find a way to deal with it.

Emily and I were comfortable with each other, but to me, she felt more like a distant cousin or someone that you only saw on special occasions and I really wanted to keep it that way. Besides picking up Mia was my most special occasion. I had very little thoughts of ever wanting Emily back in my life in any other way than the way it was. When those rare thoughts did cross my mind, I didn't let them stay very long. Even though I'd never throw it in her face, I still remember that she left both of us and I don't think those thoughts will ever leave my mind. I know that created a numbness in regard to her that allowed me to be that way, but it's the way I felt. It was the same when the units that we worked with would lose someone. We knew those guys well, we saw them and worked with them every day. It hurt so much when they died but our hearts had to build up scabs so we could keep on going.

Keeping Emily at somewhat of a distance worked for me so that's the way I wanted it after she returned. She wasn't dead or hiding, she was a recurring part of my life that I just felt I had to keep at an arm's-length for my own sake. In dealing with Emily, I always wanted to keep my own emotions in check because of our past. I think when Emily left, I was hurt a lot more than even I ever acknowledged, but I had Mia, so I had to keep moving on, scabbed or not. I simply had to use that numbness that I've mastered to redirect towards whatever pain or feelings that I thought were misplaced. Emily actually looked great again and seemed a lot like the person I first knew. I think she may have very well found her own numbness or maybe even thicker scabs over her own heart. Emily said she never told anyone what her father did to her except for me that night in the Bahamas. She was embarrassed and felt like less of a person, even though she was the victim.

When her father died, she never thought she'd get closure. She wanted to confront him as an adult, to tell him how much he hurt her life. She even wanted to try and forgive him, thinking that would free her, but she never got that chance. She said her greatest guilt came after her father left her. He remarried and had more kids, some of which were daughters. Emily knew that he was probably doing the same terrible things to them. She felt that she contributed to what she just knew they had to deal with as she did. When she left she went to see her stepsisters and her greatest fears were found to be true. Her father was murdered by their mother, a step mother Emily never knew. Her step mother killed her father because of the atrocities that she didn't tell anyone he was capable of. She didn't even tell me that part until she returned. She said she was so guilt-ridden about everything—her past, then her father's death, and then his newer crimes.

She said, she simply couldn't function with everyday life; that unfortunately included raising a newborn baby or being a wife. Back then I wished she would have let me helped her, but she didn't. She didn't know how. In many ways, she didn't feel worthy because, she blamed herself for all of those terrible things that happened to her. Every time I'd learn more about Emily's past and her trials and tribulations, I gained more respect for her mainly because of how she did as well a she did. I know that there are situations and deaths that are greater than even numbness can help handle. Without reducing the severity of my own losses, I think she may have had it even worse than I did, which I didn't realize was possible until her whole story came out. Regardless of all of our hurts and pains, we really were doing a great job raising Mia separately but together. I can tell because our little girl was happy and growing like a weed.

Emily really did deserve all of the good things that life offers because, quite simply, she'd been through enough for it to be any other way. I jokingly thought, if an old dude can add to her contentment and happiness, then more power to her. I also thought, maybe I'll find me a sugar momma someday too. I wasn't so sure that Mia would have shared me as easily but with kids you never know. I always called Joe an old dude, and to me he was, but he was probably no more than ten or eleven years older than us at best. I think I may have kept saying that because my subconscious was trying to help me promote myself while reducing the validity of anyone else in my daughter's life who wasn't me. I didn't think I was a jealous guy until that situation, but when it came to Mia, I'm pretty sure I always will be to a degree and I didn't need my subconscious to tell me that. I really thought everything was going fine after the original introduction to Joe, but evidentially, for some of us, it wasn't.

One day, as I pulled up to my apartment, Mia was once again out in the front yard of Joe's house. She saw me, and as she did the last time, she got excited and started calling out for me. Not now or ever will I ignore my child when she calls. I did see this time Joe was outside with her. I didn't think about anything other than walking over to my child who was so eagerly calling out for me and giving her a big hug. This neighborly closeness thing was still new and weird, but I didn't give a damn, my baby girl was calling for me and I was on my way over. By the time I got across the street, Joe angrily snatched Mia up in his arms. As he was grabbing her, her little neck snapped back and she started screaming and crying for me to help her. "She yelled out, "Help me daddy, help me". He then rushed her into his house and slammed the door. Emily's car was there, so I assumed she was already inside, but I didn't really know. I did know however what that man just did to my child and it made me see blood red like never before.

I was only about fifteen feet away when it happened and rage flew through me like when those this SCUD's landed. If I could have gotten to him, I honestly think I would have found a way to shove that nice shiny red Corvette right up his old ass. I literally felt my temperature go to a degree it had never been before. I then went to that same door that flew open so easily the last time and rang the hell out of the doorbell. When they didn't answer, I started pounding on the door like I'm absolutely sure I would have done to Joe's bald ass head if he would have answered. I was getting ready to kick the door in when a police car pulled into Joe's driveway. I didn't give a damn about the police or jail or anything other than checking on my daughter. It's one thing to have your buddies back in the military. That's important, it really is, but for my baby girl that protection is multiplied by infinity.

I had and will always have her back, front, side and every other part of her protected. When the police got to me, I heard the normal, "What's the problem, Sir?" I could barely tell them everything that happened because I was so out of breath from fury. No one from inside the house came out while I was there. The police told me I had to go back across the street to my own home. I talked back a little but realized I was just making matters worse for me so I left and was mentally planning my return when they left. This was far from over but I knew I had to be strategic about things then. One of the policemen walked me halfway back to my apartment while the other stayed on Joe's front porch. When I was almost to the steps of my entryway, I looked back and saw that coward had finally made his way outside to talk to the police himself. My already maxed-out temperature went even higher as I slammed my apartment door open trying to catch my breath.

I'd never been this violently angry before and I was going nuts. Once inside the phone started ringing and I thought it was going to be Emily or the police telling me that they were arresting that bastard. Sadly, it wasn't either of them. It was Kathy, my old high school friend's sister and she told me Eddie had just died. All of the day's events were screaming through my mind. I was literally going insane. Another dear friend, unexpectedly gone, and gone way too soon--- then there was the mess across the street. It was, once again, too much to handle. I spoke with Eddie's sister the best I could in the state of mind I was in. When I got off the phone, I sat on my couch and fought back tears of rage for both situations I found myself in. Since the police evidentially didn't do anything other than talk to Joe, I called Emily, but I called her from a very dangerous state of mind.

I didn't know what I was going to say other than to check on my daughter and whatever else came out of my mouth, but she never answered anyway, and I was still very much going crazy. I looked out my window to figure out what I was going to do next when I saw Emily putting Mia in her car. I could only assume they would be going back to her house where, thank goodness, she was still living. I let a little time pass and then I went to her house, too. She wasn't there when I arrived nor the many times I drove by. I eventually went back to my apartment, feeling very unfulfilled and still very out of control of my own emotions. I was also hurting from the news of another friend's death and I knew for me this was once again just too much to handle at once. Seeing that man jerk my child up in the way he did and hearing the news about my dear friend Eddie gave me old feelings. Feelings that I prayed would never return to my life. These same feelings I thought I had swept so far under the rug. I hid this part of me so well up until then.

My child was only four-years-old and all I was doing was going over to hug her after she called out for me. How could I have done anything any differently, or why should I? I thought to myself, Emily let all of that stuff happen and didn't say a word, or wasn't anywhere to be found. I couldn't stop thinking about it. I felt absolute fury and I couldn't sit back and ever take a chance on anything like that ever happening again. Another hour went by and my phone rang, it was Emily this time. She was crying and apologizing on the other end. I barely let her speak, I just wanted to know that Mia was okay and if that was what I could expect from that moment on. Emily never tried to explain or do anything other than apologize. She did let me talk to Mia that did calm me down a bit but I was still very much pissed, and felt I absolutely had to do something substantial to help me understand what was going on a little better, so I did.

Old Friend

As an ex electronic warfare specialist, one of the things we learned about were frequencies and radio waves, and how to bug things. We could bug cars and planes. We could also bug people if we needed to. Almost anything we wanted could be bugged. In this case, I wanted to bug that idiot's house across the street. I knew I had to find out what was actually going on, so I took steps to do so. In the middle of the night, I ran a copper wire across the roof of my apartment building. That wire was more than enough of an antennae for a target that close. I subconsciously apologized to Sarge before going up there again but I went anyway. I ran another wire from the peak of the roof through my kitchen window and hooked it up to a police scanner that I bought earlier that day from Radio Shack. I then connected the scanner to a tape recorder that I purposefully placed beside it.

At the time, cell phones were rare, but cordless phones were very common. Those types of phones all have their own frequencies. So, once I figured out what frequency Joe's phone transmitted from each time he used it, the call could be clearly heard through the scanner and simultaneously recorded on a cassette. It sounds kind of hard to do something like that but it really wasn't. It was illegal as hell anywhere other than the military but it was still necessary. This was something I'd done many times before but this time I did it quicker. This unsettling situation blew up out of nowhere but I was preparing as if I never left the military and I implement everything I was ever trained to do to sheer perfection. I remembered with precise clarity on how to set up everything with ease and with the help of a dark and dangerous numbness. I quickly discovered that Joe's cordless phone's frequency transmission number was 49.666.

Those last three numbers, like many other things in my life were quite ironic, *but if that devil wanted a fight, a fight was what he was going to get.* When those numbers popped up on the police scanner, I had won the proverbial lottery and it didn't take too long for my contraption to hit. This little method worked every time that magic number is used, whether he called out or when someone called him. Since I hooked it up to a recorder, I didn't even have to be there to listen; it would listen for me twenty-four hours a day, seven days a week. I don't think I was ever that proficient in the military but those missions weren't about Mia either. I told Emily that I'd start picking Mia up from her daycare instead of from her house. I felt betrayed by her and enraged by her new friend. I just thought it was best that we kept our distance for a while. I just wanted my daughter back in my safe arms every second I could. I also wanted Joe to start using his phone more often so my contraption could do its job and help me find out what he was really about, and also to help me decide what I was going to do next.

Before I picked Mia up from daycare, I called a lawyer to tell him my situation and see what he recommended. He very much reminded me of those old colonels who often risked our lives senselessly for their next promotion. He mostly wanted to talk about how I was going to pay him more than give me any useable advice. I was able to get a little information out of him before agreeing to meet him at the end of the week for his precious payment though. I would have robbed a bank if he could have fixed this mess. Obviously, I didn't tell him that I bugged that idiot's house but I did tell him everything else. I even included everything I knew about Emily's past. I didn't have any more compassion for her for the first time. Before, I felt I couldn't kick her when she was down, but this time I didn't care.

This time was different. As I spoke with the lawyer, I realized I knew more about Emily than I ever thought I did and I let it all out. I told him how we didn't have lawyers involved during our original custody arrangement. Of course, he scoffed at that, as to insinuate that was the whole problem right there. In a clearly aggravated tone, I had to remind that weasel that the actual problem was the guy that just hurt my child. I also explained how close we live to each other and how my daughter was calling out for me when all this started. I let it all out. I wanted to use everything I had to find a way to save my child from this guy, and if her mother wasn't going to protect her, I'd protect Mia from her too. It was just that plain and simple to me. I was trying to do this in the right way but when I thought about how that man jerked my child I returned to red. Thoughts of her little neck being snapped back and her being snatched up as if she was nothing plagued my mind. Her little arms were reaching out for me all the while saying, "Help me, Daddy. Help me."

It kills me that I didn't help my child that day, and I made a promise to myself and to her, regardless of what anyone else ever did, to include her mother, I would never let her down again. Things did relax a bit on my days with Mia. She was as jovial as she ever was when I finally got to pick her up after the incident. When we were together she was all I tried to concentrate on. I almost burst into tears when I saw her the first time afterward though. I thought about how she should have told me in the way she does, "You could have done better, Daddy". Instead, she just gave me her normal, overly excited, cute little giggle and a big hug. I didn't cry though, I pulled it together and that day we went to her favorite restaurant once again. I guess you could say that was a meal to help with my guilt and to apologize to her for not helping when she called.

Usually, Mia would eat as fast as she could to be able to play in those nasty balls a little longer. This time, she didn't want to leave my side. She knew her Daddy needed her help too. She was happy but I honestly think she knew something was wrong with me and she probably also knew that she was the only one who could fix it. *How did my child get so much smarter and more loyal than I was? I* thought? I didn't rush home that day, we just sat there and talked long after we both finished eating. Besides, I already knew if Joe decided to make any kind of plans, I'd know exactly what was said. Joe was the kind of guy who was too prideful to ever let this be over from his position and I knew it. All I cared about was my daughter but I knew he'd try to get a few more jabs in from somewhere. I didn't care what that man was going to try to do to me but I'd never let him make Mia cry again. We finally made it home and played on the floor for a while before her bedtime.

While I was with her, I didn't think about Joe or Emily at all, mostly because I was always so preoccupied with a miniature tea party or whatever else Mia wanted to do. I was the glad participant in all her games and stories, even the one she was getting ready to tell. As we always did, I got her ready for sleep, she grabbed a book and I laid down beside her with my feet hanging off her little bed. I was ready for her to make up a few tales about the book she picked out but this time, unlike any other, she included her mother in our pretend adventures. It was as if she knew something was wrong with her too. I think she already knew that I wasn't very happy with her mother and she was softly trying to get her back in my good graces. Mia didn't say a word this time about Joe in her story but every sentence included her, me, and her mommy. It was like, now that she had a mommy, she didn't want to lose her and it seemed like she was protecting her in her stories maybe even from me.

I wasn't jealous or mad, I just curiously listened to what that beautiful little storyteller had to say. I wanted to see where she was leading us with her tales. While reading, or storytelling I should say, Mia spoke about a beach and a lagoon, and that her mommy and daddy played on in the rain. I thought to myself that sounded a lot like our honeymoon before she was born. I just listened as she talked about how mommy, daddy and her were doing this and doing that. Many of the things she spoke about Emily and I actually did, so the only way this little four-year-old could possibly know about them is either she was psychic or her mother told her, because I knew I didn't. Mia wasn't born during any of the times she spoke about but she included herself in all of her descriptions. Since she evidentially was the reason Emily and I met, for me it was more than fine for her to include herself, because in a way, she had always been right there with us.

I thought jokingly, if Mia is clairvoyant, maybe she can shake a magic eight ball and tell me what's going to happen next. When she was with me I felt I was who I was supposed to be. I was warm, loving, and happy. All of the good traits that most everyone wants to have, she brought out in me but when I didn't have her, especially at that point, not so much. Mia would be going back to her mother in a few days and I all but forgot about my sleuthful duties and the equipment that I set up in the kitchen. When she was with me I had no reason to care about what they were doing. When Mia went back to her mother's, though, those thoughts quickly became a different story. I was still dumbfounded by her mother and also still furious with this Joe guy but I thought maybe things would settle down a bit and I'd get back to somewhere close to normal.

I should have known this was just the beginning of what was to come though, because like I said, Joe was too prideful to run into a house like a coward and let me or anyone else think of him that way. I was so tired of fighting in any manner but this time I was getting ready to fight the most important fight of my life. The next night I started listening to what was taped and the calls occurring in real time. Every single call that Joe made or received seemed to have something to do with me, as if I did him wrong. I had no idea until then that Joe himself was a lawyer, which I knew left me in a worse position than I originally thought. I never thought I'd say this, but my eavesdropping gave me a much greater respect for Emily, though. After hours and hours of listening to those original conversations, she never at any time had anything bad to say about me, and when he did, which was in almost every sentence, she'd change the subject every time. I didn't expect that and I knew they didn't know I was listening.

The conversations did start stabbing deeper and deeper though, as I listened to another man say he was going to take my daughter away from me over and over again. He talked about them getting married and moving away. Emily responded, but never really agreed, she just changed the subject. It was almost as if she was defending me without doing it directly. For some reason, she seemed even smarter than Mia was with her slick eversions. I knew she was still with him because I obviously knew they talked every night—hell, I heard all of their conversations. I was still pretty sure that they were planning on getting married, even though I couldn't wait to see if she'd come to her senses. Either way, I knew I had to go to that lawyer's office to pay him just in case. When I got there, that lawyer who was so cocky on the phone, told me that he couldn't take my money and I was overly shocked.

I never heard of a lawyer who wouldn't take money before, so I asked him why. He mumbled for a second but eventually told me he had a conflict of interest and had to pass on the case. I thought to myself, no problem, there were a hundred or more lawyers in the area. But everyone I stopped to see or call said the same thing. I got the same corrupt response each and every time. It was a conflict of interest, or they were too busy to take any more clients on at the time. I knew then that Joe had played his next hand. The thing about that emotional blanket that I call numbness is, although it usually comes in as a protectionary response to something terrible like death, it also comes when you have no other choice but to do something terrible. Even if that terrible thing is in the name of war, that numbness is required to help do what you have to do. If that's the case for war, how greatly would its help be in the name of love for my daughter?

I wasn't mad anymore, now I was saturated with a massive veil of deep, dark numbness. That veil had just been provoked to its absolute limit and my numbness was bursting at the seams. When I listened to his calls that night, I heard him talk to some of the very same lawyers that I tried to get help from. They were mostly laughing at my expense like it was some kind of a game to them. Thinking about what they did and what I was hearing, I thought back to what Sarge often told us. He said, "A lion doesn't have to tell anyone he's a lion, he just shows them." The straw that broke the camel's back and what caused this sleeping lion to roar like never before was when I heard Joe's phone ring from the speaker on my police scanner later that night. It was some judge returning his call. As I listened, I heard this side deal that finalized everything.

After Joe and Emily's wedding, Joe planned on taking me to court and it seemed the outcome had already been settled by the two men talking on the phone. Their plans included me losing custody of my most precious gift, my Mia. The judge agreed to the outcome before I even had a chance to find a lawyer. This again was too much to handle and death, once more, was getting ready to be the unfortunate and unexpected perennial theme of my life. The difference this time was I planning on giving it direction. People can only be pushed but so far. I'm sure Emily's stepmother felt the same way. Enough was enough and we were way past enough. Being in a war as long as I was, and whether true or not, we are taught that there are justified deaths. I didn't know if I believed that but I did know I was going to the pawn shop to see what they had available. The 308 is known for its power and distance and I needed both for what I was getting ready to do.

I already knew Joe's schedule and about when he'd be home. I even knew when he left every morning. In a sense, I'd been hunting that man for a while without even realizing it. The death part of this story would unfortunately be easy for me once again. When I got to the pawnshop, I realized I hadn't touched a gun since getting back from the war. I didn't plan on ever touching another one, but as we know and I have lived, life sometimes adjusts our plans for us and we have to adjust with it. You don't forget how to use a gun, you never forget. I hated guns after the military with all of that horror but that night, I was reintroduced to an old friend. I bought a Winchester 308 and a box of bullets for $300. I broke my promise to Sarge during the flood with the rats, I broke that promise setting up the surveillance equipment, and I was getting ready to break my promise to him again about ever getting back on a rooftop.

I went home and went into the kitchen to listen to the scanner a little longer. I had to add some fuel on an already out of control inferno. As I listened to Joe's past and present conversations once again. I thought about all of those great losses that that old gypsy woman told me about and by had experienced. I lost so many people in my life with the most recent being my old high school friend, Eddie. Even the thought of losing my daughter in any sort of way created this massive veil of annihilation that engulfed me. It took me to a place that I'd never been before, not even in war. This time, I myself would unquestionably be the judge, the jury and executioner. I never felt that way before but now there was no remorse and no turning back. In war, I always felt the other side was more like us than anyone really wanted us to know. They were just following orders, helping their own colonels get promoted and trying to get back to their families like we were.

They never worked out any underhanded deals to take anyone's child away, but Joe did. This time, there will be a finality in knowing he will never be able to hurt anyone again simply because he wouldn't be here anymore. After dark, when I knew old Joe should be on his way home, I climbed onto the roof of my apartment complex, which again, was directly across the street from his house. I started setting my scope. I didn't think about my promise to Sarge at all this time. My heart didn't race and my palms didn't sweat either. All of those biological apologies happened in the desert but not this time. This time, I was calculated in preparing for what was next like never before. Joe arrived right at the expected time. He roared that Corvette into his driveway and got out and looked at himself in his side view mirror way too long again. He then started walking his last walk to his front porch.

That was the same front porch where all of this started, so it was a fitting place for it to end as well. This time, when I raised the rifle I did so in a much smoother fashion than I did at the twenty or so men in the desert. I then put the crosshairs right in the middle of where his temple should be, three-fourths of an inch diagonally from his left eye. He hesitated in going to the front door. He was in his yard kicking a few leaves in a pile but I was in no hurry. I decided to wait until he got all the way to the steps and then it would be over. As he started to make his way there, I placed my pointer finger on the cold, deeply ridged metal trigger and without any resemblance of emotion I held my breath as I was taught and began to ever so slightly squeeze old Joe's life away. Before I had the chance to put enough pressure on the trigger to make the rifle fire, he stopped. This move made what I was doing even easier. I wasn't thinking clearly, all I thought about was how he had a pre-arranged deal to take my daughter away and how I had to stop his plans.

This would be a great loss I simply couldn't begin to handle. So many times, I just had to deal with someone else rearranging my life so drastically, but not this time. I controlled what happened next and all it was going to take was another pound of pressure on the trigger. I didn't think about the prison sentence that would most definitely come with this decision. I was just a man trying to deliver justice and keep a promise to his little girl to always protect her. All of a sudden, out of nowhere, a big wind came up. I readjusted my sights to compensate and I knew I still had time to make the shot. Regardless of what I thought I knew I soon learned this wind wasn't for everyone, it was only for me. Somehow, once again, Sarge saved my life and in doing so, he saved Joe's that day as well.

I literally heard Sarge's voice in that breeze say, "I pray you are not hard tested." I knew it was Sarge because he'd always say that, and he was the only one I've ever heard say it. I didn't know how he was saying it right then but it was definitely him from somewhere. I angrily yelled back at Sarge or the wind or whatever it was to mind their own damn business. Then I screamed out, "This is the definition of being hard tested!" This ethereal banter went back and forth for several minutes, which thank God was enough time for Joe to make it safely inside of his house. It wasn't exactly like an argument you'd have with an actual person, it was more of a knowing, a knowing that I shouldn't have even thought about killing anyone in that way, or really in any way ever again. I began shaking profusely after that Sarge-influenced realization. I guess the emotions that were missing earlier hit me all at once and then I laid my rifle down on the roof.

I was mortified with myself. I was so out of sorts that prior to right then I didn't even think about what it would have done to Mia. If I would have went through with my evil plan I wouldn't see her either way because I'd be in jail. That common sense was something I just didn't have. Listening to all of those tapes made me so crazy, whether they were from legitimate plans or not. I don't even know if it was Sarge, God, or angels, but someone saved me from all of that fear and rage that day. I didn't care about hardly anything at that time but I did care about Mia's Daddy not being a murderer. It just took me a little while to realize it. Again, with the irony, and how we classify killing, huh? When it's okay or when it's not, but to me, this case could never be considered acceptable. I stayed up most of that night, just staring at a picture of Mia on the wall. I don't think I was thinking about anything, just like when I was blown up in the air after the first SCUD attack, time stood almost still.

Purple Dinosaur

A s time stopped, if nowhere else but in my mind I realized that was that numbness again but, thank God, this time it was because of life, and not death again. Some time that night I did fall asleep. My rifle was still on the roof and it stayed there for over a week before I got up enough courage to go get it. I think I was scared to go before then because I still didn't trust myself and truthfully, I wasn't sure if the wind would be blowing on the second round or not. When I did go up and get it, I didn't keep it long. I didn't take it back to the pawn shop either. I destroyed it like it would have done to my life if I would have used it that night. The signs of PTSD can include hatred, hallucinations, guilt and many other things that I hadn't experienced prior to that man hurting my child, but when I did, I ceased to exist as myself for a while, and someone or something else took over. I had been stabbed in the heart so many times from the daggers thrown out during each of those conversations, even though no one other than me knew I was listening to them.

The black, soulless eyes and the horrid grey skinned couple who overdosed in Spain allowed no light in but, for me, I allowed even less. The utter darkness completely took me over. I was absolutely helpless without me even realizing it, that is, until the wind blew. I still listened to the tapes after that night some, but they didn't have the same hold over me. I still got mad and felt a certain way about the situation, but I mostly just concentrated on Mia and making the most of our time together. I talked to Emily when I needed to, but for the most part, I just kept Mia as the only topic of our discussions. This situation was far from over and I knew it, but I wasn't a murderer, and I really wanted to forget about whatever or whoever it was that almost took me there.

I was going find a way to stop what I had heard as Joe's plans. I didn't know how, but I knew it wouldn't be by killing him. I didn't stop that day on the roof because of Joe either. I've seen so many better men die much worse deaths. I stopped because I realized just in time who I was, and really who I wasn't. It may have taken Sarge or whatever it was in that wind to remind me, but I stopped it. The whole situation reminded me that I am Mia's father above everything else and her Daddy wouldn't do that. It's that simple. Love was greater than hate. My love kept Joe alive, even though he'd never know it. Not too long after that night, I completely stopped listening to the tapes altogether. I prayed more and I played with Mia even more than before. Maybe I should have done that from the start but I didn't feel threatened by Joe's deception anymore. I somehow knew if love had a way of keeping me from doing something so terrible then it would also help find a way to keep me and Mia together as well.

Not long after that night and my new mindset, on one of the days I had Mia, I got a call and it was Emily. She was whispering and I could tell she was crying as well. I knew Mia was okay because she was with me, so, to be truthful, I just wasn't that worried about her mother. She told me that Joe had just hit her and he was in the other room yelling and she was scared. In fact, she told me he had been hitting her for a while. My original nonchalant response began to change a bit, especially when Emily said she was scared for her life this time and asked me to help. Part of me originally wondered if it was a trap, but even though we weren't on the best of terms this was the mother of my child, and regardless of how much I didn't like her at the time, I felt I had to at least try and help. I told her I'd call the police and I would be on the way.

I knew the police somewhat overlooked this guy's transgressions last time but I had a feeling when they got there this time it was going to be a little harder for them to ignore. All of the animosity and hard feelings had to be set aside. For the time being I couldn't care about that, I had to go. First Emily's father, now this guy. The harsh reality is, this is what she knew about relationships. I should have suspected something when she said she was in a car accident but, to be truthful, my mind never went there. She may have felt she had too much to lose being engaged to such an obviously powerful and wealthy man, I simply didn't know. I do know her life had seemed like this terrible web of deceitful abuse and now here she was once again. All of the frustrations from the past months, in regard to Emily, disappeared as I got a sweet older lady from down the hall to watch Mia until I returned. I then started across the street once again to old Joe's house.

When I got there, he was the one with the gun this time. Unlike me, I really believe he was getting ready to use it too. This man, with all the influence, power and prestige, had his own demons out on display and they were helping him wave that gun all over the place and at everyone that night. My attendance at his house didn't make anything any better either. In fact, it made things much worse. He was yelling at Emily and then he'd turn to me spewing out some sort of incoherent drunken babble. I already called the police myself because I knew I couldn't trust him and really didn't know about Emily at the time. I definitely wanted to make sure it wasn't a trap, so I took my own precautions. All this yelling and gun waving went on for a few minutes before the police arrived. When they did, they walked in his house from where the front door was left wide-open. Then as ignorantly as it was, Joe started including the two young policemen in his threats.

The officers tried to calm him down, but once again he must have felt too mighty to listen. He had to show all of us who was really in control one last time. Like Sarge, he then put the barrel of his gun in his mouth and pulled the trigger. *Jesus*, I thought. Where does it end? All of this death, all of the time. I wasn't happy this terrible man killed himself, I was in shock. Emily was slouched in the corner, bloody, and crying by this time. Her shirt was almost ripped off and she was shaking and rocking herself back and forth. I grabbed a blanket off of the couch and wrapped it around her. I leaned down, making sure my body was in a position where she couldn't see the body of the man she was supposed to marry. A very short time later, I made sure she was still covered up and helped her get to her feet. I had seen that look in her eyes before. I saw it when her dad died, I saw it when she left, and I was seeing it then too. This, though, was a time that was absolutely not about me.

The police insisted that Emily go to the hospital to get checked out. As she was being loaded into the ambulance, I told her I would meet her there. I needed to make arrangements for Mia and I'd be on my way soon after. After the ambulance left, I was walking back to my apartment and once again, like before, I looked back. This time, they were rolling Joe's body out on a covered stretcher. This guy put me through hell. He spoke so terribly about me, he beat the mother of my child. He even hurt my daughter, but I still said a prayer and cried for him. This is somewhere I never expected this story to go, but it did. I didn't have any idea where it would go next, but I did know death, for about the umpteenth time, had been the unfortunate and unexpected perennial theme of my life. I ended up taking Mia to my parents' house to have them watch her for the night. I had no idea when I'd be back and I knew she'd be fine there.

When I got to the hospital, before I could get to the desk to ask where Emily was, I noticed a great commotion in the back of the emergency room. I could barely see anything through that small rectangular window in the thick wooden door. I could see, however, two doctors and four or five nurses grouped around a bed. Trying to see all I could, my heart dropped when I realized they were working on Emily. After Emily arrived at the hospital she tried to kill herself, too. For many different reasons than Joe, but she wanted to end what she evidentially thought was a nonetheless. As the crew dressed in white were hovering around her, I saw her blood creating an ever-growing dark red puddle on the floor. I found out later that she took a pair of medical scissors from one of the silver trays in the back room and cut herself so badly that she almost succeeded in what she was trying to do. That extremely long night ended with her alive but in a suicide watch unit on the third floor.

The doctors wouldn't let her have any visitors or calls for several days, so I went back to my parents' house to pick our baby girl up. It was early in the morning, way earlier than Mia usually gets up, but I got her up anyway. I had to hold her. I had to hear her little voice, even if it would be a little raspy from not getting enough sleep. The events of that night like so many other things in my life were simply unexplainable. Call me selfish but I knew my daughter would be the only one able to give me any relief at all. So much heartache, pain and death once again. I didn't care that they had just opened, I took her to McDonald's anyway. When I opened the restaurant door, I remembered Joe opening it. When I sat down at the seat, I remembered Emily sitting at the very same seat that I was sitting at. I remembered everything that got me to this point. Any of the things I may have forgotten for that short amount of time before I got on that roof came back to me, amplified tenfold.

Memories of my family, high school, the military and everyone who was ever in my life. Thoughts of Emily, Mia, Sammy and the rest of my family. Even Joe flooded my mind with perfect clarity. It was like life's Adderall and my flash forward was for the many people who couldn't do it for themselves anymore. My eyes were once again open to how precious life really is and how so many of us simply don't realize it, to include me, most of the time. We take the lives of others, and sometimes we take our own lives, when all life wants us to do is be there for each other. This was another day that I didn't rush Mia out of the restaurant. It was also another that she just knew something was wrong and wouldn't leave my side. A few days later, the doctors allowed visitors. I knocked on Emily's hospital door and she softly told me to come in. I walked over to her bed and we shared a gentle smile. She spoke first, then said, "Hey, what's your story?" I laughed, remembering that was almost the first thing she ever said to me. I asked her how she was, and she said, with tears in her eyes, that she needed help.

We talked and I knew she was right. She had been hurting so deeply for so long because of so many people. My biggest fear now would be that she'd try to do again what she did in the hospital or have another reaction like after her father died. I wasn't worried about Mia being cared for, I knew I could do that. I just wanted Emily to have whatever help she and the doctors felt she needed. We lived in Virginia but the doctors strongly recommended a rehabilitation program in California. It was a program for women who'd been through similar things as Emily. The location was the first issue but the length of the program was the second. It lasted a year but the doctors claimed it could have permanent results. Emily said she wasn't going to make any decisions until she talked to Mia.

I fully understood her reasoning because I knew our now almost five -year-old was always much smarter than we'd ever been. I also knew Mia had always been my best counsel in times of need. Emily came over to the apartment after she was released. She was seeking that youthful, honest and pure guidance from our little girl. Emily told Mia that she needed to talk to her and Mia, in her ever so serious way, climbed up on the couch that her feet couldn't touch the ground on and patted the cushion next to her, as to signal for her mother to sit down and chat a while. I left the room cracking up a bit because she really was so much smarter than we were. I let them talk and hopefully give Emily space to find whatever answer she was searching for. I walked back in the room at the very end of their conversation and I already knew what the outcome was going to be. I never knew what Emily's last question to our daughter was, but I heard Mia clearly say, "Oh no, mommy, you can do better." I knew right then without question Emily would be going to California for a year.

Emily stayed with us for the last few days before she left. I understood she wanted to spend every second she could with Mia before she left again for so long. She would be able to call home while she was there but couldn't have visitors or come home for the whole year. We did some research on where she was going and even talked to people who went there and it really did seem like the place she needed to be. This time, I was very careful in not making Emily feel worse about leaving. She was still pretty young herself, and if she got the help that she needed, she may just very well have a wonderful life after all. After Emily left for California, she called every time they allowed her. This time just because Mommy was out of sight, didn't mean she was out of our minds or out of our discussions.

Mia would talk about her mother all the time. All of her nightly stories included her mommy now more than ever. She even wanted me to buy another star for her mommy that was of course a hundred and ten dollars, plus tax. Mia missed her mommy, but she knew that she was away, following her own ever-so-wise directions of learning how to do better. Days came and days went, and very soon, little Miss Mia was turning five. She really was an easy child, a little curious and adventurous but overall a pretty happy kid. She'd paint my fingernails, do my hair—she took every bit of what I thought my masculinity was away, and I was glad to give it to her. I never had so much fun or been as primped up as I was from my own child. She was always full of guidance too, whether asked for or not. I think the worst thing Mia did back then was introduce me to that stupid, purple singing dinosaur. You'd think small children would be scared of something so big and purple singling "I love you, you love me, blah blah blah."

I heard that song over and over again throughout our whole house all the time. I guess her love for that purple thing made me cave because, on her birthday, I had an idea. I rented a professional Barney suit from a costume store and planned a visit to her school. The suit looked exactly like the big guy, with the big purple head and tail and even that great big green belly. It was an exact replica and she would never know it would be filled with her biggest fan. To me, it seemed I accidentally picked the hottest day of the year to do this too. I pulled into the school's parking lot without being seen and snuck beside my truck and proceeded to be engulfed in that purple silliness. After I was fully dressed, I opened the front door to the school and headed to her class. Now, every kid back then loved Barney, not just mine, so before I got to her class, I was mobbed by the other snot lockers throughout the pre-school.

I think I now know how Elvis must have felt, but in this case, it was hunka hunka burning Barney. Kids were running up from all over to get a chance to hug Barney and of course sing that damn song. I had to disguise my voice like his so that I wouldn't be recognized, which wasn't as easy as one would think. After I made a deal with the teachers to visit every class, they cleared a path, and Barney was on his way to see his Mia. It was so sweet. The same massive flood towards me happened when I entered her class but just not from Mia. She was as happy as the other kids, in fact, she was the only reason I was in that ridiculous suit, but she didn't have the same awe that the other kids did. She was probably thinking, *I'm cool, me and Barney are best friends, anyway so I'll share him.* I went on playing with the kids for a while in all of the rooms, and after an exhausting two hours, I finally got to leave. When I got to my truck I realized that once I got my fluffy purple mittens off I couldn't get my big fat purple head or the rest of that stupid suit off. Again with the two's; two zippers were stuck. Not just one.

I didn't want to go back inside the daycare and scare the kids by seeing Barney disassemble himself layer by layer. As I stood there in a purple rain of sweat, I had the bright idea to go to the closest business to see if they could help me strip that big suit off of me. The problem was, the closest business was across four lanes of traffic and, believe it or not, Barney couldn't see very well through his big fat head. I got beeped at, whistled at, but I finally made it across to a dentist office. I knew they saw me coming because everyone inside was already laughing at the idiot in the purple Barney suit who just made it all the way across the street without getting hit by a car. I mumbled my request for help and like a pit crew Barney's insides were quickly set free.

It was more than worth the brief imprisonment though, because when I picked Mia up that evening, she couldn't stop grinning. She told about how Barney visited her school for her birthday. She talked about how he played with her and with the classes throughout the school. She even told me how it was the best day of her life. I didn't know whether to be happy or remind her about all of the other stuff we did all of the time together but I stayed quiet and just listened to her talk. She was so excited about her day and that damn purple dinosaur that I just wanted to listen to her jubilation. She talked about Barney for the rest of the day and all the way up to bedtime. As I laid her down to sleep that night, I went to turn off the lights and heard the most precious voice say to me, "Goodnight, Barney Daddy. I love you." She knew, she always knows. I winked at her, told her the same back and left the room as quickly as I could to keep from tearing up. This time, it was from my own absolute joy.

That's the way we were. It wasn't weird having my daughter as my best friend, she really was the greatest blessing of my life, and with those words that old gypsy lady was correct once again. We did have our moments though. Most of those times usually had something to do with hair, food or clothing, and of course her belief that I could have done better in some way. I actually was pretty good with the piggy tail thing, but that was about it when it came to hair. She'd get frustrated with me, especially when she started kindergarten. She'd ask me, "Do you expect me to go to school looking like a raggamuffin?" I often wondered where she even heard that word from. Then I'd laugh thinking she must have watched that same old movie that Sammy picked up "Good Day...Good Day" from.

There were times she never let me forget though; one being when it was the time to talk to her mommy and the other was the time I forgot to put her underwear on before we left the house when she was three. On that occasion, we pulled up to her day care and she looked at me so seriously as she said, "Daddy, I'm not getting out." I thought she was just being sweet and wanted to stay with me for the day but that wasn't it at all. In her snappiest little voice, she said, "Dad, my whoo-whoo is hanging out." I said, "What?" I asked, and kind of laughed trying to guess what she was going to say next. She then pulled her little dress up to her waist and showed that there was nothing underneath but skin. I asked her why she didn't tell me before then, or put some on herself but that little smart aleck said, "That's your job, Dad, you can do better." "Who is this little brave kid?! I thought.

Up to that point, I was always Daddy, but when she was mad, all of a sudden, I became just Dad. I don't know about other fathers but those other "d's" and that 'y' mattered to me. That situation didn't stop there. After we went underwear shopping, I got back to the school to drop her off for the second time. This time that little punk said, "Good job, bud." Man, that kid better not turn out like Eric, I thought. She was bold. That time was pushing it – she was never disrespectful either, but she was definitely brave. I loved her spirit, of course, until it was pointed directly at me like Jacob's middle finger used to be. Mia was growing up so quickly and Emily was still as much of a part of her life as she could be. Mia understandably asked questions about her mother, questions like, when could she see her, or when she was coming home. I understood how she was feeling and would always make her mommy the hero of whatever story we were talking about because, truthfully, I didn't have all of the answers to give her.

One night during one of our nightly reading sessions, and remembering my own past, but in an extremely different context, I told her a story by using the analogy of the sky. I said, "Baby, your mom is like the sky." Mia, in that sarcastic tone said, "What are you talking about now, "Dad?" There's the "Dad" thing again but I brushed it off and said, "Your mommy is like the sky because just like the sky, she can be everywhere all at once". "When you're in the house and look up you can only see the ceiling but that doesn't mean that the sky isn't there anymore, it's still there and even bigger than the ceiling." As simple as that was it did seem to make Mia content for the time being, but it also gave me another idea to attempt to create a visualization of what I was trying to say to her about her mother being the sky.

One day while she was at school, I glued a bunch of glow-in-the-dark stars on her ceiling. As she got in the bed that night I told her I had a surprise for her from her mother. She perked up with excitement and asked what it was. I made Mia close her eyes and I cut the lights off. Then I told her to open her eyes and look at what her mommy sent her. The fluorescent stars glimmered. I said, "See, I told you she was the sky." I also told her about how the first time I met her mommy I just knew that she glowed unlike anyone else I'd ever seen, just like the sky was doing right then on her ceiling. I didn't tell her that her Daddy fell off a chair, not once, but twice trying to glue those crazy stars up there, but Mia seemed satisfied for quite a while now that she understood that her Mommy was just like the sky and now that her ceiling was so lit up every time she turned the lights off. Other than Mia's newly-lit ceiling, Emily sent our little stargazer a stuffed bear. Mia quickly named it Beary Mcbear.

Kids are so strange sometimes. I understand the Beary part, but I can only guess that the Mc part came from combining her two favorite things, McNuggets and now that fluffy little bear from her Mommy. Beary McBear went everywhere Mia did, and most of the time, it was by the hand like one of those precious Norman Rockwell paintings. Every single day when she woke up, she would wash Beary McBear's's face, pretend to brush its teeth, which weren't there by the way, and put a new outfit on its furry little butt. That thing had a bigger wardrobe than me or Mia combined. Mia even had little shoes for it. *What in the world did a stuffed animal need with shoes for,* I often thought, but still obviously bought. Regardless of all of the clothes and the unused miniature shoes, Beary McBear was Mia's most prized possession and quickly became another equal part of our family. It was kind of like Beary McBear did for Mia what Puddles did for Sammy so many years ago.

That little bear was also another piece of Mia's Mommy that I could tell she needed so much at times. Emily was doing great in her program and really became more of a part of our lives than she ever was before even though she was so far away. She talked to Mia every time she could, which was pretty often. When Mia missed her mother she'd gaze at her glowing stars or give that little fuzzy bear an extra squeeze but for the most part, I kept that little buggar of ours pretty busy. Sometimes, once I'd leave her room after putting her to bed for the night I could hear her talking to the stars on the ceiling as if her Mommy was right there with her. It was so sweet, and pretty soon, Emily would be home so she could hear her precious little voice in person. I felt different about Emily coming home this time. For one, I knew when Emily would actually be coming home, but this time, I had an underlying feeling of peace that I really never had with Emily before.

It was kind of an intuition that everything would finally be permanently well with her. This peace wasn't just for me, it was for Emily, and for our Mia as well. I felt that Emily may have just finally chased all of those evils away and that was what we all needed the most. Emily had a graduation ceremony about a month before they actually were finished with the program. She invited me and little Miss Mia to go. Of course, we went, in fact, there was no way we would ever miss it. She also asked if Mia could stay with her for the remaining time she had there because those who had kids had another recommended part of the program that included their children's attendance if possible. I realized this was very important to her, and also that Mia most likely wanted to spend some time with her mother anyway.

When we arrived in California, Emily met us at the airport like she had done for me years ago. Mia ran up to her Mommy as soon as she saw her and was as excited as I've ever seen her. Damn if that ridiculous glow wasn't back, too, and was now radiating from both mother and child. I don't know how, but I felt her healing even more than I saw or heard it. Her ceremony was wonderful, and after a great deal of catching up and all-you-can-eat shrimp, it was time for me to head home. Again selfishly, I still wanted Mia to come back with me but I also knew Mia would be okay because I knew in my heart that Emily was now too. No thanks were ever needed, even though Emily tenderly and wholeheartedly gave them. Looking at Emily was like seeing a new-born baby. She was fresh with a clean heart, ready to go out and have that wonderful life as a mother, but also as the person she was reborn to be. I was very appreciative to what that place did for her and for our daughter.

I am the Sky

I said my goodbyes knowing that I'd see them both in about a month and headed to the airport. My life has always been so unpredictable with all of these huge highs and deep lows. It seems as soon I felt like I was climbing to the top of one mountain, a new kind of turbulence would appear and blow me back down. Each time, at the bottom some of those places or events would seem so ridiculous that it was hard for me to believe they really happened, but they did. On the flight home, my next round of turbulence began and just like everything else it came with an unexpected vengeance. Literally, on the plane ride back home for some reason, I got a severe headache and my right side went numb. I thought to myself, damn, I have finally appreciated my life into an illness. When I returned home, my issues didn't go away, as a matter of fact, they got worse and almost unbearable. After two days, I finally had no other choice but to go to that stupid white house again and get checked out myself. On the first visit they didn't find anything, but my headaches got so much worse that night that I went back again the next day.

This time they sent me to a neurologist and she sent me in for an MRI. That stupid tunnel was worse than any problem I could have had, I thought. I could hear and feel a swooshing or something going around and around. It felt like whatever it was that was swirling around me was tugging at all of my internal organs. The results came in two days later and they called me back in for round three. I thought to myself, damn, this can't be good with a doctor calling back so quickly; you usually have to wait for at least a month or more, but not me. The doctor sat me down as if I had a week to live. I wasn't going to let her psych me out, though. I've lived through so much already, and besides, I still felt fairly young—hell, I was still fairly young.

Then the doctor bluntly said without delay, "I think you have brain cancer." I acted like I didn't hear her because I didn't want to hear what she was saying, that was for sure. She told me not to worry but she wanted to do a series of tests starting that day so she could come up with a more definitive prognosis. I sarcastically thought to myself "No problem, Doc. I won't worry about MY BRAIN CANCER. The doctor did say as a consolation prize it could just be Multiple Sclerosis or Lou Gehrig's disease." I thought and even said out loud, "What the hell kind of choices are these, Doc?" I even sarcastically followed up with, "Uhm, I'll take door number three, Alex". I agreed to start the test right away as if I really had any other choice, and after they were finished for the day I went to the local bar to celebrate. Raising Mia on my own left no time or desire for alcohol but with this news and being by myself for a few more weeks I thought I'd revisit that old friend too. I hadn't drunk any kind of alcohol in a long time, but just like shooting a rifle, I guess you never forget. For the few weeks before Emily and Mia came home I had to go to that damn white house every day.

Everything I personally owned was tested, poked, and prodded. Afterwards whether it was a good idea or not I'd always extend my therapy sessions at this one particular watering hole. I guess I was trying to keep the party alive, for lack of a better saying. I still hadn't told anyone and the timing to have all of these stupid tests was actually pretty good so I tried to stay as positive as I could. I did hope that I had time to clear up all of this craziness before Emily and Mia got home and I guess grab a few beers along the way. At this point I made a new best friend for those few weeks, and its name was Uber. I never used an Uber before, but with it I could go out wherever I wanted and drown any sorrow or fear I may have had and still arrive home safely after my escapades.

I still had to be somewhat careful in not letting Mia know that anything was wrong so I always made it home early enough to catch a quick nap to clear my head before she called, but I pulled it off. At that bar I thought I could all but fully escape like I did so many other times in my life when things got tough. Besides, it was so close to the hospital the place itself almost seemed to be calling my name. I probably should have thought about my situation a little more at the time but by then I had long mastered running away and alcohol and new places just made it that much easier. Sometimes I'd actually talk to other people but I soon found out that most were just like me. They all had their own stories. Some were retired looking to pass the time away, some were escaping themselves, while others were looking for a cure to their problems. Even though it was short lived, those daily trips I was making to forget about my new problems seemed to push me further towards many of my older ones. It seemed the more I tried to drink and forget, the more sober I actually became and the more thinking I actually did.

All of these thoughts were coming to me, whether I wanted them to or not. This ambush of memories was from my past but also towards this new unexpected and unwelcomed news. I knew deep down that I had the wind on my side but I was still scared. So many times I didn't care about life, but things definitely changed. When the results finally tallied, they were shocking, but I didn't expect anything any different because, over and over again, death in one form or another has been the unfortunate and unexpected perennial theme of my life. This time it was tapping me on the shoulder without question. That damn doctor could have lied to me, but she didn't. She could have softened up the news a little, too, but she didn't do that either. She was wrong, though. I didn't have Lou Gehrig 's disease and I didn't have Multiple Sclerosis either.

I didn't even have brain cancer. With a great and mighty strike three, you're out, she said I had stage 4 pancreatic cancer," and to add to my gift, my troubled cells had broken away from some hidden mass and spread to my brain among other places. Two weeks ago, I was healthy as two horses and a goat. I didn't even think I had any health problems at all, but evidentially, now I have a big ass problem and for me I don't think it gets much bigger. I guess because I've always done things a little bigger than most, I had to do it once more because this wonderful disease that I had no clue about had graciously entered my bloodstream and evidentially spread all over my body. All of her medical babble basically meant she didn't know how long I had left. I knew they didn't make shovels big enough to dig my way out of this one. The doctor didn't know if the root cause of this terrible disease was from a chemical exposure from all of those oil fires that we so often inhaled while being in the desert or what.

She assumed that was the cause but what she was positive about was whatever it was, was coming to get me at a ravishing speed. I can remember what my grandmother said before she died from cancer. She said, "I am not afraid to die. I'm afraid to leave my family," and that, especially when thinking about my little Mia, sums it up for me as well. I couldn't imagine not being able to see my daughter. That would be the real hell for me. She has been the absolute best part of my life. My great blessing just like that old gypsy woman said she would be, but the reality of my situation is my cancer had gone too far too fast without me knowing it or even having any sort of a chance with an attempt at chemotherapy. The doctor didn't feel chemo would even touch it at this point anyway. She kept talking but all I got out of it was my dreams were really going to have to be left for another.

I have to say as bad as my situation was and as quick as it came on I tried not to think about myself. If this was going to be the end I wanted to do like my mother did when she ended our Christmases growing up. I wanted to find a way to give them all one last big gift and I wouldn't hide it in anyone's bathroom either. I know this was my way to avoid reality but it worked for me. I knew I had a way too because one of the only good things about being extended so many times in the desert was, each time we had to stay a bit longer, the military allowed us to increase our veteran's life insurance. We didn't have anywhere else to spend our money and everyone else was doing it, so I did it, too. I kept paying on it after I got out, even though I really never thought I'd ever need almost a million dollars in life insurance. It now appeared that I did and I knew exactly what I was going to do with it.

Being that I was surprisingly just declared terminal I was allowed to get the majority of the proceeds from my policy before I actually croaked and since the veteran's hospital helped push it through, I hit that jackpot in less than a week. I then went back to that same lawyer, the first one who had a conflict of interest. I even paid another to make sure that genuine human being did what I directed him to do after I was gone. He didn't have any problem taking my money this time as we wrote out my last will and testament. I left some money for my parents, and for Jacob and his family. I loved them so much and they helped me so much with Mia long before I had a clue what to do with her. I put aside enough for Mia to go to any college she wanted. I also bought her and her mom a nice little house in a quaint neighborhood a long way from my apartment and my old neighbor's house. They deserved a new start, even though this time, I'd be the one leaving.

It's just going to be Mia and Emily rather than her and her Daddy this time. I also bought Emily a newer and nicer Corvette. Jokingly, I thought I wanted to make sure it was a two-seater so it would just be them for a while this time, but in reality, I knew Emily was ready for anything life brought her way. She deserved the nicest and best that anyone could provide so I gave it. I also left them enough money to go on some of the adventures that Mia always talked about in her stories. I'd be there, I'd just have to be the one in the sky this time.　The night before Mia and Emily came home, I sat on my balcony. I wasn't looking at the neighbor's house this time. It wasn't because I knew he wasn't there, it was because now it didn't matter. All he put me through didn't matter at all. I still prayed for him but this night had to be about me. I stared at the moonlit heavens, just wondering what was going to happen next. I never really asked why, if for no other reason than I didn't have the time.

While sitting there I remembered how at the end of Sarge's meetings, Eric's silly ass often said, "Okay boys, let's go hit em' in the pancreas." I'm fairly sure none of us actually knew what a pancreas was but we did know that getting hit there was a bad thing. It seemed like such a random thing to say at the time but that's exactly where life hit me. Sitting in the moonlight was calming. I didn't know how much time I had but I knew it couldn't be much longer. The doctor did get the excruciating pain to stop with the help of Gabapentin and other drug cocktails but that was replaced with bleeding from just about every orifice I had. While sitting on the balcony, I had an extra strong flow of blood pour out of my mouth and nose, so much that it made me dizzy. The blood coming from my body reminded me of that great flood in the desert. It had the same biblical persistence, but instead of thinking I was going to see Noah, this time it just might be St. Peter.

I calmly collected myself. I took a very deep breath for a very different reason this time and called an ambulance to take me to the hospital. This was to be my own final trip to the white house. I made it to the door to meet the men who came to get me. I was weak and dizzy but I made it to the ambulance on my own. Just a few weeks ago, I had seemingly been as healthy as anyone, but not now. It didn't take long after getting to the hospital to have all those wires and tubes put in me. Wouldn't you know it, I had another one of those hose like catheter's in me as well, and I didn't even have to fall off a damn building this time. I did feel, however, that life was making fun of me one last time. When Emily and Mia arrived the next day, they had no idea I was sick, and definitely not as sick as I was. I talked to them every day as if nothing at all was wrong. They came as soon as they found out. At first, I was a little worried about Mia coming in the room, but how could I leave without seeing her, or really both of them, at least one last time?

I'm sure that my daughter wouldn't fully understand but I prayed so hard that someday she would. My life's mission was over. It was time for her mother to fully take over and I knew now more than ever that both of them would eventually be more than fine. When they walked in to see me, instead of just Emily glowing, they both were again. This was my definite and absolute signal that everything would be okay. I didn't have to say goodbye because I'd always be there. I'd be in their hearts, I'd be there in the sky, and just maybe I'd also there for them when the wind blew. It was a short life compared to some and even though I took it for granted so many times, what a blessed life it was. My last words to Emily were me trying to lighten the room by saying, "Tag, you're it," but my last words to Mia were a little heavier.

New Skin

I looked at my baby girl one last time and winked and said, "I am the sky, you know, and the sky loves you with all of my heart." I didn't know what was going to happen after I closed my eyes but regardless, I knew I'd always be with her in some way, and she would definitely always be with me wherever it was I was going. Then I closed my eyes and simply stopped being a part of the world in the way they were. Once and for all, death in one form or another was the unfortunate and unexpected perennial theme of my life. I've heard people say that you can see your soul leaving your body or that there should be some sort of bright tunnel that you need to head to but for me, that wasn't the case. I can't say I've woken up from death or if I even knew exactly where I was, but I do know it at least seemed good; maybe even a little more than good -- I don't know for sure yet.

I felt like I had been here before, even though I had absolutely no idea where "here" was. I was told that after you die, you should see some sort of magnificent bright light, and I did see a light, and it did seem amazing, but it was off in the distance, appearing to be quite far away. I could also faintly hear the most pleasant music. That comforting hymn was so glorious that it was beyond anything I could adequately describe with my limited earthly comprehension. I thought it came from the same direction as the light, but I wasn't sure about that either because it sounded like it was delicately pouring in from everywhere. If it wasn't for those two, what I can only define as heavenly signs somehow engulfing me in assuredness, I would almost think somehow, I ended up in that other place. The one most commonly described as quite a bit hotter and possibly not so welcoming. My instincts and that beautiful music were definitely telling me that I didn't have anything to worry about, even though I was stirring up my own emotions.

I guess I was doing that because as my memories were flashing through my head, I could see with perfect clarity that I didn't have what most would consider an easy life. I lost so many friends and family member's way before anyone would think their expected time should have been and those visions were flashing through the sky of wherever I was now at. Many of those closest to me died in a terrible war. Some of them took their own lives and many others had their lives abruptly eliminated by whom we considered to be the enemy. Life just didn't seem to give any of us the cards that any of us could expect to win with. Standing there, wherever 'there' was, I was reliving those recollections in full view but this time it was more as a spectator. Admittedly, in many ways my life resembled one of constant struggle, but in one very special way, I will be the first to say that I was blessed beyond measure. I think I was just beginning to realize how much of a gift I was given but for whatever reason I had to leave.

I remembered and actually saw everything, regardless of where I was with perfect clarity. The prominent thought on my mind as it always was and always will be was of Mia. Mia was such a great and unexpected gift, I often questioned if I ever came close to deserving such a wonderful responsibility. Up until her birth I felt the only constant in my life was death, but not with her. She brought life, a real life, a life that finally made me feel blessed for having but then I had to go. I will say though, that little girl enlightened me about how great of a connection that kind of love can bring. From day one, and in so many ways she raised me every bit as much as I ever raised her. I don't think I ever fully realized the magnitude of this truth until I got to that place, and right there in that place, I could still feel that eternal link to her.

I realized I was gone in a sense but I didn't feel gone from her at all. This was a connection that I pray is never taken away no matter where I am. Not all fathers allow this acknowledgement but those of us who do, or did in my case, fully understand that the bond between a father and a daughter begins at the first knowledge that such preciousness is in the womb. That blessed bond grows into a love that for the sake of the child's safety, happiness, or even for an innocent smile of contentment will cause a father to do just about anything. As I stood wherever I was in a self-imposed trance pondering what was and questioning what I am now I had three very distinct realizations. The first thing I noticed was there was some sort of path that was almost hidden and somewhat covered up underneath my flower-garden-like surroundings. It nestled itself a very short distance from where I was standing and it appeared to be leading towards where I thought that sweet music and the majestic bright light originated from.

The path itself didn't seem much different than any other you'd see at a local park or in a larger well-groomed backyard, but it did seem to be strangely inviting me towards it for some reason. When I tried to move though, it was like my body was being pulled towards it, but my mind stubbornly wouldn't let my feet or the rest of me move an inch in its direction. I felt as if I was in one of those dreams where you absolutely know with certainty you're as completely awake as you've ever been, but you're not awake at all. You're just dreaming that you're awake. With those types of lucid dreams you can't move a muscle or snap yourself out of it either. You usually just have to wait it out and see what's next, kind of like what I felt I was going to have to do here. I have to admit, this constriction gave me an unsettling feeling that I didn't have before.

What made those feelings worse was my second realization. This was something else that I was always told when I was alive but definitely wasn't experiencing in any shape or form for myself in this place. From an early age I was taught that when you die you are instantly reunited with your family and friends that passed before you. They are the ones that you missed so much while you were left behind. What I definitely noticed was I didn't see any of them, anywhere. In fact, I didn't see anyone at all. I was in some sort of motionless stupor in the middle of some gigantic garden all by my damn self. The more I looked around the more it just seemed like I was standing in someone's nice backyard instead of anywhere I expected to arrive at in the great beyond. I did have an underlying feeling that there wasn't any reason to be overly distressed but I still wouldn't allow myself to move for some strange reason. As my uneasy feelings kept escalating my third and strangest awareness came to light.

This realization was so odd but at least thinking about it took my attention away from the two more serious acknowledgements. I got to the point where I felt so strongly that death was such a perennial theme of my life that every time another person I loved died, I would get a tattoo of some sort. I got them on my right arm to serve as some sort of a permanently etched remembrance. I felt my heart was always in the right place with my painfully inked memorials, but more so, I genuinely thought I was giving those that I missed so much a visually lasting place in my life once again. My justification for anything I ever did was somewhat questionable at best and I guess tattoos were no different for me in that regard. That self-prescription always gave me just enough courage to help rationalize most of what my misdirected actions were.

The problem with all of my well intentioned chiseling's was not one of them ever brought any of my loved ones back. If anything, those tattoos often made things worse because every time I got a glance at my arm, whether on purpose or inadvertently, I'd often feel the pain from their loss all over again. For me, the many tattoos I got over the years ended up representing my losses more so than the positive memories they were intended for. Tattoos are complicated too, they definitely hurt but at the same time they are somewhat addictive. Strangely enough, every time I'd arrive at a tattoo parlor to get another a big part of me wanted that physical pain. For me, it was almost a deserving punishment for my life continuing while those I thought I was doing it for didn't. Now, my third realization, as unexplainably as it is, was, they were all gone. There was nothing on my right arm, no tattoos at all. Nothing but unblemished skin. As a matter of fact, every scar or other imperfection I had anywhere on my body was gone too.

My skin itself had changed to a more unified shade of amber, kind of like a pale golden tint and it seemed almost regal. I really don't know how else to describe my new skin because I'd never seen that color before. Now for some reason I don't have any tattoos or punishment marks anywhere. There was nothing but a naked arm with new skin and a lot of confusion about what's really going on with me in this place. I don't know why every time I think I know how something should be it never quite turns out that way. Life and now death once again highlighted how little I actually know about anything. That's the way it was in my life and evidentially that's going to be the same for me in death as well. Right before I worked myself up in a total tattooless frenzy, I started hearing something or should I say someone whistling in the distance.

At first I couldn't see anything but as the high pitched tweeting became louder and more pronounced I began to make out the silhouette of what appeared to be a little old lady. She was wearing a big floppy hat and dark over-sized sunglasses. Those glasses were so big that they hid half of her face. She slowly shuffled her way to me through what seemed like millions and millions of flowers. As she became closer all of the flower petals that she was shuffling around blew up in the air to make me think a rainbow was headed my way. They say this place has many mansions and for a second I thought maybe I was just dropped off on the wrong floor because for the life, or death of me, I had no idea who this elderly woman was. When she finally made it all the way up to me I greeted her with a cautious yet welcoming, "Hello." She didn't say anything back at first. She just slowly kept circling me as if she was looking for any unwanted scratches on a brand new car.

That little old lady walked around me four or five times. I guess she felt that she had to thoroughly check me out before she'd offer up any sort of final approval. After at least five full minutes of her invading way too much of my personal space she warmly giggled and finally introduced herself as Ms. Grace. She then said "Hello, Grampy." I may not have known her but she sure acted as if she knew me, so I played along. I didn't have a clue why she was calling me Grampy but out of respect for my much older inspector general, I kindly responded back and told her my name was Israel. I wasn't alone any more so being called by someone else's nick name didn't seem to bother me too much at the time. This lady may have been old but I have to say, she had the warmest hazel eyes hidden underneath those extra-large sunglasses. Her glasses really were way too big for her face and crookedly pulled down on her nose. It was almost as if she was trying to hide her eyes for some reason.

It didn't matter though, I couldn't miss those pronounced golden rings around her delicately aged pupils. She also had the most distinguished looking white hair that was flawlessly tucked to perfection underneath that silly hat of hers. Her eyes, her rosy cheeks, and her somewhat plump little body gave her what I felt was a genuinely trustworthy appearance. I guess my legs trusted her too because before I realized it we were both headed towards the path. That was the same path I wouldn't let myself go towards on my own earlier. I guess for some reason I was meant to wait for her. I don't know if I expected guardian angels, St. Peter, or even seventy-two vestal virgins to meet me at the pearly gates but that's definitely not what I got. Instead, I was tardily received by someone that looked more like one of the Golden Girls in a ridiculously floppy hat and over-sized sun glasses. I have to admit this situation was kind of funny because this little lady evidentially really was my divine tour guide to, I guess literally, God only knows where. After what seemed like just a very few steps on the path I began to see a beautiful cast of light come over her.

Her skin was originally very similar to my new skin but now for her at least, there was an additional glimmer that softly spread to all of our surroundings. It was almost as if it was lighting our way. It wasn't an overly bright glistening but it was just enough to let me know that there was something very special about this little old lady. The funny thing is, I actually thought I'd seen such a glow come over someone like that before. When I met Emily, I could have sworn that she had a very similar glow to her as well and then later for Mia as well. It may not have been as pronounced or spread out as far as Ms. Grace's but I definitely believed it was a signal to me from above. For Emily, whether I was right or wrong, I thought that it was God's way of showing me who he wanted me to be with.

I guess that happened that way because I was probably too slow to figure it out for myself. For Mia, I knew it was so I'd never forget how much of a blessing she was, and that was something that I did achieve in life. The hat that Ms. Grace had on was still ridiculous and her glasses still covered too much of her face but her soft beautiful extra glowing appearance brought me to such a peace. It was a peace that permeated throughout my whole body and definitely reached every inch of my soul. I guess I could only come to the conclusion that this time, there was no denying that Ms. Grace's glorious radiance was unquestionably real. Although I didn't know where we were going, we were definitely heading somewhere together and she was most definitely leading our way in more ways than one. As we walked on the path for a while she seemed to already know all of the stories about my life that I was attempting to tell her.

I thought to myself, "Can this lady give me a break? I just croaked here for goodness' sake". She listened to me but was very selective with her responses, almost as a person would be when they didn't want to give any secrets away. I still didn't know where everyone that I was supposed to see in such a place was, but every time I'd try ask, she'd quickly redirect our conversation towards more of whatever she wanted me to know about instead. It was a little frustrating to be truthful but I politely listened to her describing the many different flowers that surrounded us instead of what I really wanted to know about. She also kept calling me "Grampy" for some reason, especially when she wanted my attention directed back towards her. Her voice was so nurturing that I couldn't be overly mad at her because even I wasn't brave enough to get too snappy with a woman who had a definite glow about her.

Our walk seemed more like being on a treadmill than any other sort of path than I'd ever been on. With a regular path you at least feel like you're making some headway towards reaching an intended destination but not with this path. This stroll felt more like it went on forever without us truly ever gaining any ground. I think Ms. Grace sensed my frustration even though I did the best I could to hide it. Even though I still wanted to ask her a million questions she told me that we had walked enough for the first day and for me to go over in the field next to a specific tree and get some rest. I immediately thought to myself I wasn't tired and I didn't want to rest either, but again I still wasn't brave enough to refuse the orders that were given by an old glowing woman. I reluctantly yet respectfully followed her directions and departed from the path to make my way towards the field and that particular tree she spoke of.

When I arrived at the tree I noticed that she had definitely been there before because she had already made me a make shift bed out of flower petals. I never thought anyone had to take naps in a place like this or even that you'd ever get tired but I was doing exactly both of those things. Lying under that tree made me think about my past life once again. When I was younger my brothers and I would spend hour upon hour just lying on our backs pretending that the clouds were animals, cars, people, or of course those infamous women's body parts. We made those puffy white canvases of our imagination into just about anything that we wanted them to be. As I laid there this time I think I just wanted the clouds that I'd never expected to be looking at again to tell me something instead of me trying to direct what they could become in my imagination. The clouds never seemed to let me down and as I drifted off to what I guess was the greatest sleep of my life or death in this case those beautiful clouds didn't let me down this time either.

At first I dreamed that I was a young boy again. I didn't have a care in the world. I ran around playing with my brothers. In these visions my parents always seemed to be around too. This was a lot different from reality because in life, my parents worked almost all of the time to provide for their three adventurous knuckleheaded boys. We were nowhere near being close to angels back then either. I mostly had a wonderful childhood though, that was up until my grandparents and then brother died. I was in college when my brother passed and something inside of me just snapped. For some reason from that point on and for a long time afterwards I just kept running away. I ran away to college, I ran away to a foreign country, and then, I even joined the military to solidify my attempts to run away as far as I could.

For me, those thoughts were more like hauntings. No matter how far away I ran I just couldn't get away from them. None of that ended until I went back to where they all started, really until I went back home. I eventually turned things around and became what I felt was somewhat stationary again even though there would always be a certain very special part of me missing in multiple places. I managed handling those feelings by telling myself that Sammy was in a much greater place doing much greater things. I honestly had to completely buy in to that thought to get a handle on him being gone and then I had to do the same for so many other people. I don't think taking a stroll with an old lady, glowing or not, down a flower laden path was exactly what I expected for him or for me either for that matter. As I sprawled out further in the pile of flower petals I mostly dreamt about all of the wonderful things that occurred in my life but I also clearly saw the not-so-wonderful as well. I vividly revisited the war. I once again saw all of my friends that didn't make it home.

I saw one that I absolutely loved take his own life, and I also saw many others die in so many other ways too. I could even see my own death and later my little girl's reaction at my funeral. My heart, asleep or not, was crushing as I saw her crying at my grave site. She was only six when I left and now her daddy is gone. This time gone really does seem like forever. It was happening again, I felt like I was awake and directly experiencing these visions in real time but I wasn't awake at all. I don't know how long I slept under what I am going to call my own personal tree of remembrance but when I woke up the rest of me felt like my right arm now appears. I have to admit I felt refreshed and a little different too. I was cleansed during that sleep somehow. I guess, this is what being made anew means. Maybe Ms. Grace was right, I did need to rest for a while but that rest, I believe, was supposed to be more like a final good bye to many of my earthly concerns.

I then knew that nap had to happen so I could be cleansed for whatever journey lay ahead. Possibly now I can truly realize that I may actually be in a much greater place and just maybe I too am here to do much greater things. That nap was like a release of all of my leftover emotions from an existence that was no more. I didn't forget my life as it was, I just evidentially had baggage that Ms. Grace knew I had to file somewhere to be able to continue on to wherever it was she was taking me. I don't know why I expected my death to be any less confusing than so much of my life was, but I did, and once again my expectations were wrong. The one thing that I was sure about was it seemed pretty apparent that regardless of where I was or regardless of what I was doing, whenever God wanted me to learn a lesson he always provided some sort of teacher to lead the way.

I would have to say that realization started with my parents, then Sammy, then Andy, and Sarge, then of course Mia, but now it's pretty apparent this little old lady in a floppy hat is leading me somewhere too. Similar to the first time we met, my current floppy hatted professor, Ms. Grace was approaching and once again her jovial and very much out of tune whistling gave her arrival away. This time, as she did the last, she greeted me with a "Hello, Grampy", and then let out a cute little mischievous giggle so much like Mia used to do. *This lady is nuts*, I thought. I don't know who in the hell or this odd version of heaven, or wherever I am, this Grampy is, but it was obviously someone that Ms. Grace had a great adoration for, so I guess that would have to be enough for me.

As we made our way back to the path she asked if I felt like I had an unfinished life. Without hesitation I quickly responded that I absolutely felt that way, how could I feel any other way about myself and about all of the others in my life that died too soon. I began to tell her about, my brother, my friends, and family members that died before me. She was finally letting me speak a little so I told her that I felt the same for them as well. Our conversations finally began to have some meat on their bones instead of just talking about flowers. I wasn't feeling sorry for myself, I wasn't mad either, I just didn't understand why any of those that I spoke about, to include myself had to leave their lives and the one's they loved so early and in some cases in such a terrible manner. Ms. Grace listened to what I was trustingly confiding in her about. She appeared to be profoundly internalizing my words as if she was reliving them herself. She didn't provide any overly insightful response but she was definitely showing signs of a true heartfelt remorse.

Glowing or not, I could see that what I was saying was reaching somewhere deep inside of her and it was hurting her more than I was willing to let happen. Her emotions were coming from an obvious and sincere caring for me and from the stories about the one's I loved and lost as if she was right there with me. As we walked we both became quiet, then we just looked around for a while in silence. I had no idea what she was thinking about but I knew that I didn't want to cause her heart anymore anguish at the time. I also didn't want to run off the only company that knew where we were headed. It was never in my original nature to want to hurt anyone anyway. Even in the war, I thought about the men on the other side and their families a lot. I just never saw how they could be but so different than us regardless of what the news, politicians, or colonels wanted us to believe at the time.

It's not that I have ever been an overly sympathetic person but I did know that everyone that we came in contact with in such a manner had a story of their own. I knew that they had their own families, their own joys, and their own sorrows just like I did. I just didn't see how one side could be so different than the other regardless of what classification world governments placed upon any of us. Make no mistake about it, I also saw evil, it just seemed to be mislabeled many times. But no matter, whether it was labeled right or wrong, I still did what I was ordered to do and I lived with that constant guilt that stayed afterwards. I guess I'm seeing for myself that I left the world with the ability to feel that feeling still. When Ms. Grace and I started talking again, out of the blue she strangely said, "You know I've always been with you, and I always will be too". I really didn't know how to respond to her then because like I said, I've never seen this lady before now.

Fire Eyes

Even more peculiarly I almost felt Ms. Grace was saying those words for herself as much as she was for me. I think for some reason she was trying to ease her own guilt about something even though I didn't know why or what it was. Again it was kind of like she was hiding something and wanted to let me know but just couldn't. I didn't think she was God but because she blurted out something so strange I had to ask. She let out another one of those cute little giggles and said, "Oh heavens no, but I really have always been with you, and like I said, I always will be too". I think this walk upset her so much because even though I didn't know it at the time she had a job to do and very much like mine in the war she wasn't completely sure how to do it either. If nothing else, I surely felt that I'd be all rested up after Ms. Grace once again told me it was time for another intermission of sorts. This second involuntary round of rest came with accommodations that were even more beautiful than the last. Instead of flower petals there was a hammock that was tightly stretched out between two towering palm trees.

Those trees stretched so high in the air I couldn't even come close to seeing their tops. The hammock was made out of these huge fuzzy auburn colored leaves that warmly enveloped my body once I reluctantly decided to get inside. It was like an unfinished cocoon that was purposefully left open just enough for me. It's positioning seemed to be purposefully forcing me to direct all of my attention to this the beautiful waterfall a very short distance away. As I settled in to the only place my swaddle allowed I couldn't take my eyes off of the glistening stream of water that was gently trickling into a pool at the base of that waterfall. What made everything even more wonderful for me was the fish that were jumping all over the place.

I wanted to ask Ms. Grace for a rod but I wasn't sure that was allowed there. My surroundings were hypnotizing and another holy reference that I was still very much in need of. Without me realizing it at first, Ms. Grace's planned step-by-step cleansing was leading me somewhere specific, which was exactly what she intended. Once again at the time, I didn't know if I was asleep or awake but I do know that as I laid there peeping through the small visual allowance in my hammock, I saw a stout young man dashing out through the back side of the waterfall. I can remember rubbing my eyes and pinching myself to see if I was a dreaming or not. Again, this was someone I'd never seen before. This young man was definitely coming towards me but in a much different manner than Ms. Grace did. He was getting to me in a hurry too. He didn't have any rainbow flower petals floating around either. This guy appeared to be in his early twenties at the most and he had flowing goldish-brown hair like the actor in the Hercules movies. As he got closer I became very frightened because of his eyes. That feeling that I once had of having nothing to fear instantly left.

I believe I lived with the knowing that someday I'd have to pay the piper for some of the things I did in my life and this definitely seemed like it was going to be that time. His eyes looked like something straight out of a horror movie or where I didn't think I was, in hell. Actual fire was raging out of the sides of each of that devil man's eyes. The flames fluttered all around his face and very much unlike Ms. Grace's peculiar welcoming, this evil dude jumped at me as to solidify the danger he was delivering. I tried my best to fumble my way out of that cocoon thing that I was once so impressed with. I did finally fall out on the ground but that was only after it spun around a few times like you'd see happen to the more ignorant characters in the cartoons.

Once I regained my bearings, for some reason, I began to tense up as if I was going to actually try and defend myself against that hellhound. Not very long after my bluff was called. I didn't know exactly how you die after you die but I was doubting very seriously I could win that fight. Instead of a pancreas this time Fire Eyes was going to get me. As I began to think maybe I wasn't exactly where I originally thought I was, this inferno man started laughing and flexing his huge biceps at me. Then the idiot said, "Good day, Good Day". I was all but trembling in fear but his voice, that flexing, and his overly British greeting were all so familiar. Right in front of me he changed his eyes to eyes I have definitely seen before but I just couldn't figure out where with all of the excitement going on. Once my heart stopped jumping and started pumping somewhere closer to a normal pace, I noticed by the way the man was moving his muscles all around, he wanted me to notice his chiseled physique.

Then, instead of calling me Grampy as Ms. Grace seemed to do all of the time, he called me out by my real name. "Israel, Israel Rain," he yelled in such excitement. This young man seemed so happy to see me and now that he put the flames in his eyes out, I could try to figure out who he was. He was definitely still laughing about how he literally just scared the hell out of me but I was still as I've been since I got to this odd place- confused. He grabbed me up like a sack of potatoes and gave me this huge bear hug. It was one that virtually took all of the air out of my lungs in a hurry even worse than the SCUD in the desert. I just saw this guy's eyes on fire so I was extremely uncomfortable to say the least. I didn't care if he was just kidding or not, but I've never seen any crap like that before. He held me so hard that my feet actually came off of the ground and I honestly felt like my face was turning blue from a lack of oxygen.

While I separated from his massive grip as politely as I could, I moved my head back away from his and looked directly into his eyes this time. I did it gingerly at first just to make sure he wasn't going to blow my face off with those fiery devil eyes again but secondly because I had to signal to guy that was enough hugging man. It was when I finally got a good look at his eyes that I knew exactly who he was without a shadow of a doubt. I didn't know how it was him, and I didn't know how that crazy fire thing with his eyes was happening, but I knew it was Sammy. I've missed those eyes and the rest of that boy so much. It was my sweet-sweet brother, Sammy. Once he knew that I actually knew it was him I don't think neither one of us wanted the next hug to end. After the hug and our own joyous waterfalls of tears and joy finally stopped we sat on the rocks near the waterfall and talked and talked.

We talked about our parents and grandparents and how wonderful of an upbringing we felt we had. We also spoke about our other brother Jacob and all of the trouble we used to get into as children and about my greatest blessing, Mia. I also asked this new Sammy about where we were and what was going to happen next. He let me know that where I was, was more like a life in between lives, in his words. It was a place most likely temporary if I chose it to be. He then sarcastically told me he lived at the destination and assured me that with time and patience we'd most likely be roommates once again. I didn't know if that part of the story was good or bad but either way he disclosed that I'd only be given a little at a time and this life in between lives is like the last life in many ways. There may be times that aren't always easy but it would most definitely be worth it at the end of the journey.

He then, as he was doing ever since we reunited, flexed his muscles up and down and all around once again. He wanted to make sure that I saw him doing it each time too. Once he finally stopped playing around with his new body he pointed to the pool of water at the base of the waterfall as to signal for me to look down. He told me it was just like tuning in the rabbit ears of an old television set once I learned how. We had to find the "higher frequency" as he called it to get the picture. The frequency thing sounded familiar too as Sammy explained how certain frequencies gave us the ability to see all of the people that we knew and loved no matter where we were. He told me with the right frequency we could see, hear, and in some cases even interact with those that were still alive. Sammy's directions worked too. I couldn't do it myself yet but he could and he showed that ability off too.

It was as if we were watching a movie screen draped across the pool of water at the base of the waterfall. He tuned into our parents and later our other brother, Jacob, and his family. We also saw our friends and those who were such a big part of our lives from the past. Who I wanted to see the most, Mia, was nowhere to be tuned into though. I asked Sammy about her and he assured me that she was fine but it wasn't time yet, I wasn't ready for that, as he said. Time is a funny thing in this place, it's like it's barely moving here but it's jumping all around for those who are still there. Also the events that are happening in their actual time are much clearer for us to see than those in the past. We could still see the past and even the future in some cases but I didn't think Sammy had perfected that ability yet because those visions were quite fuzzy compared to their current time. I was happy to see everyone, I really was and everyone looked like they were getting along as great as they could but who I really wanted to see the most was Mia.

Sammy, in his efforts of getting my mind off of not being able to see her asked me if I wanted to mess with Jacob. This really was like old times where Sammy and I would team up in hopes that we would come up with something at Jacob's expense. In truth, Sammy always played the middle and sided with both of us. By doing so, in reality he was the only one who actually ever won. When we were younger, Jacob and I fought a lot but once again, God only knows what Sammy was playfully stirring up to do to Jacob now. When Sammy so called "tuned" into Jacob in efforts to enact some not-so-divine intervention, we happened to catch Jacob the clearest as he was reading a bedtime story to his children. We listened carefully to see if what he was saying would give us any ideas about our next move. We were just like our old immature selves but this time, I didn't think we had any chance of our mother catching us. We even became a bit giddy thinking about the extreme upper hand that we had on Jacob this time. We were honestly getting excited about doing something that we knew we shouldn't but definitely were going to do anyway.

Just like times of old I once again had Sammy, the other little trickster, to help influence my agreement with a plan that may be somewhat questionable. As Sammy and I mischievously listened in we heard Jacob slightly adjust the words to a book that he was pretending to read to his children. Almost like Mia did but he replaced what was actually written with some of the true stories about him and his eavesdropping brothers. He used different names but Sammy and I knew who he was so lovingly telling his children about. Jacob in his own way was telling the actual stories from our shared past. Jacob started this one story out by speaking about three fisherman who were attacked by a fierce pirate ship named the Armageddon.

Immediately Sammy and I started laughing because there was more truth to Jacob's story than his kids would probably ever know. The more Jacob spoke to his children the more the sometimes unbelievable true tales of our childhood came out. After a while we could tell that Jacob was simply telling stories about us to his kids because he was obviously still missing his two older brothers pretty badly himself. Jacob was always more like our father than we were. He was a little more serious and usually a lot more responsible than we were too. He was definitely much more selfless than at least I ever seemed to be. Now he has a family of his own and he's still the same with them too, if not more so. In his stories he was simply giving one of the kindest, most loving secret eulogies to two more of his own loved ones that seemed to leave his life way too early. After seeing Jacob barely be able to make it through his own stories and hearing his loving words about us I guess Sammy and I thought he deserved a little reprieve from whatever we may have thought that we were going to do to him.

That little glimpse into Jacob's life made our hearts feel somewhat weighted even there because we could tell how much Jacob loved and appreciated his children just like our parents did us but also how much Sammy and I meant to him too. In a way it felt like a million years ago but in another more special way hearing those stories the way Jacob told them made it feel like they just happened yesterday. After we "untuned" as I guess you call it to Jacob, Sammy hugged me way too tight again, he assured me that we'd see each other very soon, and once again said "Good day, Good Day". As quickly as he appeared he was gone again. My very-very special brother went back through that heavenly waterfall as quick as he came.

My heart was full, really full for the first time since I got to that place so I did what I probably should have been doing the whole time and I thanked God. I thanked God so much for both of my brothers and for the blessings from this wonderful day. I also thanked him for the very important lesson that Sammy taught me. One I hoped to learn for myself in a very short time. I don't know whether it was on purpose or not. It may have been his way of looking out for his big brother once again but he did teach me that everyone seems to have a frequency, and evidentially it was an energy that I had to learn how to tune into. It was the way that I, in some way could see and hear my Mia again. Before I got too wrapped up in Sammy's tutorial, incidental or not, I began to hear a terrible fluttering noise coming down from the sky. It sounded like it was coming from somewhere near where I would think the tops of those huge trees would be. As I looked up this time I didn't see fiery eyes, thank goodness.

I wasn't scared for my life either because this time it was an angel, an actual angel like so many people have on the top of their Christmas trees and more so of what I expected to see when arriving in such a place. It was coming in with its wings plumbed out just like the tattoo I got on my arm after my old boss died in the war but these feathers were real. This angel, however, unlike any I have ever seen inked on myself or in the movies appeared to be beaten up and tattered as if he himself just returned from a war. He wasn't scary looking though, he looked honorable and proud. When he landed I stood at attention as if I was back in the military for some reason. I don't think I knew what else to do and that kind of came naturally. As I was standing there with my arms and legs locked in place several other angels came down behind the first. Unlike the larger original one, the followers were completely clean and glistened from the light in the distance.

It looked like they had the same kind of new skin that I did. They looked more like what I thought an actual angel would look like. This time however regardless of any wings or ruffled appearance I fully realized who he and the others were almost immediately after everyone settled in. Unlike Ms. Grace, or when I didn't originally recognize my smart aleck brother with those stupid fiery eyes, I knew who these very welcomed visitors were right away. It was Sarge and behind him my other buddies that died in the war. At first I was somewhat apprehensive at the feathers and their general appearance, especially Sarge's, but I couldn't help myself. I broke rank and ran over to each one of them as if I were a lost child who just found his family again. I hugged each one as hard as I could and almost as hard as Sammy hugged me. He had more of those new muscles than I did so that comparison was probably a bit unfair to myself. I think this time Sarge and the other guys were probably thinking "Okay, that's enough man" for themselves, but I couldn't help it. All of these men looked the exact same as I remembered with some very definite exceptions.

In life, Sarge, who I strongly considered my second father was a black man and of course he didn't have tattered wings or couldn't fly at the time to my knowledge. I never really thought about it before and the only reason I did now was well…. he wasn't black anymore and neither were a few of my other friends who used to be. Just like the tattoos that once riddled my right before my arrival to this place, my color, my shade and my pigment were all gone and so were theirs. It was all anew for all of us. I have as much respect and admiration for Sarge as I've ever had for anyone. He was a good man that definitely had some terrible things happen to him and in response he did a pretty terrible thing to himself as well. Along with my grandparents and brother, Sarge's death was one of the hardest losses of my life. I love that man and even after his death he somehow kept saving my life over and over again.

As strange as it sounds, during my most trying times he was always there. After I personally saw his own life end he spoke to me in the wind, he visited me in my dreams, and he persistently sent me small but very effective reminders that I originally thought were just coincidences to let me know he'd always be there for me. This wonderful man saved my life over and over again even if he or no one else could save his. There is a common belief about what happens to someone if they take their own life and after seeing him I now realize that love put him in that position and I guess love must have also gotten him out too. As our own prolonged hug ended he held me by my shoulders and looked me directly in the eyes as a father would do. He then said, "look what we have here! 'I Am the Sky'," Sarge then let out that same old barrel laugh that we used to hear so often from him.

As he was trying to stop laughing and regain his composure I made my way around to my other friends who just wanted to come out to see me before going back to wherever it was they came from. That just left us, a father and his son alone to talk. Sarge, smiled as he let me know that he noticed there were no tattoos or blemishes on my body. He then moved his own arms around and said, "See, I already knew we were the same underneath anyway". Make no mistake about it, Sarge was rightfully proud of his heritage but even more so about the confirmation of what he always knew and often taught us. Our outer appearance was now unmistakably seen as a true and holy commonality all the way around. It was just like our insides always have been whether some would ever admit it or not. The real beauty of our new attire was how strongly it signaled the "oneness" with something that is so much greater than any of us could ever be on our own. Sarge stayed for a while longer. We laughed and we cried together, and as Sammy did, he assured me that we'd see each other again and began to leave.

I was so grateful that his blessed visit reminded me about just how much that man helped me even after his own death. He spoke to me in the wind, he visited my dreams, and he persistently sent me small yet very effective reminders that I originally thought were just coincidences. If he could do that for me there had to be a way for me to learn how to do the same for Mia, I thought. Before he left I had to know why he looked the way he did. I respectfully asked Sarge why he looked so beaten up compared to the others. I already knew what could possibly be the reason so I was somewhat scared that he was going to say it was from some sort of punishment, but that wasn't the answer he gave. He just proudly winked at me and said, "Saving souls like yours, 'I Am the Sky,' is hard work, and I guess I wear my work on my new sleeves." He then, as strange as it is to say, flew off way above the tress until he was completely out of sight.

What a beautiful man, I thought, and what a great gift to be allowed to see Sammy, my friends, and my second father once again. I then did the only thing that I knew to do once more, and I thanked God for such a gift. I was so grateful for those visits but there were still other people that I wanted to see, especially my grandparents who I felt had to be at this place somewhere too. I was the oldest grandchild and I had a very special relationship with them. As far as people go, my grandmother and grandfather couldn't have been any different from one another. My Nanny as me and my brothers called her, could chew us out for something I'm sure we did but for some strange reason we'd feel better afterwards. She must have had that loving correctional gene that none of the rest of my family seemed to inherit. She had the darkest hair all of the way up into her later years and she had eyes that were every bit as beautiful and nurturing as Ms. Grace's were. They were same shade of brown too. She was a rather small woman herself in contrast to our grandfather.

Papa as we called him, was a huge man. He was more like a gentle giant in many ways but he was also quite a bit of a task master. He liked things his way and that was it. It's not that he couldn't bend at times, it's just that he rarely did. The thing that both of my grandparents had very much in common was the love that they had for their entire family. When I was younger their house was my favorite place to go. Over the beach or the mountains or anywhere I just wanted to go to Nanny and Papa's house. As I became a teenager and started doing my own things as teenagers sometimes do I for some reason regrettably forgot how much I loved being around them and I didn't see them as much. It wasn't too long into my teen years that I heartbreakingly realized that I wouldn't get a chance to anymore. My Nanny died first and then my Papa. That big old tough man didn't live much more than a month after she passed away. He let us all know that he didn't want to live without her. With all of the death that surrounded me in my life, they were the first two and some of the most painful to experience.

As a teenager I was definitely one of those kids who believed my grandparents would live forever but as I'd learn so many times afterward, life and death both usually have their own plans and there is very little anyone can really do about it. When I went to both of their respective funerals I made sure that I held each by the hand as a final good bye. It was my way before tattoos to try to remember something that I felt I could keep with me forever. I didn't ever want to forget the hands that provided so much love to me and my family throughout our lives. My Nanny's hands were small and soft. When I held hers in mine they still seemed to be as warm as they ever were. Not even death could diminish the warmth of that loving lady's heart. When I held my Papa's gigantic hands, mine in comparison were still as small as it ever was when I was a little boy.

His hands were not only powerful but also chaliced with several mangled fingers. He always told us it was a reminder of how hard he worked to provide for his family in his own way. No matter where ever I was, whether in college, the military, at another funeral, or wherever, anytime I needed my grandparents I'd close my eyes and feel the love that my grandparents and their hands provided. I can still do it now. I don't know why I chose there left hand to hold. It may have just been the closest to me at the time. But just maybe it may have been the one that I thought was the most direct path from their hearts to mine. Either way with my eyes closed tight I felt them with me once again. I think maybe this is as close to that tuning in that Sammy was talking about because now not only could I feel their hands I could also see both of them right in front of me as well. Much different from the last very-appreciated visitors my Nanny and Papa were almost translucent. Not ghost like or scary but more comparable to a loving spirit visiting me. My Papa's body may have been semitransparent but his hands surely weren't as he bipped me on the back of the head like he used to do when I was a child. He then laughed and said, "Boy what are you doing?", as if I just woke him up from a nap or interrupted his dinner.

Just like when they were alive my Nanny started fussing at him and said, "Don't hit that boy in the back of the head," as if it could still hurt me now. It wasn't ever an aggressive slap, it was just a little grandfatherly welcoming that he loved to give and my Nanny absolutely hated seeing. I think he did it to mess with her as much as he did to toughen me up. They too had changed in one way but not in another. They were very recognizable but in a younger, smoother, non-descript skin sort of way just like my skin but even clearer. Their faces that once carried lines and wrinkles of aging were now smooth and fresh looking. My grandfather jokingly rubbed his face and sarcastically asked me how I liked his new digs.

During my grandparent's visit I could almost swear that my grandmother wanted to talk about whether or not she wanted to bake a pie. If she actually did she held off because they mostly talked about how proud they were of me and my brothers. I didn't think my heart could become any more-full but if anyone could have maxed it out it would definitely have been my grandparents. They also let me know that before long I'd have some pretty big realizations to deal with and in their seasoned wisdom they reminded me that free will was invented in this place so I better use it wisely. Just like all of the others, they began to leave to wherever the next place is. Before they totally disappeared my Papa called me over as if he wanted to give me one last hug. When I ran over to him as I would have when I was a child I should have known better. Even in this place that wasn't the case and another bip on the back of the head and chuckle is what I got. He deservingly got fussed at again by my Nanny though, so it wasn't too bad. With them, they'd never say a regular goodbye either. They had a unique farewell of their own. They'd always say "See ya later," and this time they did the same and left from sight. As for me, after they left, I thanked God once more.

Everyone I saw that day left with definite promises for more visits in the future. I guess that had to be enough for now and besides this little glowing lady was whistled her way to get me once more. Just like with my grandparent's Ms.Grace seemed a bit different. She was still fully recognizable but a little more youthful in appearance. She still had those big goofy sunglasses on and she was still wearing that ridiculous hat but I could tell that something was different. With all of the visits I was feeling a bit bolder and maybe even a little more full of myself so I asked Ms.Grace if she was feeling a little like Benjamin Buttons. I wanted to see her reaction but I should have known what the answer or lack thereof would be because once again she giggled and as usual avoided my question. All she did say was, "Let's get a move on, Grampy," and off we went.

Nasim

Now there was no way that I wasn't going to talk about my visitors from that day so as we walked I told her about Sammy, Sarge, my other friends, and of course about my Nanny and Papa. Unlike the last time where I seemed to sadden her with my words this time she was sharing in my excitement and appreciation for the wonderful gifts that I had been given. Thinking about that I came right out and asked her, "Where is God?" She got this huge smile on her face and stopped. She pointed at herself and then at me. She then pointed at everything that surrounded us and said God is here, he's there, he's everywhere, and he's in everything. It wasn't quite the answer that I was expecting because I didn't know any more than before I asked but in a way I knew what she was talking about, he is in all of us. Her answer kind of reminded me about how I told Mia that her mother, then I was the sky. She then went further though with her explanation and said, God is similar to that water. Without water nothing can live and without God nothing can either. Some people think they can, and actually some people seem to for a while but in reality nothing or no one ever really does on their own.

After that for the first time she actually told me where we were going. She said our next destination was a church, and according to her we were almost there. I laughed a bit after she revealed where we were headed because in a way I thought this whole place was the ultimate church. In fact, I thought it was the big Kahuna of churches. She smiled and this time she turned the conversation away from what she just told me as if she let the cat out of the bag too early. This time she changed our conversation back towards Sammy, Sarge, my friends, and my grandparents. She spoke about them as if she loved them every bit as much as I did. Ms. Grace was on a mission herself even though I didn't realize it at the time.

Her mission was not only for me but it was for her as well. This time our steps seemed to be progressing towards some place closer to the light and that sweet music. Before we got all the way there though, we arrived at an old dilapidated concrete building. This building was off of the path and it blocked much of the light that I thought we were getting closer to. The building also seemed to muffle a lot of that beautiful music out as well. This wasn't like any church that I'd ever seen before. As a matter of fact it looked more like the bombed out building that I was forced to stay several nights in during the war. The same one with all of those nasty rats. I almost think it really was that same horrible building. I was hoping we'd walk right past it, but I should have known, we didn't. When we arrived at the steps of that so called church Ms. Grace told me to go inside and settle in and then as she always did, hugged me and then disappeared into all of those flowers once again. As I walked through the door of the building I noticed that she hadn't been inside prior to my arrival this time.

There was no make shift bed made out of flower petals, there was no fuzzy hammock hung between the trees, in fact there was nothing on the floor or on the walls at all. This really did seem to be exactly like that same damn cold concrete building that I prayed I never had to see again. If it wasn't the same it was at the least an exact horrid replica. *This life in between lives is so flippin' odd*, I thought. I tried my best to see where Ms. Grace was trying to take me but I hardly understood anything even though almost everything looked familiar in some way. As I crouched in the corner I dropped my head towards my knees to try and rest as quick as I could to hopefully help this part of the journey be over with as soon as possible.

As I began lowering my head, I saw a line of men forming outside the building. Once they were in order they started filing in that terrible building and one by one began making their way to me. As each man entered they walked over to me and individually placed their hands on my head. I was still crouched in the corner as each person touched me and confusingly told me they forgave me. After that without haste those same men left out of the same door they entered from. These men didn't have wings like Sarge, or my other military buddies. They didn't have an extra glow like Ms. Grace and they weren't translucent like my grandparents. Thank goodness, they didn't have those fiery eyes like Sammy originally did either. They seemed more like me than any of my others visitors. Their skin was like mine and their other features were made up of what I feel sure were their earthly characteristics. I knew there had to be a million things that I needed to be forgiven for but I didn't have any idea why these men felt like they were the ones who had to give it right then.

There was exactly twelve men who riffled through that building and came over to me at first. I originally thought at least the pats on the head from those men were a lot less painful than the playful one's from my grandfather, but this time there wasn't any playfulness intended by the men. This time those pats were very serious and carried a very deep meaning for all of us. As the last man came in, the thirteenth man, instead of touching my head or forgiving me as the others did he sat down on the floor beside me. The man introduced himself as Nasim Amari. After our introductions we just sat on the floor next to each other for a while in silence. I guess he was trying to give me time to figure out where I'd seen him and the other men before. As politely as I could I finally asked if I was supposed to know who they were.

He proudly assured me that we were all a very big part of each other's lives. Although his complexion was very similar to my new skin when I really looked at him there was no doubt at one time he was of Middle Eastern decent. As I sat there thinking about where I could have possibly known these men from it didn't occur to me where the obvious place should have been. I spent so much time blocking that place and those horrors out of my mind that I guess I was still doing it then. Once I let my mind return to that hell neither one of us had to say another word to confirm our connection. My heart sank because although I may have not recognized them at first, I did now. There's an old saying that the eyes are the gateway to the soul and I've seen these souls before. There was a time where I could have sworn I saw the souls of all of these men leave their bodies and unfortunately in the case of those thirteen men it was from own hands and the rifle I held.

This has definitely been the source of most of my debilitating guilt. I knew no one was worthy enough to take another's life but that didn't stop me from doing it thirteen times. This unworthiness has in many ways consumed my life since the war. Mia's birth gave me the first ounce of relief since those smothering feelings began but with Nasim sitting next to me now offering his forgiveness I am more-sure than ever that we are more alike than most would ever admit to include me in my past. Nasim confidently shook his head as to say he approved of the completion of this part of the mission. This was evidently part of the journey that had to happen for all of our eternal sakes. It was also one that had to be completed together, or not at all. Before Nasim left he asked me if he could give me a present. I already felt that I've been given more than I ever deserved, especially from those particular men but I graciously said yes.

He then asked me if I was having trouble seeing my daughter from this place. Somehow he knew what I wanted more than I could get across to anyone else. Not only that, he wanted to be the one to help me. What I once felt was my greatest curse is now helping me with my greatest blessing. I knew I didn't know how to tune in to the living like Sammy did but Nasim was evidentially going to show me. Nassim was probably the last person that I ever thought I'd see again and justifiably one that I never thought would want to help me with anything either regardless of where we were. Although I tried my best to fight back tears, it was no use. I was getting ready to see Mia again due to the great power of forgiveness and love. Nasim then grabbed my hands, the very hands that were just forgiven by the thirteen men and asked me to bow my head.

When he did, he smiled and simply said, "Now pray, pray to see her." I opened one eye as wide as it would go while still keeping the other shut and kind of looked up at him with my eyebrow stretched towards the sky. I was hoping my eyebrow, now that they are full again was saying, "Come on man, that's it?" He laughed and said he promised that's all I had to do. That just seemed too easy and I could have done that all along if that's all it took. I told him about Sammy and all of that tuning in and the higher frequency stuff which made Nasim let out a huge laugh. Once he gained his composure he said, "Yeah, I have four brothers myself," and shook his head as I always did. After I got over the shock of the simplicity of being able to see Mia and the unheavenly feelings I was having about punching my little Herculean brother out, Nasim and I interlocked our hands. We then bowed our heads and prayed. This time I kept my eyebrows down and followed Nasim's directions. As we prayed to see Mia, just as Nasim said would happen, I could finally see my baby girl.

Sammy came out of the waterfall, Sarge and my other military buddies flew from the sky. My grandparents appeared from what seemed like the ether, but where I could see Mia from made the most sense to me. Mia appeared to me from what looked like a projection that was shown directly from my heart. I could finally see my little girl. I may not be able to have quite the same interaction with her as I could with the others but I could finally see her and that meant so much to me. With what I felt my curses were, I never felt that I could justify being overly religious. But no matter what feelings I may have been about my own unworthiness there wasn't a day that went by that I didn't tell my little girl that I thanked God for her. She helped me become a person that I didn't think I could be anymore and she somehow did that before she could even talk.

I buried all of that guilt and any of the other negative feelings that I may have had as deep as I could inside of me. I kept all of that death and resentment as far away from Mia as I knew how. I might not be with her now but I could finally see her again. Although I'll always feel that connection to her, seeing her gave me an assuredness that I still need regardless of where I was. Now that I could see how sad she was without me even there my heart was breaking. I knew something was wrong but I couldn't see her before to confirm what I already knew to be true. I was so happy to see everyone but Mia is who I needed to see the most and I knew that I am who she needs too. I don't know why I had to leave when I did. I don't think anybody ever does but there has to be something I could do for her from here. I understand now why everyone kept saying that I wasn't ready to see her but when your child hurts you hurt too no matter where you are or what you're doing.

I was thinking this place is so much like a casino. There aren't clocks or calendars around anywhere and up until now with all of my recent visitors I thought maybe I hit the jackpot myself but I don't feel that way anymore. I know that Sammy in his own playful way was just trying to help but when it comes to Mia I'd rather hurt than not know somethings wrong with her. When Mia was really little if she didn't have the best of days we'd watch her favorite movie to cheer her up. That movie was Mrs. Doubtfire. There's an unwritten rule about letting a child jump on the bed but after seeing Robin Williams and his children in the movie and all the fun they had that rule simply never applied to us. No matter where we were in the house if we heard that song come on Mia's eyes would light up and we'd stop whatever it was we were doing and run to the closest bed to jump on it.

For me it was like being a kid again but for Mia it was much more. Not only did her daddy let her break the rules, I was breaking them with her. Mia cackled and cackled watching her daddy act like a little kid jumping all around with her. We never missed any of our opportunities to jump either because if it happened when we were out somewhere instead of jumping on a bed we'd more or less jump in place wherever we were. I think one time in Toys R US the other shoppers had to be thinking they were witnessing a dual father and daughter seizure session, but we didn't care. We just did what Mr. Williams and Everlast directed us to do, we jumped around. We were also like Mr. Lennon said to be, we were happy, very very happy. This prayer thing is simple I thought, and in this place it seems like we have more of a direct line than I would have ever thought so I decided to do it myself. As I watched Mia sadly dredging around her room I saw her pick up some of her favorite toys and play with them for a minute or two and then put them down.

The toys didn't seem to be helping her with what she was feeling very much. I also heard the radio on in the background. I didn't think a prayer could be wasted on a little jumping around so that's exactly what I decided to do with my prayer. I tried and tried but for me nothing happened. I didn't know how much time I really had so I decided to ask for help once more. Nasim graciously obliged and as the music started, Mia's eyes popped wide open in excitement as they always did and then heartbreakingly she looked around as if she was waiting for me to run in the room and start jumping with her. That was not what I intended and when she realized that I wasn't coming she started crying. I know now as much as ever when your child hurts you hurt too no matter where you think you are.

Just before things got too sad for me to bear Ms.Grace returned. I was grateful for all of Nasim's help and I let him know it as he departed. This time Ms. Grace wasn't whistling or even smiling like she always did before. Her emotions seemed to mimic mine. She knew what I saw and she also knew how I saw it too. As I left that building that I felt was one of the most terrible places I've ever been I realized that I had a mixed opinion about it now. In one sense, I was grateful for the forgiveness that it housed, but in another after seeing Mia like that, I resented it again. I then turned to Ms.Grace and sarcastically asked, "How could that building ever be considered a church?" Although a little more somber than usual she still gave out another cute little giggle and said it's never the building, or any building for that matter that makes a church, it's the forgiveness, love, and other gifts that happen when people come together at any place that make a real church.

I knew then without doubting any longer that the forgiveness that I received and at least the ability to see Mia with Nasim's help in that old concrete building qualified that place to be as much of a church as any ever was. As we walked I realized there was no question that the path that Ms. Grace led me down had deliberate resting spots along the way. Those were times for me to be still and let the plans that someone else had for me to become enacted. Those times not only cleansed my soul a little at a time but also began adding clarity. Those places also helped me realize that Mia was still just as big of a part of my after life as she ever was. I refuse to ever let that go regardless of the consequences. As we were walking I noticed that Ms. Grace appeared to be even younger than she did just the day before and we were also getting even closer to the bright light and that beautiful music.

Before I could make another Benjamin Buttons joke she turned to me and yelled out, "Look, look!" Her once shiny glow now turned to a more pale shade as if she saw a ghost. The way she looked at me this time startled me because I couldn't imagine what a real ghost would look like in this place. I didn't know if we were in some kind of trouble or what was going on. As she finally gathered her words, she kept telling me to look down. When I followed her directions I saw all of these green balloons floating through what I thought was the ground and then through the air in every direction. There were so many green balloons surrounding us in such a short period of time. There were so many that I could barely see the multitude of flowers that were usually the only thing we saw on the path.

I didn't have any idea why we were being invaded by so many green balloons or why they seemed to be coming from everywhere but Ms. Grace did and she was beyond shocked to see them. To me they were just green just balloons floating through a very strange place. This place was already so odd to me that a bunch of balloons didn't really shock me as it did Ms. Grace. I did know that green was my favorite color but I really didn't have any other connection that I could think of to the balloons that were absolutely floating everywhere by then. Ms. Grace said over and over that she'd never seen this before, she then yelled out, "It's Mia! It's Mia! She's doing this for you!" As I, with Ms. Grace's help this time directed our prayers to see my little girl, it was her. She was releasing one green balloon after another while saying her own prayers for her Daddy.

It's more than obvious to me now that prayer works in all directions, everywhere, and although I don't know if she'd ever know it or not but it was working for her too. I've been trying to signal to her and she was doing the same for me. With her much purer heart it was working to the amazement of Ms. Grace and to me as well. I knew that time was a little confusing here and what I thought was only a few days was obviously a few years for Mia. Unlike Ms. Grace she was aging as you're supposed to. When I looked down to see Mia, if I had to guess I would think she must have been about ten years old now. The one thing Sammy did tell the truth about was that I could see the past as well. When I looked back at Mia's past, again with Ms. Grace's help, it was a little fuzzy but I did get to see what had been going on in her life. I saw her call my phone over and over again to hear my voice. I watched her hold on to everything that was mine as if it was me, and I also saw rivers of tears stream down her little cheeks day after day.

Green Balloons

Even though we were separated, I wasn't separated from the earthly pain of seeing Mia in so much pain. I had to come up with some way that I could help her. It wasn't that she didn't have her good days it's just there weren't enough of them. She carried those dark clouds around with her like I did before she was born and it was tearing my heart to pieces. When Mia was little, obviously younger than she is now we'd play what I called the Claim-Game. It was a way to pass the time in the truck but also a way to make the ride more enjoyable. When either of us saw a corvette whoever saw it first would yell out, "Claim it." We were pretending that we'd actually own the car if we yelled out that we claimed it first. Since there weren't a whole lot of corvettes around where we lived many times we'd spend a full trip just looking around in hopes of beating the other for the much desired fictitious prize. She was so funny, when I won she'd always come up with an excuse like she was looking at something else, or she had something in her eye.

At times she sounded like one of those slick lawyers trying to defend her reasons for not winning but other times, when she'd win, she'd do her best version of a touchdown dance right underneath her tightly strapped seatbelt. I have to admit I did let her win sometimes just to see her seat celebration but not all of the time. Her youthful justification for not claiming a passing corvette first was almost as comical as her seat dance so either way the game was a success to me. I know it's such a little thing but I believe I'm going to get some help in praying for some more corvettes and two-dollar bills to enter her life pretty soon. The two dollar bill thing was just another game I made up too. Because we didn't see too many of those either I told her every time we got a two dollar bill back as change or in a birthday card, or from anywhere, she got a wish.

That kid was so smart on the week I came up with the game she figured out how to cheat right away. She knew enough to ask my mother, her grandmother, to take her to the bank to get a bunch of two dollar bills and in doing so she'd get all of the wishes she wanted. Once I finally got through to her that the game didn't work that way and I laid down some ground rules she bought into it all the way. From there she seemed to be satisfied with just getting the two dollar bills and with what we called in-house wishes. I learned my lesson to be very clear with that little girl because she was definitely much smarter than her father ever was. One day she hit the proverbial jackpot herself. We were at McDonald's, her favorite restaurant when a corvette parked outside while we were ordering our food. She yelled out "Claim it" so loud that she scared the cashier. Once the worker realized that my kid wasn't robbing the place she unknowingly gave us two, two dollar bills back for change.

Mia got three wishes and a convertible corvette that day. I thought she was actually going to try and kick the owner of that sleek little ride out of his own car when we left because she took that game pretty serious at times. On that double prize day after she finished her chicken nuggets and French fries she told me that she made up her mind about what she wanted for her wishes. It was as if she'd been planning her wishes for quite a while and just had to wait for the arrival of the next two dollar bill so it could come true. Once the next one made its way to her she looked up at me with those big brown puppy dog eyes and said, "Daddy, my wish is for us to be together forever." Now I don't care how big and tough any father thinks they are those words from your little girl are pretty special. Her wish was so special to me that I was pretending that I had something in my eye so she wouldn't see me proudly choking up.

I know I couldn't help it, or even do anything about it, but I do feel to a degree I broke my promise to her. I felt the same way with Sammy, and with Sarge, but this is my daughter. She knows I didn't want to get sick and she has to know I didn't want to leave her, it wasn't my decision, and it damn sure wasn't my choice either. I could barely stand there and watch her hurt for me like all of those green balloons were telling me she still was. My original circumstances as a father was kind of like the first time that we entered an actual war zone. It had to be all in or not at all, and doing nothing never crossed my mind when it came to her. I've had massive issues with guilt before and much of that was released by Nasim and his men in that so called church but I would never be able to absorb the guilt that I would have by not giving Mia my best regardless of where I am.

I know my thoughts are so dramatic but so was my life. All of these constant highs and lows even here. For some reason my lows always seemed to involve someone dying, which to me was the lowest of the lows but my highs included growing up with an amazing family and having some of the truest friends a man could have. The kind that would literally lay their own life down for you. My greatest high however is that little girl below praying and releasing all of those green balloons up in the air. This place is definitely not like anything I was ever was told or expected it to be. I missed Mia so much and I had to help her in some way even if it had to be from a distance. While all of this was going on and I was standing there ranting and raving to myself Ms. Grace seemed to disappear. I knew she said the physical communication upward was a rare thing but she never knew how Mia and I were together.

This time instead of Ms. Grace coming back it was Sammy again. I guess she needed to call in reinforcements because of the rarity of the situation but I was also hoping she didn't go anywhere to tell any sort of heavenly policemen either. Besides, I owed Sammy a punch in the nose for not explaining this tuning in or prayer thing better but I also knew I'd never actually do it. He was flexing all of his parts up and down just as much as he did the other day as he got to me. Sammy told me Ms. Grace would be busy for a while and that I'd see her later but in the meanwhile he'llbe taking over babysitting me. I asked him jokingly, if she had a fingernail appointment or had to get her hair done or something like that because I didn't know what could possibly be more important than taking me to wherever it was we were going.

Sammy must have learned a thing or two from Ms. Grace because he basically ignored my comments and we did what we always do when we were together. We joked around and thought about ways to mess up stuff. I was still upset about Mia but damn if that boy didn't distract me enough to give my mind a little break. Like I said before, time is a funny thing at this place and when Sammy told me he wanted to play a trick on Mia's boyfriend I about flipped. "Boyfriend?" I asked. I just saw her and she looked to be about ten years old she better not have a boyfriend. Sammy laughed and prayed and somehow I started to see my now teenage daughter below. I was speechless as Sammy smiled and said let's go boyfriend hunting. To me in my mind Mia was still a little girl. I didn't want to hear anything about a boyfriend but once that kid came into our sight Sammy hardily laughed at my expense once again. This kid had one of those stubby dog tail looking things on the back of his head. I think they're called a man bun or something idiotic like that. I was an ex-military man and definitely from a different era.

I had no idea what Mia could ever see in a guy with a pony tail sprouting out the top of his head, besides it felt like just a few hours ago she was ten years old. We figured out that this kid's name was Payne. I immediately started to rant, "Who the hell names there kid Payne?" *This kid's definitely not John Payne or Payne Gretzky, or even Payne Stewart*, I thought sarcastically. To me I was still replacing the W with a P and it was more like Payne-Payne go away and don't come back another day, that's it, the microphone has dropped, leave my little girl alone, or I'm going to come down and haunt your ass when I figure out how to do it myself. My little girl was so young last week and now. This may have been the hell I originally expected to go to. I was getting a little ridiculously worked up but Sammy wouldn't stop eggin' me on. I know that flexing jerk is loving this because once again he's getting me and that kid at the same time.

"P-A-Y-N-E," I said in my slowest whiny voice, seemed so damn awkward it was almost a shame to do something to him but hey if Sammy said it was a good idea who was I to argue him? I was the rookie here. I was still pretty new at what I could do or couldn't do from this place so once again I had to rely on my brother, the same one that I should have tuned into punching but he was the only option that I had. Again with time being somewhat funny we could tell that the poochy-headed kid was getting ready for some kind of fancy event like a prom or homecoming. As Sammy and I watched him brush the stub on the top of his head several times I asked, "How hard it would be to blow up his house from here?" I was just joking about that but I do think what we decided to actually do was almost as detrimental to that young man's plans for the evening as anything could be.

When Sammy was alive everyone he met instantly loved him. That meant everywhere without exaggeration, he was just one of those types of people. I'm glad for us now that every animal did too. I'm pretty sure with his current higher influence they still will too. I think the plan was set without the real need of working out any overly specific details. Animals, especially dogs have a keen sense and are very good in most cases at following directions. We watched for a little while longer until P-A-Y-N-E finished primping himself up. Then he headed to Emily and Mia's house to where I was hoping all of the festivities would begin. This boy was driving a huge Toyota truck with massive tires and the most obnoxious horn ever installed. As the funny named kid arrived to pick up Mia, he leaned over in the seat looked at himself in the mirror and sprayed some kind of spray in his mouth, I guess to disinfect his breathe, but if it's up to me his breathe wasn't going to be anywhere near my daughter.

Anyway, I don't think Sammy ever stopped laughing as he once again mysteriously contacted one of his earthly four-legged friends. This friend was something I guess you could call a dog and one that was just a few yards away from where P-A-Y-N-E had to go to pick up Mia. Sammy has always been over the top and this prank was no different. He could have picked a beagle; he could have even picked a labrador retriever. They're common dogs in the K-9 world but not for Sammy. As Payne rang the doorbell Mia and Emily came out on the front porch. Mia was in this beautiful gown and she looked so grown up. She had this long flowing purple dress on and she looked almost exactly like her mother did when I first met her. She was almost grown and finally she seemed so happy... even if she was dating this P-A-Y-N-E idiot. I almost forgot Sammy and I were on a mission but he didn't.

After that boy reached in to give Mia a hug everyone on the porch jerked their heads around in a hurry to see what was approaching with such a clatter. It was as if they heard train coming their way but this train had slobber slapping out of both sides of its mouth. I think if Sammy could have used a dinosaur he would but this dog was pretty close. As the porch dwellers started shuffling for safety Sammy's new buddy, a humongous Saint Bernard was headed their way. I say their way but he was most definitely directed solely at P-A-Y-N-E. Before that mammoth dog made it all the way to the porch I confirmed with Sammy that his new Cujo looking friend wasn't actually going to kill the kid. Without giving me a clear answer once again, Sammy laughed and just told me to watch. That dog acted like Payne had a prime rib in his pocket and sloppily bit down right around his crotch area.

I don't like cussing like in a place like this but even I had to say "D-A-M-N," out loud. The dog wasn't hurting him or his boy-parts but it sure did a number on his finely pressed yuppie pants as they ripped off from that dog's slobbery grasp. To both Sammy and my amusement it left that man bun kid standing on the front porch with nothing on except his underwear and more importantly, triggered his running back to his swamp buggy to head back from where he came from. That kid screamed louder than his obnoxious horn could blow. Mia and Emily tried not to laugh but it was funny, so there was ample laughter from above and below. After they went back in the house and Payne went home to change, Sammy decided to continue to stalk him. We could tell he was still embarrassed and when he tried round two at getting ready for the dance he began talking to himself in the mirror. His words were mostly about that big old stupid dog as he described Sammy's new pet. He also fussed about being all but molested right there on Mia's steps by the thing.

Sammy and I laughed at the kid's commentary about what he thought he experienced almost as much as we did about the attack. The thing is after a while of listening to his blubbering I could tell this kid really liked Mia. I don't care if I was there or here I had to check any boy out that was going to be around my daughter. Sammy finally caught his breathe from all the laughter and let me know that was his favorite prank of all time. I had to agree but I really wanted to know more about this boy and more about how Sammy actually got the dog to do that too. I wanted to be able to interact with her too if I felt I needed to, even if that help had to be delivered through some huge horse-looking dog.

After that kid primped again he jumped back in that over-sized truck and headed back to try and pick up Mia for the second time. Sammy asked me if we should start planning the second round but something inside of me felt like he had enough for one day. This time when he went to the door he was as nervous as I've ever seen anyone wearing a man bun but that's understandable I guess. I did however make sure Sammy had that big St. Bernard on standby just in case. When Mia opened the door they both laughed and he politely walked her down the steps making sure her dress didn't drag on the ground. He was definitely looking all around for a certain four legged intruder and he was definitely pulling at his pants to make sure they stayed on this time but most of his attention was where I thought it should be. He even opened the truck door for Mia and gave her a boost up in that ridiculous thing. He may have known I was watching from somewhere because he even watched the placement of his hands while helping her. This kid at least scored one point with me and he's definitely not a quitter, I thought.

When I was his age if a massive dog tried to bite my parts and pants off I would have definitely seen that as a sign to stay away from any girl but not him. I wondered at first, mainly because Sammy was whispering doubts in my ear, if this guy was as genuine as he seemed. Watching them at that dance was truly heart-warming. He never stopped being polite and he did seem to be real as anyone could be at their age. As they sat down to drink what I hoped was a non-alcoholic refreshment I listened in as everyone seems to always do to me. They definitely were still talking about the front porch assault but both of them spoke about their fathers. Payne spoke of his and Mia about me. Although I didn't know Payne's father and hadn't met him here yet I soon found out that he was one of the young men that didn't make it home from the same war I was in. I thought to myself, dammit now I have to like this kid.

But the more he and Mia spoke the more I actually did like him. Sammy didn't catch on yet at first. He was playing the air violin in the background and still flexing. As the night went on I realized that Mia was almost a woman and this guy almost a man himself. But the respect that he showed my daughter turned any anxiety that I may have had towards him into appreciation. By the end of the night even Uncle Trickery liked the guy too. As Payne dropped Mia off, he was just as cordial and he helped her out of his truck and back to the house. They hugged and kissed each other on the cheek but that was it. *I might be able to handle these Hallmark-moment kind of dates,* I thought. He still looked in every direction when he headed back to his truck but this kid really a good guy and I was proud of him and the way he handled himself with my daughter even though he'd probably never know it.

When Mia went inside she excitedly told her mother about her night and how much fun she had. This was the happiness that I always prayed she'd have. I was kind of hoping I was the one that caused it but Mia's okay and this kid is too. Emily then told Mia about the first time we met, which was very different and in a bar but she left out those kind of details out as she told our story. She said she can see herself in Mia. I thought to myself slow it down now but I understood what she was saying. Emily was very happy when we first met but she had family problems that ended up consuming her and our marriage. I got Mia in the process of her mom trying to find her way back from her past and that gift was my greatest blessing by far. Emily's obviously a wonderful mother now and Mia seems so happy.

She does seem very mature for her age and with the exception of his hair, so does Payne. I guess losing a father makes you grow up faster than seems fair, *but these kids are going to be just fine*, I thought. Now that we've finished playing tricks on people I'm not going to let Sammy go anywhere until he helps me become a little more Houdini like myself. Even though Sammy plays a lot, he knows when I'm serious about something. At least now I'm somewhat at ease about how Mia is doing. So now I want his help for more positive reasons than I probably would have ever wanted it for before now. I understand that prayer and belief is key but I couldn't pray that dog into biting that boy in the crotch when Sammy could. I want to know what he knows and this time I'm really not going to let him leave until he shows me. When I asked Sammy to teach me all of his mystical ways he laughed and asked, "Did Houdini tell his secrets?" I don't know about what Houdini did or didn't do but I knew who I was going to make spill the beans before they could leave.

Like I've been thinking and even saying since I got to this place, it's still so much like home and for whatever reason I'm still the big brother in this situation. Sammy never cared before about telling me any secrets, in fact he was the worst secret keeper there ever was and this time was no different. It's not that any of it was ever a secret anyway it was more of a process. I simply had to take it in a little at a time. Maybe I wasn't ready before now but I am kind of accepting where I am and I just want to be able to do a little more while I'm here, more for me but more importantly more for Mia too. In truth, I'm even beginning to understand the life in between lives thing to a degree. With almost everything to include a meal there has to be a cleansing and preparation stage to prepare for the main course.

Those forced naps that Ms. Grace made me take and those visits that I was so blessed to receive, and even what seemed like a never ending path all have a purpose. That purpose was to prepare me for whatever is at my own final destination. There's no question that we all have a say in how that is constructed. Look at Sammy, Sarge and my buddies, and even my grandparents. They all came to me in a way that after I thought about it for a while I could somewhat understand. Even the way Mia projected out of my own heart made more sense to me now. I knew I wasn't ready to be completely engulfed in that light yet but hopefully I'm more ready than I was. Nasim and his men also really helped me take leaps and bounds in that direction and I'm grateful for that as well. Soon I may even be worthy enough for such a blessing. Believe it or not, that kid with the man bun, and seeing Emily as she was, and Mia so happy helped me so much. From the moment I got here most of my thoughts were on Mia and her sadness.

Now most of my thoughts are still on Mia but there's a relaxation in my heart that was sporadic at best before. She's mostly grown and seems to be having a pretty good life whether I'm there or not. That's all I ever wanted. I guess this is that letting go that people talk about. The harder we seem to fight against something the more it seems to persist or resist what we're trying to do. My life was such a battle at times that I seemed to still have some of that resistance in me here. I think that's why it was so hard for me to see Mia myself at first, and why I couldn't be the one that befriended that huge Saint Bernard was because I was never clear-headed enough on what I was asking for and I didn't feel deserving enough to get it. Maybe none of this is as hard as I'm making it out to be after all. This rambling was a conversation that I was trying to have with Sammy but after I finished, he said, "See there, now you're Houdini too."

My eyebrow wanted to come up again as it did when Nasim told me all I had to do was pray to see Mia. Of course this was after Sammy misguided me with all that tuning in mess. But maybe, just maybe they were both right. I guess another way of putting it is letting go is actually the same thing as having faith and tuning in has to be the same as cleansing to prepare yourself for your request. I told Sammy this life in between life thing is pretty deep. He smiled at me and said, "Naw, only as deep as you make it". I wanted to confirm that I had everything straight so I said, you mean all you have to do prepare yourself for the prayer, pray, have faith that your prayer will be answered, and to top it all off give thanks for when it is. Sammy said, while half- heartedly listened to my description, "Yep, that's it." I was expecting a little more expansion on the subject but I didn't get it. He just kept calling me Houdini and flexing his muscles thinking about what we did to that poor kid.

He did mumble something about their being one more little thing to it but it wasn't a big deal. I had this thought before but at that point I really began to notice that even though Sammy looked like a rugged and chiseled man on the outside he was really still that same little boy I grew up with on the inside. I guess here, once you learn how, you can look like whatever you want. He was just fifteen years old when he died and I'd be willing to bet that somewhere underneath all of that that masculine puffiness, he still is now. His innocence gave him the preparation, his loving heart gave him the faith, and our wonderful parents taught him how to pray. His light-hearted view on life always gave him assuredness so it was no wonder he thrived so well here. I think he was trying to hide it but when he got ready to leave that day instead of him telling me a secret I told him how proud I was of him.

Not about the new muscles or flowing locks but about the stuff inside, that made him, him. I looked at Sammy and said, "Thank you." He then smacked me on the arm and said, "We can play pranks on anyone you want, just let me know." I said, "No not for the pranks, even though that Saint. Bernard thing was funny, but not that." Well for what he asked. I said for being my brother no matter where we are. That Brutus-looking man got tears in his eyes. The innocent kind of tears that fifteen-year-olds get so easily when something touches their heart. Instead of flexing anything up and down this time he appeared to me as he was on earth, Down syndrome and all, and gave me a hug every bit as strong as his muscled-up version of his self ever could. He taught me so much in life and now he was here as well without even really trying. As he walked off all I heard was, "Houdini... Houdini... Houdini," but once again all I could do was thank God for so many things but today I gave a little extra thanks for my very special brother.

Cerulean Blue

By this time I was realizing that Ms. Grace seemed to be slacking on her tour guiding duties because I hadn't seen her in a while and I kind of missed that sweet old lady. I jokingly thought to myself, I guess she must have gotten held up in St. Michael's hair salon or maybe at Abraham's antiques. I had no clue where she was but for the first time since I've been here I was going to have to find my own resting place. I didn't realize it at first but I almost got to where I looked forward to those little breaks. I was never tired but to me it seemed that each resting spot brought something that always seemed to get me a little closer to that light and the music, and to whatever my final destination was. Along the way I was able to be reunited with so many of my loved ones here and even a few from where I was, especially Mia. I was fairly sure that any place I chose to rest would be considered safe in this neighborhood, so off I went. I wasn't looking for any particular place but like everything and everyone else here it found me.

As I walked I once again began thinking about my life and like so much of it, my thoughts settled back on Sammy. Before he died we were in a boating accident that hurt him pretty badly. He already had so many health problems towards the end and I felt I added to his problems. Instead of sticking around to help out I went to Israel on a summer study abroad program. A whole lot happened in that country but one of the biggest things that I did was paint something that I couldn't take the credit for. Don't get me wrong it was my hand and my time, and I was actually the one that put the paint on the canvas but that was about it. It was like every idea and image flowed to me completely from somewhere else so effortlessly. When I was finished I had never seen anything like what that painting was. Its features were just as special as Ms. Grace's eyes or even her glow but different.

It was almost as pure as our skin is now but with as many colors perfectly blended around the other rather than one unified shade. When I started painting I didn't stop until when I felt the channeled masterpiece was finished. After Sammy died I didn't really paint anymore and out of rage from the loss of my brother I destroyed something that wasn't mine to ruin. It wasn't too long after that I joined the military. When Mia was small I bought her little art sets and although we did have fun with them we didn't do much more than doodle out cartoons. I started painting to teach Sammy how to do it for himself and without him I didn't think it was fair for me to continue. I don't feel that way anymore now that I see how well he's doing. I also see a full-fledged art-set sitting in the middle of the woods.

Ms. Grace isn't fooling me, she may be pre-occupied but she's not busy enough not to give me another gift and directions about where she wants me to head next. When I got to my obvious next destination like so many years ago once I started painting I couldn't stop. I don't know how long I actually painted that night but I do know I only stopped when no more paint would fit anywhere on the canvas. The result this time was every bit as magical as the last, if not more. I've learned that I shouldn't expect anything less from this place, so I won't. Once again, I really couldn't take credit for this one either but it didn't matter. I had that old feeling of true accomplishment that I hadn't had in such a long time. I can remember the last painting and even the color that most often permeated throughout what I felt I had inherited. It was Cerulean Blue. That shade of blue is a little like a deep sky blue or maybe even the color of a clear sea, the kind you can see all of the way to the bottom of. It was mesmerizing then and even more so now. I didn't want to stop painting but it was time.

I finished all I was given to do on this part of my journey. To me this day was a glaring metaphor for my life. Many times it was messy, similar to paint that I spilled all over the forest floor but other times it produced something far greater than I could have ever imagined. With both Mia and those paintings they were so much better than anything I could have ever created on my own. So without hesitation once again I thanked God but this time it wasn't just for the outcome. For the first time ever it was also for the spilled paint of my life as well. All of it, the good and the bad which has made this painting and my past life as amazing as it was and I'm finally realizing that. Life was so funny at times but death is so odd as well. There is really very little difference so far between the two for me at least.

As I did when I was young, and not having Ms. Grace to direct me any differently I laid on my back again and just looked up at those magnificent clouds. Not one of those puffy canvases in their own right contained even the slightest ounce of darkness. Lying there, I looked over at my painting that I had propped up next to a tree. Every now and then the painting itself seemed to become even brighter than it originally was. It was almost like a heartbeat of color pulsing to signify how special it was for itself. I felt like I was that same kid from my youth too. That kid that didn't realize he'd ever have a worry in the world and right then neither did I. I have known pain and I've seen so much death, but I've also seen where it all ends up, here. If the destination is better than this place I can't even imagine how glorious it will be. Finally, I hear the leaves rustling again, I'm going to get on Ms. Grace for abandoning me, I jokingly thought. But it wasn't Ms. Grace coming this time, it wasn't Sammy or Sarge either. It was a little brown headed girl.

I knew it wasn't Mia, but she looked very much like she did around the time of my death. Just like Ms. Grace always did this little girl came up to me as if she knew me forever and said, "Hey, Grampy." This kid was just as sassy and funny as Ms. Grace too but in a miniature much faster way. She noticed my painting and ran over to it. I didn't have a house here, and I'm guessing I'm what you'd call a transient, so when she asked me if she could borrow it I didn't see any issue with her request. Besides, I remembered it really wasn't mine to keep anyway. She looked deep into that painting for a while like she knew what every brush stroke meant. It was a lot like that young man in the wheel chair did in Israel. I could tell she appreciated the painting and I thought about asking her if she wanted to paint something together but I already spilled most of the paint that I didn't use and there really wasn't any left to speak of.

She said we didn't have time to paint anyway because we had to get a move on. We had a lot to do, and we didn't have a lot of time to do it either according to her. This little girl cracked me up because she was bossier than Mia ever was. I guess she thought she was Ms. Grace's personal secretary or some other sort of important confidant that had to live up to a certain responsibility. Just like when I wasn't bold enough to refuse the orders from my glowing elderly chaperone, I didn't have guts to deny the directions from a sassy little girl either. I rapidly followed her directions and went to grab my painting to take it along with us. I didn't mind if she borrowed it or even kept it. I figured by now I'd be able to paint another anytime I wanted but she wasn't having any of that. She wanted to carry it herself. The painting was almost as big as she was and as we made our way back to the path she'd peak over and around the edges of the canvas every now and then to make sure she didn't run into anything.

I asked her where Ms. Grace was or if she even knew her. I've learned there's no guessing about anything in this place so I at least had to ask the questions even if they often got ignored. She told me she was close and she would always be with me. I've heard those words before directly from the horse's mouth but obviously their definition of being around or with me and mine are very different. As strange as it sounds and being that Ms. Grace seemed to be aging in reverse a weird thought came over me in this odd place so I asked, "Are you Ms. Grace?" I got a very similar reaction similar to when I asked Ms. Grace if she was God. That little girl laughed while shaking her head and then she said, "My name is Abigail. Abby, for short". Now this still didn't tell me where Ms. Grace was or why this little girl was now my very active chauffer, but she evidently was and per her demand off we went.

I guess carrying around that painting finally got a little awkward for Abby because she told me she'd be back in a minute and disappeared through the flowers that still inhabited almost everywhere. When she came back just a few minutes later she didn't have the paining with her. She assured me that she just put it in safe place but we had to keep moving. Now, Mia could be strong willed when she wanted to be but this little girl, Abby, was definitely bold to say the least. She was so cute and confident that I really didn't have any other choice but to do what she asked. On the path this time I could tell we were getting extremely close to where I was guessing the end was. As we walked, it was refreshing to be around a little girl again. She, unlike Ms. Grace went on and on about everything she saw but also that she thought she saw too. She had such amazement with everything.

Abby's age and above was the part of Mia's life that I missed. It was so peculiar how comfortable we were around each other once I got used to her confidence. There wasn't an ounce of shyness about her; just a curiosity about everything to include me and I had the same interest in her. She was the first child that I'd seen since I've been here and thinking about Sammy I wondered if she chose to look that way or if someone changed her appearance for her. I didn't know how to ask a little girl a question like that so I decided to leave it as a mystery. Abby asked me if I knew what her name meant. I had a blank stare on my face because I really didn't know what my own name meant and my name was Israel. So I felt I should at least know that, and said, "Why don't you tell me?" She gave this big grin and said, "Abigail means the bringer of joy." I smiled back because as happy and energetic as that kid was I could definitely see that in her. She'd walk for a bit, then almost jog with a skip thrown in every now and then. I may have never been tired before with Ms. Grace but keeping up with Abby was another story.

If I'd fall a little behind she'd look back and say, "Pick it up, Grampy," and I'd do my best to catch up with her as fast as I could. I even tried to make up conversations so she'd slow down a bit but she kept up with the conversation much better than I did with her pace. I could tell that she felt we had to be somewhere at a specific time but I didn't know why. This was the first time that time itself seemed to be a factor here. Jokingly I thought, there was no way for me to be late for my own funeral because that already happened. After a while as kids her age do, and all at once, she seemed to get tired herself, really tired, as if she wore her own self out. I asked her if she wanted to take a break but she said we couldn't and asked if she could ride on my back.

I felt I was past the point of falling out too but without hesitation I kind of felt like it was an honor that she even asked. I missed things like this with my own daughter so I proudly scooped her up and spun her to my back. She didn't feel like she weighed much more than a feather so it wasn't that difficult to keep on the path at pretty much the same pace as before when she led or maybe a tad slower. I walked for maybe ten steps and then she rested her little head on my left shoulder and shortly thereafter she was asleep. I forgot how quickly kids her age crash. It's sixty to zero in three point three seconds sometimes. I decided to keep walking in the direction we started just in case she woke up. I didn't want that little girl fussing at me again. Like everything else that has happened in this place I'm sure whatever it is we're supposed to see will find us long before I even know that I'm looking for it. I think Abby was dreaming as she napped because every now and then I'd hear a faint little murmur. It was so cute and this walk just felt so fatherly. This was the kind of thing I missed so much and I wasn't so sure that I wanted to her to wake up for a while.

She slept on my back for about thirty minutes and just like when you put a car battery on a charger she woke up as energized as she was when I first met her. She may have been a little embarrassed about falling asleep but when she climbed down she didn't quite walk as far in front of me this time even though she definitely talked as much as she did before. I didn't mind though, it was cute seeing how animated she'd get about everything. When she gave me a chance to get a word in I asked her why her and Ms. Grace always called me Grampy. She laughed as if it was some state secret and basically did what Ms. Grace always did and completely ignored my question and kept talking about whatever it was she wanted to talk about.

That little buggar was outsmarting me too. I figured maybe I'll get some answers out of her because she's a kid but that thought didn't work either. When I asked where Ms. Grace was again with a little more insistency in my voice, Abby scrunched up her little nose and said, "She told you she'd always be with and always would be with you too, man." Her answer didn't "answer" anything and I was beginning to think this little girl might need a time-out. When I thought about those words, 'time out', I immediately thought back to Mia and the one and only time out she was ever given one. I can't say that Mia was ever that bad. I never had to spank her, not that I could anyway but the one time she did receive that sentence you would have thought I sent her away for thirty years to do hard time. I really don't think she understood what was going on but I had to do something so she wouldn't see me vent and then laugh at her attempt to get her point across.

One afternoon, I was fixing dinner and she was playing in her room. All of a sudden I heard this terrible pounding coming from the back of the house. I ran back there as fast as I could to see what was going on. When I saw what my child had done, Tim the tool man may have been proud, but I was a little upset to say the least. Mia evidentially saw me cooking hamburgers for dinner. She never had any problem with eating hamburgers before and I thought she liked them so I was making that meal again. Hamburgers and macaroni and cheese, that's a good meal for anyone I thought. When I looked around this little girl's room it didn't take but a second to realize that she nailed two hand drawn pictures of a cow with a red X through it on her wall. I don't know what she was thinking. I didn't know what to say. I didn't even know that she knew where my hammer and nails were, or how to use them correctly, but she obviously did.

Most of all I didn't realize that she knew hamburgers were made from cows in the first place. I was absolutely speechless and she seemed overly proud of herself. I still don't know how at her age she knew what putting a red X across something really meant but to her I soon learned that it meant eat more chicken. I didn't know to laugh, to get the putty for the wall, or really what to do or what was going on. I did know that my little protester was evidently watching way too much television, and most definitely too many of those dumb Chic-fil-a commercials. That, for her is what led to her one and only time-out. Thinking back to Mia and my mother, I fully understood that times had changed since I grew up. If Jacob, Sammy, or I would have done what Mia did, my mother, quick-draw-McGraw would have definitely handled the situation a bit differently.

In her defense though we did so much wrong most of the time we left her very few other choices. Walking and talking with Abby has been so enjoyable. She has many of the same mannerisms that Mia did but also the boldness and confidence of Ms. Grace. This little thing is a mess as she's kicking at my feet while I walk. Before long she smiled again and said, "We're here" I looked around and asked, "We're where". The beautiful music was louder but we weren't all the way to the light so I don't know where that 'here' is that she's talking about. Besides I thought it was Ms. Grace's job to get me to the destination or the light or wherever it was I was supposed to end up at. Abby grabbed me by the hand and led me over a small hill that was hiding the 'here' that she was talking about. When we reached the top of the hill there was a hundred or more people just about twenty yards or so away. As we reached the middle of that crowd, Abby seemed to be showing me off like I was a new baby doll or the shiniest penny in a shiny penny contest.

Before I could introduce myself, she beat me to the punch and introduced me as Grampy. It was a whirlwind event, meeting one person after another until I believe we got around to just about everyone. The gathering reminded me of one of those country family reunions where you know you're related to most everyone there in some way but you really don't know who most of them are. This place was no different. I did know, or at least thought I knew some of these people from the past. I saw my great uncle and a few older cousins. I saw other kids there too. Surprisingly enough, I even saw old Joe, who like me had no idea how he could end up in such an oddly wonderful place. After I saw my dear friend Eddie, I thought maybe this really was the destination or at least the check in line for it but I still realized as wonderful as these visits were Ms. Grace, my grandparents, Sammy, and Sarge weren't there this time.

I just knew that list of people would be the first ones in line with me. They'd be right there letting out huge sighs of relief that I actually made it that far and evidentially on time too. Since Sammy wants to be roommates again, and God I pray that's not possible, he'd probably be at the front of the group with a sublease in his hand. No, this gathering looked more like a giant pizza party without the pizza. There was just fellowship and laughter. The kids to include Abby were running around playing too, so if the others were here this would be more like what I expected, I guess. Another thing I noticed was there was a long table where the oldest people were sitting. This place never ceases to amaze me and the similarities to an actual family reunion kept piling up as well. When Abby took a break from playing with the other children she once again grabbed me by the hand and led me over to the elders as she called them. Now I didn't recognize any of these people

Once again, Abby introduced me as Grampy and this time she was doing it to those who fit that bill much more than I, plus some. If you could be anything you wanted here I never understood why they stayed old but as they welcomed me they all told me who they were in relation to me. Some of those men and women went back four or more generations and they, like everyone else was since I got to this place, were so glad to see me. We all visited for a while and Abby once again told me we had to get a move on. I guess the party was over because when Abby said we had to do something it didn't take too long before we were doing it. As we got to the other side of that hill I saw another first for me in that place. It was an animal. In fact it was dog, not just any dog either, it was our old dog Puddles and he was way happier to see me than any of the people I rekindled with were. I think if people knew how to love the way that dogs do then the world would be a much better place. Puddles, made me think of the old Jon boat I had growing up. I always heard having a boat without a name on it was bad luck, so I let Sammy name it.

I reminisced about how after going out fishing one rainy day that little boat started collecting puddles of water underneath our feet. That's what happens to boats in the rain I guess but that was enough inspiration for Sammy to figure out what he wanted to name my boat and his new puppy when he got him a few weeks later. Sammy was wild back then and obviously still is with all of his pranks, but Puddles' tail looked like it was going to shake off as he lathered up both sides of my face with that humongous tongue of his in his own excitement after seeing me for the first time in so long. Abby reached down to pet him and she started playing with him too. Puddles was the sweetest dog but I guess being influenced by three brothers that were always into something wore off on him.

I remember when we got him from the local shelter and for whatever reason Sammy picked him out because he peed on him. I also remember that little thing not only chewed but ate any and everything he could get his fuzzy little mouth on. I can't count how many times we had to help his backside release a sock or an extension cord, and that part of dog ownership was nasty. How he lived through all of that was still a wonder to me. Looking at him now I also remember my father got up really early for work every morning. He always got dressed and tried to leave the house as quiet as he could because the rest of us were still asleep. He always put his shoes by the door and I couldn't count the times that we were woken up at 4:00 a.m. by hearing the words "That damn dog." Sometimes Puddles would just hide one or maybe both of his shoes but other times he'd fill them with slobber or even chew them to shreds.

I don't know why my dad wouldn't stop leaving his shoes by the door, but he didn't. Not that it matters now, but I really thought that dog's life was in danger many times. Puddles was a jokester too for a dog. Our favorite meal like many younger peoples' was pizza. That dog probably took a hundred slices out of our hands and even right out my mouth one time before I could get a good bite on it. He was definitely as much a part of our family as any of the rest us were, especially after he learned how to leave my father's shoes alone. I then heard a whistle and Puddle's ears perked up. He then left towards the sound. I didn't exactly know where it came from but if we're talking about Puddles, I knew Sammy couldn't be too far away. Sammy used to be the only person Puddles would ever leave me for. After our furry little buddy left I saw that little Miss Abigail was bouncing off the walls after playing with him. That dog had that effect on everyone, especially with children.

True Grace

This was a pretty long day I thought, regardless of the funny time here. I knew Abby was glad she stashed that painting somewhere before we went because she really would have crashed after carrying that around all day. Thinking about how funny time is between here and there I knew when I got a chance I had to see Mia again. I thought to myself, she's probably a senior citizen by know like those elder's I just met. I don't know if me thinking about her triggered something or really how that connection works but I got this overwhelming feeling that I had to find a way to look down on her right then. Abby acted as if she was greatly honored that I asked her to help me, so we did. As I saw Mia again, this time she wasn't on a front porch getting ready to go to a dance, or even jumping in the house to avoid a Saint Bernard. She was driving down a highway. A little older version of that daggon same boy P-A-Y-N-E was with her again.

Thankfully this time he had a hat on, so I couldn't see if he still had that man bun pony tail thing or not. As they drove I could tell that things must have gotten a bit more serious with them. I was unexpectedly eavesdropping on a grown up conversation about where they'd like to live someday and how many kids they may want. Abby was giggling at me and I shook my head. I think they were even playfully picking out baby names. I felt like this time I was tuning into to some sappy soap opera but then it registered with me that this was my own daughter spewing out this Hallmark-moment stuff. I can't say I didn't want these things for her but like everything else that ever happened in life and yes again in death I definitely wasn't ready for it. With no exaggeration, I feel like I've been at this place for no more than a week or two and now my child is talking about having children and traveling across the world with a new husband.

I'd ask where did the time go, but it seems it went here and this place is slowly collecting it all. Abby then tugs on my shirt to get my attention to something I didn't see before; it was a silver Honda. After I saw it I knew something wasn't quite right. The car looked as if had been in three or four wrecks already. It had deep scratches and fresh dents down both sides. It also had a spider webbed windshield and it was missing one of the side view mirrors. When it slammed into Mia's car entering the highway I knew why I had the feeling that I had to see her. My heart sank again because this wasn't just a little fender bender it was a horrific accident that caused Mia's car to flip over several times and catch on fire with Mia and Payne still inside. I felt I knew what to do in a way but nothing would work because what overwhelmed me more than anything else was fear for them and rage for the driver of the silver Honda. Rage and fear were things that I thought I got rid of at this place, but obviously not.

Abby held my hand as tight as she could and wouldn't let go. No matter how hard I tried to help from above in any way I could think of I was helpless. Besides, I really still didn't know how to do much and no one except Abby was around. I was going to have to be forced to see Mia and her friend burn up inside of a car, I thought. I didn't know if I could ever forgive anything like that. This would have been the worst thing I would have ever had to see and I've seen pure evil before. Not once did it register with me where she would most likely go if she didn't survive the accident. I just wanted her to be safe and to live. All I saw was every vision I had of her life flashing before my eyes now. Like so many other terrible events the car seemed like it was rolling in slow motion and I could feel the heat from the flames on every inch of my own body. Watching this was hell to me.

Abby didn't leave my side as she closed her eyes with every roll of the car and she tucked her little chin down at the flames. She evidentially couldn't help either because she was so scared even though she was trying every bit as hard as I was. There was just nothing we could do except watch in horror. I just knew that my baby girl was dead after the car settled and the flames continued. Other drivers began getting out of their cars and running over to where they had to feel they'd be witnessing a fatality. People tried to get close to the car to see if there was any chance for those inside to be freed but no one could help, the flames were just too high. When I felt all hope was lost I saw a black man in tattered clothes and an old fatigue military jacket. Somehow the flames and the carnage of the wreck didn't affect him and he was able to drag the motionless bodies of both, my beautiful daughter and that young man away from the wreck.

After a few more minutes the ambulance and police arrived, a few more minutes after that Payne sat up. He was still in shock of what happened but when he gathered enough of his bearings he ran over to Mia. He leaned over her lifeless body and prayed, that boy prayed so much and so hard that his prayers even echoed to where Abby and I were. Not being smart enough to make my own prayers work at first, Abby and I joined in and started praying with him. Then every person, or angel or whatever they were from the reunion on the hill came almost instantly by our side and started praying with us as well. Then Sammy and my grandparents came too. There was already a mass of people praying for one common goal when my military buddy's came to join us. The last to person to get to this glorious congregation was a black man in an old military fatigue jacket, it was Sarge.

What he did for me a hundred times before he also did for my precious daughter that day as well. We all prayed like we never prayed before. They say where there are two or three gathered in His name, He is among you. Now, I've heard a lot of things since I got here that wasn't exactly like what I was originally told and I've seen things here that were completely different than what I ever expected them to be. But instead of two or three we had what looked like hundreds or maybe even thousands praying for Mia and on that day everything was just the way it was promised and our prayers were answered. No words spoken or ever created could adequately express the gratitude in my heart for everyone who helped pray for Mia. I never felt this full of what I can only describe as pure love and appreciation before. This wasn't a numbness at all, this was gratitude in its purest form for an answered prayer. I never thought for one second if the accident would have gone another way that she'd be with me again. I wanted her to live and have a life that for whatever reason, I wasn't able to finish with her.

She had a concussion and minor bumps and bruises that healed in a short amount of time but she was okay, she was alive. Sarge didn't stick around after our prayer gathering too long, I guess he had to change his clothes again but even here he's what he's always been in my life, my favorite angel. That accident solidified Mia and Payne's fate in a much different way than I saw coming. I guess they had so many things in common to include both being saved by a man in an old fatigue military jacket that neither one of them could imagined not spending the rest of their lives together. Payne decided to ask Mia to marry him. After seeing him pray for Mia, and doing something there that I couldn't even do for her here by myself I knew she'd always be in good hands.

Whether they'd ever know it or not, this father gave his blessing in more ways than one on the day of that proposal. I laughed to myself as I thought about how what started as a dog attack before a dance got to where they are now. I don't know why things happen the way they do, either here or there, but sometimes they really do end up better than any of us can actually plan for ourselves. I'm more humbled by my surroundings than ever before. I don't seem to have one foot in the other world and one in this one as much as I did before. It almost feels like I'm literally feeling a heavy coat coming off. This place's cleansing methods may not be easy at times, but they sure are working. In fact, not as much as Ms. Grace, but just maybe I believe I may have a little extra glow about myself now too.

Since meeting her, other than stashing that painting, Abby rarely left my side. We played in the fields and on the path. I told her stories almost like a father does, really exactly like a father does to his beloved daughter. She'd listen as if she was the main character in every tale, especially when I told the story about the great pirate ship the Armageddon. We'd even come across some more paint and easels in the woods now and then and we'd just let the cerulean blue take us where it would. I knew Mia was more than fine now. I felt like everybody I used to worry about were as well, so I just felt a freedom come over me that I never let myself feel before. Abby drove a lot of those feelings with her curiosity and interest in everything. Mia brought the best out of me there but it seemed Abby was doing the same for me here without question again as well. The best here is different from the best anywhere else though. A person's best here is ridiculously good. The kind of good that creates paintings, waterfalls, angel's wings, and even old military fatigue jackets out of nothing except faith and love.

Speaking about faith and love, as far as weddings go, I guess it was bound to happen at some point. In truth I'm really happy for Mia that it's with a young man like Payne. If it's possible to feel old in this place I guess that's what I should be feeling. Payne did everything and even more so than anyone would have ever expected of him. He asked for Emily's permission for Mia's hand in marriage, he asked my parent's and he even asked my brother Jacob as well. That had to be an uncomfortable situation for him. Without me being there, Jacob graciously did many of the fatherly duties throughout the years for Mia and I can't imagine how that conversation went. Well yes, I can, because I can see it. Jacob even being a little older now is kind of an intimidating looking fella. He's like our grandfather was in a sense because he's the more gentle type despite not looking like it.

He wasn't as chiseled as Sammy's newer appearance, or as plain old big as my grandfather but I think if he wanted to be, he could be quite a force to be reckoned with. As Payne arrived at Jacob's house the questioning began almost as soon as he came in the door. It was all out of fun but I don't think Payne realized that at first. My brother asked the normal questions that were really none of his business but were asked anyway. He asked, "Where are you going to live"? Where are you going to work? Where did you meet? etc., etc., etc. He asked all of the where are you questions until he ran out of them. Then, Jacob made it to the question that meant the most. This question stumped Payne at first, he even had his own eyebrow raised to the sky trying to think of a response. Jacob asked if he was ever going to give Mia's heart a tummy ache. Payne was stumped at first thinking about the human anatomy I guess, but once it registered to what Jacob was asking, he smiled with absolutely surety in himself and said, "Never."

That young man didn't say no, he didn't hesitate with his answer once he understood the question, and he didn't doubt the truth of his words. Jacob didn't just ask that question out of the blue either and he was dead serious when he asked it even though it really was an odd question for most. On the many days after I died, Jacob would pick Mia up and take her to her favorite restaurant, McDonald's. He'd do that as often as he could just to make sure she was as okay as she could be. Jacob knew how Mia was feeling in a way because of how we all felt after Sammy died. Mia definitely felt safe enough to open up to Jacob when she needed someone throughout the years. Once I learned how to look down at the past too, I saw Jacob break down a hundred times in his car on the way home after dropping Mia off. A lot of this came from another question that he'd often ask my little girl.

On many occasions before he left he'd ask Mia if she felt better and nine times out of ten she'd say no Uncle Jacob my heart has a tummy ache. Those words would melt anyone's heart as it often did Jacob's. Jacob wasn't joking around when he asked that question to Payne, he was as serious as he's ever been. Jacob appreciated and believed the confidence that Payne had in the young couple's future and with tears in his own eyes looked up at me as if he already knew I was looking down on them. He shook his head up and down as to show me that he was giving the approval for both of us. I think we all knew some things are just meant to be even if we don't understand how they became that way. With both of these young people losing their father's at such a young age it confusingly helped in a way. It helped those two create a bond from a commonality that they may never have been able to happen any other way. Another shared lesson they learned together was after the accident.

They both learned with absolute certainty that prayer can help them and anyone else find their way through any challenge that life may present. I even think that Payne realizes that there is no greater bond than family himself, regardless of where some of them may be. Abby heard the news about my daughter getting married and she ran around like she was going to be attending the nuptials live and in person. She told me that she needed to find the absolute perfect gift for the occasion. I didn't have the heart to tell her that I think we'd be watching the wedding from the cheap seats so I let her continue to run around and do what she was doing to find that gift. I don't think anyone has ever considered this place as the cheap seats before but I really did in this instance. If I couldn't be there in person, I wanted to do something so special for Mia that she'd finally understand death itself couldn't stop me from being a part of her very special day. That's the connection that kind love brings.

It didn't take but what felt like a few minutes in their time for it to be their wedding day. I still hadn't completely figured out what I was going to do for Mia but once again Jacob did for me. When I got married, we were a new kind of broke. We didn't have much of anything and obviously at times we didn't seem to do very well. Jacob as he often did, understood that money, whether people want to admit it or not is a factor in a young marriage, and he had an idea. Some call it a dollar dance, I'm glad he didn't use those terms because I didn't want his efforts sounding like a strip club but what it is, is exactly how it's named. During the newlyweds second dance the attendees pin dollars to the brides dress or the groom's tux in hopes of giving the young couple a little stronger financial start. It was a good idea and Jacob knew everyone could afford a few bucks.

Jacob had his own little twist though. In his version of the money dance, he used two dollar bills. He set up a hidden table like a horse racing bookie and gave everyone in attendance two-dollar bills for their singles and loose change in secret. It must have been about five or six thousand dollars' worth of two dollar bills that were getting ready to be distributed to the unknowing couple. Jacob knew I made up the $2 game for Mia and he did the same with his own kids so it really was a wonderful plan. I didn't think I could come up with anything any better but I still knew it wasn't from me. I was trying not to sound petty, but I wanted my gift to Mia to truly be from me. It didn't have to be an expensive gift, it didn't have to be new or blue or any of that other stuff, it just had to be from me so she'd know I was still with her no matter where I am.

Abby, from wherever she got it from, put on the cutest little dress as if she was actually going to be one of the flowers girls. Her prior excitement for the day was now replaced with a calm, almost guilty look, as if she was hiding something. I thought her and Mrs. Grace with those guilty looks. When Mia started to walk down the aisle she had that look on her face that I'd always wished she have. She was completely and thoroughly happy. Her mother walked her down by the arm. She had been her father and mother in many ways for so long now that definitely made the most sense and great gift to Emily as well. As she approached Payne his knees might have been knocking a little but Mia's smile eased his nerves as they began exchanging their vows. Mia was so grown and beautiful but more importantly so happy. As the final I do's were said and the rice or whatever is thrown nowadays was tossed there were plans for the reception to be at the military club down the street from the church. Payne thought that was a fitting place to honor both of their fathers on their special day.

As the newlyweds left the church, Mia jumped in excitement for what she saw that Payne rented to drive to the reception and beyond. It wasn't a limousine, and it wasn't a stretch hummer or anything like that. It was a little red convertible corvette. Payne knew all of Mia's stories about our claim game, and the fact that her mother used to have one of those magnificent ones too. My heart filled again as I heard my daughter's new husband tell her to, Claim it, girl. Claim it". As they sped off I knew this day was great, more than great, it was blessed. Mia and Payne drove that sleek little convertible corvette around for a while to give everyone time to get to the reception hall before they did. I wasn't watching where they went but wherever it was they switched drivers in route because it was Mia that pulled up in the driver's seat when they finally arrived, and the tires on that thing looked a little slicker than when they left.

After the first dance Mia was noticing that everyone was digging in their pockets for something. That something meant it was time for the money dance. When Mia saw all of those two dollar bills being pinned to her and Payne's attire she cried with a humble appreciate and also with an everlasting remembrance. She knew I couldn't help when I had to leave but she also knew that I was never very far away either. Jacob and the rest of their guest outdid themselves and the happy little bride became even happier. I could have sworn once again that she was so happy she glowing. Most new couples need money, that's a given, but Mia didn't care about how many two dollar bills they received. She cared about what they stood for. She felt, as her Daddy once told her, with that many two dollar bills her wishes in life would be limitless. As the couple moved to the gift table there was a big rectangular box leaning across the back of the table with a table cloth laid across it.

It was covered instead of being wrapped with wrapping paper like all of the other presents. I'd been a little nosy before, so I knew what most of the presents were but even I didn't know what was underneath that table cloth and inside that big box. Mia went over and tugged on the corner until the covering slid to the floor. After the table cloth fell to the ground, she put both of her hands up to her mouth in astonishment of what I'm guessing is the same reaction I had the first time I saw cerulean blue. It was the painting I just painted. I knew it, and my little partner in crime Abby knew it too because she was the one who made sure it was there. That guilty look that Abby was trying to hide before turned to one of extreme satisfaction with herself now. It was a deserving look too because I was just as grateful for her thinking so much about Mia but also about me too.

What I couldn't do myself my new little buddy did without me having a clue. I was so grateful for this little girl who seemed to be with me all the time now. I might not have found the perfect present for Mia's wedding but Payne, Jacob, and Abby sure did. Mia never knew the full story of any of my paintings to my knowledge but seeing her reaction and tears she definitely knew I was the one who painted them. I think that gift brought tears to the eyes of everyone in attendance because although they may not have known who brought it there, they all knew who it was always meant for.

Grampy

I have no right feeling any other way than grateful, not a bit, but I do even with all of those beautiful gifts from such beautiful people. It's just that I wanted to give Mia something directly from me. I know it sounds selfish, I really do know it does, but I feel I need to do it for both of us. I was so happy for Mia, but I just couldn't get past the fact that I couldn't make something happen for her on my own. After I stopped wallowing in self-pity I noticed the reception hall had two sides. One of course, is where Mia's and Payne's wedding reception was, the other was another large room that was already being set up for a birthday party, a little girl's seventh birthday party to be specific. The event crew already started bringing in the games and the cake and all kinds of things that a seven-year- old would like. As another delivery truck pulled up the driver got out and asked the man who was obviously in charge where he wanted that load dropped off.

I could tell that the boss man was stressed and evidentially working on a deadline that he might not meet so he barkishly yelled out, "Door number two, take the stuff to door number two, and hurry up!" Once the man backed to the entry doors and opened the back of his truck, I knew what I wanted my special wedding gift to my precious daughter to be even if I had to borrow it from a seven-year-old. I still didn't know if I could do it myself and I knew it would be such a little thing compared to the many wonderful things the others did that day, but for me I just knew Mia would have to know this gift was directly from me, no matter where I am. The delivery driver didn't take kindly to being yelled at or to be told to hurry up so when he made his delivery he just opened the door and started flinging out what he brought inside the first door he came to.

He threw one huge mesh bag in after the other until they were all inside. Then he drove off in disgust about how he'd been treated. Now this part I didn't do, that was just the part where something or someone else was looking out for me again, but the next move was all mine. The reception hall had these big fans in each corner because although there was air conditioning it could still get pretty hot with so many people inside dancing, and in some cases, jumping all around. They were so loud that someone went around and turned all of the fans off. After the frustrated delivery man left his load in the entry way to Mia's reception instead of inside of door number two, I decided to spiritually interact with some of those fans so they'd crank back up. It finally worked too. It seems that little girl who was getting ready to have a birthday party loved balloons, I mean *really* loved them. There must have been a thousand of those things already blown up and ready to go just falling out of their huge mesh bags.

Where I was helped once more and the most was that birthday girl's favorite color must have been green too. They looked just liked the one's Mia released when she was praying for me so many years ago. When I got those fans to kick in they produced enough air to push all of those green balloons to where everyone was at the wedding reception through a few open doors in front of the dance floor. There were hundreds and hundreds of floating green acknowledgments of my eternal connection to Mia floating around the room everywhere. There were so many balloons that they seemed to be coming up through the floor and pleasantly invading almost every inch of that joyous gathering. But to me and Mia, it was a definite present that told her that her Daddy was still with her, and always will be too.

Mia looked in amazement because she remembered what she had done for me so long ago in a very similar fashion. Now she knows with certainty that her prayers were answered. It may have only been balloons but I don't think I couldn't have given her a more fitting or conformational present. As the couple finally got to the door to leave, Mia at first acted as if she never wanted that particular time of that magical day to end. Then she remembered as she gathered all the green balloons that would fit inside of that little red car that her daddy would always be with her wherever she went. Mia tweaked the tires of that red jet car one more time while both husband and wife were waiving to the crowd. Mia of course waived from the driver's side and my new son-in-law Payne, was proud that she was. Have you ever had those days where you're almost too happy to move? This was similar to when I got to this place because once again I was definitely in some sort of self-imposed trance. But instead of having any feelings of doubt or confusion, all I felt was overwhelming joy.

There was no question about where I was anymore because there couldn't be any other place that could provide such a blessed day as this place just did, so, once again, I thanked God. I thought we'd all had more than enough for the day when Abby spoke up and said she had to take me somewhere else again. The last time we had to go to a specific place at a specific time we ended up in a family reunion with eons of different generations in attendance so there was no telling where we'd be headed this time. As we went to get back on the path I noticed there wasn't a path to get on, it had ended without me even realizing it. I was so used to the ever growing brightness and the music that I didn't realize that this part of my journey was over.

I understood enough to know that the journey was the real destination, but *what could be next*, I thought. I thought back to when Miss Grace told me God was everything because in everything was his love, so was I going to meet *everything* next? I too, along with everyone around me had been glowing a little more for a while but when we arrived at our next destination it was as if everything to include myself was pure light. Instead of calling this spot a resting place, like the others, Abby called it a "thanking place." I asked if she meant "thinking place" and just said it with a country twang but she just giggled and said, No Grampy, it's a thanking place. She didn't tell me what I was supposed to do. I think she wanted me to figure out for myself as she left me alone to do so. I guess she figured by the place's name even I could figure out what I was supposed to do there. This place was so radiant and bustling with brilliance. It was so peaceful too with this particular hymn softly bellowing everywhere.

I didn't have a problem dropping to my knees to give thanks again, so I did. I gave thanks for my brothers and Jacob's family, I gave thanks for my grandparents, and parents. I also gave thanks for Sarge and my buddies, and for my many family members from the reunion over the hill. I gave thanks for Nasim and his men from the church. Of course I gave thanks for my Mia and her new husband. I thanked God so much for any and everybody I ever knew and for the one's I didn't. I also thanked God for everything that ever happened to me, and for me. I could have gone on all day because for one, time here is funny, but also because I had so much to be thankful for. I was finally completely lost in that place but the good kind of lost where you know the outcome is going to be so much better than anybody, to include yourself, could have ever planned.

When I opened my eyes everyone that I was on this journey with was surrounding me. Sarge and his tattered wings, Sammy with what looked like a sublease contract in his hands, my grandparents, Nasim and his men. They were all there. It looked like when everyone came together to help pray for Mia, but this time there were even more in attendance and it appeared this meeting was called for me. In the back of all of those gathered people, and all of that brightness, stood the holiest of holy lights. I hadn't seen Him before even though somehow, I could tell we were related too. As He called me over to Him I felt like a tiny star heading towards the largest planet. When I got to him everything shook as He placed His hands on my shoulders but it wasn't anything to be scared of at all. It was like Sarge used to do but this time with even more fatherly love. I didn't think that was possible but it was.

At first I thought He was going to call me "I am the Sky" but that's not what He did. As His hands were on my shoulders every single thing that ever happened in my life and after life, both good and bad, flashed through my mind all at once. All of the memories that I ever had were gone after that for a brief time. They didn't leave my mind forever but they had no place around such greatness. I was in total peace surrounded by total love. As my memories slowly returned they didn't have the same control over me. They were there but like the tattoos I used to have, they were diminished when they came in contact with that amazing light. This was to be my final welcoming of sorts. The actual acceptance and approval for being able to be where I am. Strangely enough, I was in full acknowledgment that it wasn't me who had to do anything at all. If I thought green balloons were the ultimate gift for Mia it was absolutely nothing compared to knowing what was given to me now and to everyone else through true grace.

As we concluded, the light that so lovingly held my shoulders left and went out of sight. I knew He left because I saw Him leave, but I still felt His presence as if He was still completely there with me. I learned that day that He always would be too. I looked around to find Abby and I was sure that Ms. Grace had to be there somewhere too but I didn't see either one of them. I jokingly thought, *I don't know what else these people could be doing that could be more important than what just happened,* but they weren't there. None of the others that gathered seemed to want to leave though. Again, this place is so strange because everyone just sat around and talked as if we were having another family reunion. During that time I did make sure Sammy didn't think we'd actually be moving in together though. As Sammy and I were standing together my grandparents came over. This again, would be just like back at home with just a few very important people missing.

As my family surrounded me there was another light that came from where the brightest light stood. This light was a bit different though. It almost looked more like the brightest sparkler and it floated and spiraled all around eventually landing in my hands. I looked at my family as to say I didn't know we had fireworks in this place. I could tell my grandfather wanted to bip me in the back of the head again but instead they all just smiled and said it was time to see Mia again. This time I led us to see her and instead of having any fear or feelings that anything was wrong. I knew the plans for her life were greater than even this father could have ever had for her. As I looked down with my family and friends that by then had all tightened around, what I saw put me on my knees in thanks once more. That sparkle that just left my hands lovingly blended in to its future and my precious daughter Mia went into labor. Payne was right there by her side being exactly who I knew he would be. As that precious little sparkle breathed its first breath, both looked up again and smiled.

Their thanks weren't directed at me or even to Payne's father who was also in our attentive crowd of onlookers by this time. It was lovingly given to He who gave that truly perfect little package to them. They already had the baby's name picked out. I'm sure they probably came up with it on that original ride that I eavesdropped on but for some reason nurses always seem to feel they need to introduce the new little babies to their parents. This wonderful nurse was no different as she said "Mommy and daddy. Meet your new little girl, Miss Grace Abigail." All of the light, love, and music exploded at all at once. It was like the fourth of July had a fourth of July and I thanked God once again. I may have been slow at times but I knew this little girl was my granddaughter and I knew little Miss Grace Abigail, or Abby for short, would always know it too. As I saw this beautiful new addition to my family in the arms of my greatest blessing, I knew more than ever, I was with them and I always will be too.

Dear Friends,

Thank you for choosing our inspirational products! We'd love for you to visit our website at www.inkwillpublications.com to check out our full range of offerings. We hope our products will help uplift your spirits and inspire you on your journey. So in closing as Sammy would say, "Good Day, Good Day"!

Best regards,

M. A. Cole
Inkwill Publications